NO HOME LIKE NANTUCKET

A SWEET ISLAND INN NOVEL (BOOK ONE)

GRACE PALMER

JOIN MY MAILING LIST!

Click the link below to join my mailing list and receive updates, freebies, release announcements, and more!

JOIN HERE:

https://readerlinks.com/l/1060002

ALSO BY GRACE PALMER

NO HOME LIKE NANTUCKET

A SWEET ISLAND INN NOVEL (BOOK ONE)

Nantucket was her paradise—until reality came barging in.

Mae Benson was happy—a beloved wife, beloved mother, beloved neighbor. But even she wasn't ready for the tragedy looming around the corner.

The accident that claims her husband's life rocks the whole family. And it's not the only thing stirring up trouble.

Mae's oldest, Eliza, is facing an unexpected pregnancy with a fiancé she no longer wants to be with.

Her daughter Holly is caught in a marriage on the rocks.

Headstrong daughter Sara is reeling in the throes of a forbidden workplace romance.

And her youngest son, Brent, is drowning in sorrow and guilt after his father's passing.

Take a trip to Nantucket's Sweet Island Inn and follow along as Mae Benson and her children face the hardest summer of their lives.

Love, loss, heartbreak, hope—it's all here and more. Can Mae find a way to bring herself and her family to the light at the end of the tunnel? Or will her grief be too much to overcome?

Find out in NO HOME LIKE NANTUCKET.

PART I

SPRING

1

MAE

Mae Benson never ever slept in.

For each of the one thousand, two hundred, and eleven days that she'd lived at 114 Howard Street, Nantucket, Massachusetts, she'd gotten up with the dawn and started her morning the second her eyes opened. It wasn't because she was a busybody, or compulsive, or obsessive. On the contrary, snoozing for a while was tempting. Her bed was soft this morning. The first fingers of springtime sunlight had barely begun to peek in through the gauzy curtains that hung over the window. And she was in that perfect sleeping position—warm but not too warm, wrapped up but not too tightly.

But force of habit could sometimes be awfully hard to break. So, being careful to make as little noise as possible, she slid out from underneath the comforter, tucked her feet into the fuzzy slippers she'd received for her sixtieth birthday last year, and rose.

Her husband, Henry, always called her his little hummingbird. He'd even bought her a beautiful handblown hummingbird ornament for Christmas last year from a glassblower down by the wharf. It had jade-green wings, little amethysts for eyes, and a patch of ruby red on its chest.

She loved how it caught and refracted the winter sunbeams, and she always made sure to put it on a limb of the tree where it could see the snow falling outdoors.

"Flitting around the house, are we?" Henry would say, laughing, every time he came downstairs from their master bedroom to find Mae buzzing from corner to corner. She would just laugh and shake her head.

He could make fun of her all he wanted, but the fact remained that each of the little projects she had running at all times around the house required love and care from the moment the day began.

She ran through the list in her head as she moved silently around the bedroom getting dressed for the day. She needed to water the plants on the living room windowsill, the ones that her daughter, Sara, had sent from her culinary trip to Africa and made her mother promise to keep alive until she could retrieve them on her next visit. Crane flowers, with their gorgeous mix of orange- and blue-bladed leaves; desert roses, with their soft blush of red fading into the purest white; and her favorites, the fire lilies, that looked just like a flickering flame.

She had to check on the batch of marshmallow fluff fudge—a Mae Benson specialty—that she'd left to set in the freezer overnight. Her friend Lola, who lived down the street, had just twisted her ankle badly a few days prior and was laid up at home with a boot on her leg. Mae didn't know much about ankle injuries, but she had a lot of hands-on experience with fudge, so she figured she'd offer what she knew best.

She should also start coffee for Henry—lots of cream and sugar, as always. Henry had an outing planned that morning with Brent to go check on some fishing spots they'd been scheming over for the last few weeks.

Mae knew he was excited about the trip. He'd been exhibiting trademark Happy Henry behavior all week long—eyes lighting up with that mischievous twinkle, hands rubbing together like an evil mastermind, and the way that he licked the corner of his lips, like he could already taste the salt air that hung on the wind and feel the bouncing of the boat as it raced through the waves.

Just before she turned to leave the bedroom and start her day, she looked over at her husband.

He was sleeping on his side of the bed, snoring softly like he always did. It was never enough to wake her, thankfully. Not like Lola's ex-husband, who'd been a snorer of epic proportions. Henry hadn't bothered a single soul in the six and a half decades he'd been alive on this earth. Matter of fact, she couldn't think of a single person who disliked him—other than Mae herself, whenever he took the liberty of dipping into the brownie batter, or when he insisted on sneaking up behind her while she was cooking, nipping at the lobe of her ear, then dancing away and laughing when she tried to swat him with a spoon and inevitably sprayed chocolate batter all over the kitchen.

But the truth of the matter was that she could never bring herself to stay irked at him.

It wasn't just his physical looks, although he certainly wasn't hurting in that department. The same things she'd fallen in love with at that Boston bar forty-plus years ago were still present and accounted for. The long, proud nose. Full lips, always eager to twitch into a smile. Bright blue eyes that danced in the sunlight when he laughed, cried, and—well, all the time, really. And that darn shock of hair that was perpetually threatening to fall over his forehead.

She reached over and smoothed it out of his face now. Time had turned his sun-drenched blondness into something more silvery, but in Mae's eyes, he was all the more handsome for it.

But, even more than his good looks, Mae loved Henry's soul. He was a selfless giver, an instant friend to every child who'd ever come across his path. He loved to kneel in front of an awestruck five-year-old and present him or her with some little hand-carved trinket, one of the many he kept in his pockets to whittle whenever he had an idle moment. He laughed and cried in all the wrong places during romantic comedies and he knew how to cook—how to *really* cook, the kind of cooking you do with a jazz record crooning through the speakers and a soft breeze drifting in through an open window.

She let her hand linger on Henry's forehead just a beat too long. He didn't open his eyes, but his hand snaked up from underneath the sheets and threaded through Mae's fingers.

"You're getting up?"

"Can't waste the day away."

It was a ritual, one they'd been through practically every morning for as long as either could remember. For all that he'd become a proud father to four children, a state-record-holding fisherman, a much-sought-after contractor and builder on the island of Nantucket, Henry loved nothing so much as to stay in bed for hours, alternating between sleeping and poking Mae until she rolled over and gave him the soft kisses he called her "hummingbird pecks." There was a perpetual little boy spirit in him, a playfulness that another six or sixty decades couldn't extinguish if it tried.

"Stay with me," he murmured. "The day can wait a few more minutes, can't it?" His eyes were open now, heavy with sleep, but still gazing at her fondly.

Mae tapped him playfully on the tip of the nose. "If it was up to you, 'a few more minutes' would turn into hours before we knew it, and then I'd be scrambling around like a chicken with my head cut off, trying to get everything done before Holly, Pete, and the kids get here tonight."

Holly was Mae and Henry's middle daughter. She and her husband, Pete, were bringing their two kids to Nantucket to spend the weekend. Mae had had the date circled on her calendar for months, excited at the prospect of spoiling her grandkids rotten. She already had oodles of activities planned—walks downtown to get rock candy from the corner store, sandcastles at the beach, bike rides down to 'Sconset to ogle the grand houses the rich folks had built out on that end of the island.

Grady was a little wrecking ball of a seven-year-old boy, and Mae knew that he'd love building a massive sandcastle and then terrorizing it like a blond Godzilla.

Alice, on the other hand, was still as sweet and loving as only a five-year-old girl could be. She let Grandma Mae braid her long, soft hair into fishtails every morning whenever they were visiting the island. It was another ritual that Mae treasured beyond anything else. Her life was full of those kinds of moments.

"It ain't so bad, lying in bed with me, is it?" Henry teased. "But maybe I just won't give ya a choice!"

He leaped up and threw his arms around Mae's waist, tugging her over him and then dragging them both beneath the covers. Mae yelped in surprise and smacked him on the chest, but Henry was a big man—nearly six and a half feet tall—and the years he'd spent hauling in fish during his weekend trips with Brent had kept him muscular and toned. When her palm landed on his shoulder, it just made a thwacking noise, and did about as much good as if she'd slapped a brick wall.

So she just laughed and let Henry pull her into his arms, roll over on top of her, and throw the comforter over their heads.

It was soft and warm and white underneath. The April sun filtered through the bedsheets and cast everything in a beautiful, hazy glow.

"You've never looked so beautiful," Henry said, his face suspended above hers.

"Henry Benson, I do believe you are yanking my chain," she admonished.

"Never," he said, and he said it with such utter seriousness that Mae's retort fell from her lips. Instead of poking him in the chest like she always did whenever he teased her, she let her hand stroke the line of his jaw.

He pressed a gentle kiss to her lips. "Stay with me for just a few more minutes, Mrs. Benson," he said.

She could feel him smiling as he kissed her. She could also feel the butterflies fluttering in her stomach. Forty-one years of marriage and four children later, and she still got butterflies when her husband kissed her. Wasn't that something?

"All right, Mr. Benson," she said, letting her head fall back on the pillows. "Just a few more minutes."

Henry grinned and fell in next to her, pulling her into his embrace. She could feel his heartbeat thumping in his chest. Familiar. Dependent. Reliable. Hers.

"You just made my day."

"But I'm warning you," she continued, raising one finger into the air and biting back the smile that wanted to steal over her lips. "If you start snoring again, I'm smothering you with a pillow."

"Warning received," Henry said. "Now quit making a fuss and snooze with me for a while, darling."

So Mae did exactly that. Sara's plants could wait.

2

BRENT

Dang tourists.

Nothing made Brent's life quite so hard as the sightseers and summer residents who flocked to Nantucket as soon as the weather turned warm. When the island was quiet, the waterways were empty, or close enough to it that Brent didn't have to worry about navigating around drunken partiers or the overly serious amateur fishermen who liked to come through the no-wake zones blazing all four engines at full tilt and causing a big stir.

But this time of year—with a sunny, clear weekend on the horizon and the sun lighting up the water with a warm blue glaze—was prime time for everybody to head to the docks and the boats.

Naturally, that meant chaos.

Not that he minded *too* much. Brent was a people person if ever there was one. He might get a little annoyed with some of the more excessive drinkers or first-time fishermen out on the water, but he loved meeting new folks and hearing stories about where they'd come from. Other people's homes always amazed him—the more exotic, the better.

Twenty-two years of living and he could count on three fingers how many times he'd ever left the state of Massachusetts. Eliza, his oldest sister, always rode him for it, saying that he was Nantucket's version of a homegrown hillbilly, but the truth of it was that Brent didn't really see a reason to leave. Eliza called him hardheaded, but their dad just said Brent was like a husky dog—if you want him to do something, you had to show him why. Otherwise, no luck. If Brent didn't see a reason for something, he more or less just didn't do it.

Which was part of the reason he wasn't going to wait too much longer for his dad to get his rear end down to the dock. He'd been waiting on him for nearly twenty minutes. But Brent knew as well as anybody that Henry Benson did things on his own time. It was Dad's world, and they were all just living in it.

So far this morning, it had all been the usual suspects at the docks—charter fishermen, the marina employees—along with a few ambitious go-getters from out of town trying to hit the water early. But the traffic was starting to pick up, slowly but surely.

Brent looked around. The marina was old and worn but still charming in its own salty dog kind of way. The building was crying out for a fresh coat of white paint, though Brent knew that Roger, the marina owner, was in no rush to do anything of the kind.

The concrete boat ramp sloped down into the waves, which lapped gently at dock pilings, boats, jet skis. Overhead, the sky was a crystalline blue, nary a cloud in sight. It was a good day for fishing. Maybe even a great one. If only his father would get his rear in gear.

Just then, right on cue, Dad's truck came trundling around the corner, spewing smoky exhaust, just like it had since Brent was a little boy. Brent spied his father in the driver's seat, arm hanging relaxed out the window, whistling a happy tune.

Dad never changed for anybody. The only person who could get him to fall in line for even a minute was Brent's mother, and even she had to try awfully hard to get that much done.

Dad was an ex-Marine, but some of the habits he'd learned in the military had stuck better than others. He still made the bedsheets every morning tight enough to bounce a quarter off of, and he still wore his dog tags around his neck on a chain. But when it came to the Marines' sense of timeliness—well, Dad had left that in the rearview mirror.

Brent smiled ruefully to himself. He could already picture how it would go if he tried to lecture his dad on punctuality. He'd make a few choice sarcastic remarks about his lateness, and Dad would just laugh them off. That was how the man operated.

"Life is meant to be enjoyed, isn't it?" he'd inevitably say. When he said it like that, it was sure hard to disagree.

"Nice of you to join me," Brent said wryly as Dad parked and clambered out of the truck.

Dad's boat, *Pour Decisions,* was tied up on the slip next to Brent's. The boat was his father's pride and joy. He loved nothing more than to while away the hours tending to every nick, scratch and tiny blemish on the craft. God help any barnacle who dared consider *Pour Decisions* a potential home—Pops was ruthless in keeping the hull spic and span.

"Ah, my youngest son, here to greet me as we go to conquer the wide-open ocean!" Dad boomed royally in the worst British accent Brent had ever heard. Always, always, there was a hint of laughter in his voice. He didn't take much seriously. In his presence, it was hard not to do the same. "What more could a father ask for?"

"I'm your only son, Pops," Brent shot back with a grin. "And I don't know what a *father* could ask for, but a *son* could certainly ask for his dad to be on time!"

"What's the rush? Fish ain't going anywhere, are they?"

"Every Joe Schmo in the Commonwealth is coming to catch fish today," grumbled Brent. "We'll be lucky to reel in someone else's chum at the rate you're going."

Dad ambled down to where Brent was standing, leaned up against a dock piling, and clapped him on the shoulder. "Good thing I have my master fisherman son here to lead us to victory over the Schmoes then." He gave Brent a wink.

Brent sighed and smiled again. His dad was definitely laying it on thick this morning. No wonder Mom had finally insisted on booting him out of the house while she got everything cleaned up and ready for Holly and co. When Henry Benson got rolling, he was an unstoppable force of nature.

"Yeah, yeah, whatever you say, Dad," Brent said. "Now, you gonna make me do all the work here, or can you lend a hand?"

"Lead the way, O Captain my Captain." He chuckled. "Let's go catch some fish."

3

SARA

ONE WEEK EARLIER

"Scooby, take the trash out. Yuri, scrub down the countertops and the knives. And Larissa, check on the mother mix for tomorrow's baked goods service—it was acting funky earlier in the day. Might need you to feed it some more starch."

"Yes, chef!" came the booming response from the kitchen staff gathered around Sara. She gave them a curt nod to signal that she was done with her orders, and they all dispersed to take care of their respective tasks.

It was the end of what had been an excruciatingly long dinner service at Lonesome Dove, the Michelin-starred restaurant in New York City's Flatiron District where Sara Benson worked as the sous chef. After nearly eight hours of work, Sara's eyes felt heavy in her skull, and her fingers were chapped and sore. But despite how drained she felt physically, her soul was on fire. Nothing brought her alive quite like cooking. And not just any cooking, but the kind of cooking they did at Lonesome Dove—fast-paced, bordering on reckless, with a sense of flair and spontaneity that made it her favorite kitchen she'd ever worked in.

The accolades that had come pouring in during the four short months they'd been open were nice, too, of course, but that was pretty much a given, seeing as how the restaurant's owner was a well-established wonder boy in New York's fine dining scene. Gavin Crawford, owner and operator of Lonesome Dove and a dozen other wildly successful restaurants in the northeast, had seemingly been born on a magazine cover. Lord knows he'd certainly graced enough of them during his climb to the top of the culinary world. It seemed like every other weekend, he was jetting off to collect another lifetime achievement award or "Best New _____" something or other.

Sara still wasn't quite sure how she'd landed this gig. Sure, she knew she was talented, and she had the grades at the Culinary Institute of America to prove her chops. That helped, as did several glowing recommendations from her stints in some other famous establishments around the city. The icing on the cake, though, was almost certainly one hazily remembered night of tequila shots with Gavin's assistant, Kelly. That had been enough to finagle her the interview six months ago when word got around town about Gavin's new passion project.

Sara could still remember how nervous she was last fall when she'd walked into the empty guts of what would become Lonesome Dove. She had gone there for her one-on-one sit-down with Gavin. All around them hung plastic sheeting and wooden scaffolds. Workmen were hauling in stainless steel kitchen appliances and sheets of glass that would encase the kitchen like a fishbowl, so that diners could watch the art and magic of their food being prepared. Painters were painting, plumbers were plumbing, carpenters were ... carpenting?

And there, seated in the middle of it all like a king on his throne, was the one and only Gavin Crawford.

She'd done her research—no one would ever accuse Sara Benson of being a slacker—and she could list his industry rap sheet like the words to her favorite song. *America's Best Restauranteur, 2017. Bon Appetit 40 Under 40, 2014. International Food Critics Association Golden*

Lion Prize for Outstanding Achievement. One after the other, with no end in sight. Sara wondered idly where he kept all his trophies.

He stood when she entered and gave her a smile that made her heart flip.

Sara knew right away that she was in trouble.

Gavin was six feet, two inches of pure man and looked like he was practically carved out of marble. His plaid shirtsleeves were rolled up above his elbow, exposing brawny forearms that rippled with veins. His grip was firm and warm, enveloping her fingers in a handshake that sent sparks racing up her arm and short-circuiting her brain.

And that smile. Oh jeez.

This was no good at all.

Even now, months later, she still wasn't sure how she'd made it through that interview. It felt like her mouth was completely disconnected from her mind, like she was just floating around above herself like an out-of-body experience. It was hard enough to focus on the words coming out of Gavin's lips, much less formulate a response of her own to each of his questions. But somehow, she managed to plow through without face-planting or otherwise unduly embarrassing herself.

When it was over, she'd levitated herself out of the work-in-progress restaurant and walked straight to a coffee shop to try and caffeinate some sense into her wonky brain. But it wasn't even half an hour before her phone buzzed. Kelly was on the line, telling her that Gavin had loved her and the job was hers if she wanted it.

Sous chef, at a brand-new restaurant concept being launched by the infamous Gavin Crawford. What a day *that* had been.

Hard work had followed, of course. Sara had expected that— welcomed it, even. There was nowhere in the world that made her quite so happy as the kitchen. In there, everything was clean and orderly. Well, not quite "orderly" in the way that most people normally thought of the term. There was far too much heavy metal music blaring and chefs cursing in ten different languages to really be as neat and tidy as the word "orderly" implies. But there was an order to kitchens that was unique, like they operated on their own kind of physics. You set up your mise-en-place, and you yelled "Behind!" when walking behind someone, and when the head chef barked out an order, you knew with one hundred percent certainty that the entire kitchen staff would rise up and respond, "Yes, chef!" unanimously. It set her soul at ease to cook. It felt like home.

And, slowly but surely, success had followed their hard work, just like it always followed in Gavin's footsteps. Critics trickled in, and when they trickled out, they invariably trailed rave reviews in their wake. *Sumptuous. Delectable. An out-of-this-world home run.* Sara would never admit this to any of her colleagues, but whenever her mom sent her another newspaper clipping of a Lonesome Dove review, Sara stashed it in a binder she kept under her bed. It felt pretty darn good to receive praise for the work she was pouring herself into.

It finally felt like she was *earning* it. For as long as she could remember, Sara had done things her way. She'd gotten her ears pierced at eleven and her nose done at fifteen. It had taken only that and a couple of small, innocuous tattoos to kick off a historically volatile Benson family argument between her and her mother, one that had ended with Sara spitefully smashing a white china plate that her mother dearly loved. That memory still made her cringe. She was twenty-nine years old now—no longer a child by any stretch of the imagination, but still young enough to remember the scene vividly and feel guilty about it. She didn't like thinking about her mother crying on the kitchen floor, surrounded by shards of china.

"Sara?" came a voice from around the corner. She turned around. Benny, one of the food runners, had his head stuck through the doorway. He jerked his chin towards the back of the building when she saw him. "Gavin wants you," he said.

Sara's heart did a quick backflip. At this rate, it would be ready for the 2020 Olympics, because at no point in the past four months on this job had it stopped doing gymnastics anytime someone so much as mentioned Gavin's name.

"Did he say what for?" she asked breathlessly. She realized she looked like a fool, so she straightened up and put on a more serious face.

"Nope."

"Oh. All right. Thanks, Benny."

He disappeared back around the corner, leaving Sara standing there with her heart pounding.

It was stupid, she knew, but she just wasn't willing to admit that she was in love with her boss. Besides being unprofessional, not to mention offensively stereotypical—*female chef falls in love with handsome restauranteur; give me a break*—it was also just bad for her career. Everyone knew that Gavin had an on-again, off-again girlfriend, Melissa. And, although no one was quite sure about the exact nature of their relationship, it seemed like a fair bet that Melissa wouldn't take kindly to one of Gavin's employees crossing the boundaries of workplace conduct. That being said, the food scene rumor mill—one of the most active swamps of gossip that Sara had ever encountered in her entire life; savage enough to make high school look like a tea party—seemed confident that Gavin was a playboy to the extreme, despite the Melissa Question. Everyone said he was a "different girl for every night of the week" kind of guy. That didn't bother Sara overly much. Gavin was a grown man, after all, and she was a grown woman. Who was she to judge if he didn't want to settle down? And if this Melissa woman was trying to rein him in when he didn't want to be, why should Sara automatically take her side?

Whether she genuinely believed those things or was just telling herself that to justify her attraction to her boss, Sara wasn't sure. But either way, none of those thoughts were particularly helpful in calming her down as she strode along the dark hallway towards the small office that Gavin kept at the back of Lonesome Dove.

She took a second outside the door to steel herself. She smoothed down some flyaway hairs, licked her lips to get rid of the chap, and wiped her flour-covered hands on her apron. Only then did she count down backwards from three and knock on his door.

"Come in!" came the friendly reply. Gavin didn't look up as she slunk through the door. "Close that behind you, will ya? Smells like fish out there. Sit, sit. Give me one sec. I'll be right with you."

Sara perched on the edge of the visitor's chair and took in the sight. Gavin was leaning all the way back in his leather chair, boots on the desk, as he tapped frenetically on his phone. His strong brow was furrowed in concentration, and he had a habit of gnawing on his bottom lip when deep in thought. Sara found that little quirk to be irresistibly cute.

She looked around his office while he typed. It was mostly bare-bones—a rickety desk, a chair on either side, a small, cluttered bookshelf. Some framed awards on the walls. A few pictures, too: Gavin holding up a monstrous redfish and beaming wide. Cooking in his younger days, full chef's regalia on, hands a blur as they chopped and sliced and julienned. In a tux, standing with Melissa.

Ugh. The smile fell right off Sara's face at the sight of that last one.

Finally, Gavin made one final swipe of his thumb and Sara heard the whooshing sound that indicated a message being sent. She wondered who he was texting or emailing. A distant, stupid, silly part of her brain hoped that it was Melissa. *We're over. Sorry.* She shook the dumb thought out of her head and gave him a smile.

"Sara! Sara, Sara, Sara," Gavin said by way of greeting. He plunked his boots on the ground and leaned forward over his desk towards her. His sleeves were rolled up over his elbows, just like they always were. And, like she always did, Sara couldn't help but notice the deep tan, the light dusting of auburn hair, and the veins that wound themselves up towards his bicep before disappearing beneath the folded cuff.

"Gavin," she half-said, half-giggled.

"You've been killin' it out there. I really mean that. Like, where'd you come from, and how can I get a dozen more of you?"

She giggled again and immediately admonished herself for sounding like a lovestruck high schooler. That wasn't far from the truth, but still, it was unbecoming of someone trying to make it as a chef in the cutthroat NYC fine dining scene, much less as a *woman* trying to do that. Heck, it was unbecoming for anyone over the age of sixteen. And yet, she had the hardest time not laughing at every little joke and gesture that Gavin made.

"It's easy when you're having fun."

"Therein lies the secret to success, I suppose," he said sagely. "I wanted to ask you something: how are you liking everything?"

Sara straightened up in her seat. "Uh, great! Loving it. It's my favorite job ever."

"Good, good," Gavin mused. He rubbed his cleft chin between thumb and forefinger, another deep-thinking habit of his. Her father did the same thing whenever he was reading one of his WWII history books by the fire during a long Nantucket winter. Sara wondered for a moment what her dad was up to right this second. It had been— what, two, maybe three weeks since she'd talked to her parents? She'd just been busy, and when she wasn't working, she was sleeping, and she hadn't wanted to call home because whenever she did, she and her mother ended up bickering ... Then, just as suddenly as the thought had arrived, she shook her head and forced herself to focus back on the moment.

"Why? Is something wrong?" she asked.

"No, no! Not at all. It's great to hear," Gavin replied. "I was hoping you'd say that. Here's the deal: I have a little thing next week, up in Boston. Sort of a banquet-type deal—they're giving me something to commemorate I-forget-what, blah blah. Just boring industry stuff, you know?"

"Yeah, totally," Sara said. She most certainly did not know, but it didn't seem like the kind of thing to admit in this particular moment.

"Anyway, I need a—well, a date, I guess you could call it. Or rather, I have an extra ticket to this little shindig that's got your name on it. Think you'd be interested?"

It took Sara several moments to catch her breath. Was it unbearably hot in here all of a sudden? The cooling system had been on the fritz lately, courtesy of a sweltering NYC summer heat wave. Sara would have to tell Louis, the head of maintenance at Lonesome Dove, to check it out.

"Uh, yeah! I mean, yes, sir. That'd be amazing."

"Sir?" Gavin laughed. "Jeez, Sara, c'mon now. I'm not that old. It's salt-and-pepper still, isn't it?" Sara guiltily raised her eyes to look Gavin in the face as he ran a hand through his thick, auburn hair. They both knew that there wasn't an ounce of salt *or* pepper in it. Just a rich, deep red, long-ish and curly, that she'd spent months dreaming of running her hands through.

She shouldn't be having these thoughts at all. Gavin and Melissa had had lunch together at Lonesome Dove barely two weeks ago. They'd certainly seemed all lovey-dovey at the time—touching hands over the tablecloth, laughing intimately at whispered inside jokes. The Melissa Question Meter was pointing firmly at *Yes*. It had made Sara's insides curdle at the time. But it seemed like a distant memory now. And here, in this office, with the scent of Gavin's cologne wafting over her like a summer breeze, and those forearms crossed as he leaned over his desk again and considered her with his amber eyes ... well,

Melissa didn't feel very real at all. She felt like a distant dream, half remembered and long forgotten. Certainly not threatening.

Besides, no one was saying that this was a real date. "Date," the way Gavin had said it, was just a turn of phrase. "Partner" would work just as well, wouldn't it? That felt much more innocuous to say. She'd be Gavin's partner for this banquet affair. That wasn't so bad at all.

"Earth to Sara? Do we have a problem? All systems go?"

She laughed again and brought herself back to reality. "No, no problems. It'd be amazing. I can't wait."

"Perfect," Gavin said with a grin worthy of a toothpaste commercial. "I'll have Kelly email you all the details. It'll be fun, I promise."

He winked.

Sara melted.

This trip might be dangerous indeed.

4

ELIZA

Eliza Benson was having a panic attack.

Christ, how long had it been since she'd last had one of these? Not since college at UPenn, probably. If then. She thought she had this kind of thing handled. Locked down. No longer a problem. Just like everything else in her life—solved.

Stuff had been going well.

Really well.

So well.

Too well?

She had the job she wanted, in the city she loved, with a man she—admired, she guessed? "Loved him" was what she'd say if she, for some bizarre reason, ended up on a daytime talk show and the host asked her how she felt about her fiancé, Clay Reeves. But it might be a stretch. Still, she was a firm believer in the idea that love could flourish over time if watered and cared for, and if that wasn't true, then maybe love wasn't the end-all, be-all, great prerequisite to life happiness that everyone claimed it was. As a matter of fact, screw love. If what she had with Clay wasn't love, then who needed it? What she had with Clay *worked* for her. It *served* her. It served them both.

They worked at the same investment bank, Goldman Sachs, in the Leveraged Finance Capital Markets group. They shared a fancy apartment with a ludicrous monthly rent and stocked it with ludicrously expensive furniture and art, courtesy of their ludicrous salaries. They worked the ludicrous hours to match, of course. That was a given. That was expected. But, like everything else in Eliza's life, that was also fine.

They rose to the same alarm and drank the same coffee, ate the same breakfast and took the same black car service to their office building every morning, six or seven days a week most weeks. They worked on the same floor and kowtowed to the same clients and came home each as exhausted as the other. Sometimes—not too often—they had fast, punctual sex. Eliza couldn't say for sure, but she figured that she and Clay probably thought about that the same way, too—they could take it or leave it.

It worked for her. It served her. It served them both.

Until today.

Clay had had a client meeting in Brooklyn, so he'd left the GS building early with a couple of their colleagues who were staffed on the same project. Eliza had stayed back to work on a slide deck that was due for review to Marty Fleishman, the firm's managing director, by seven a.m. the following morning. She'd had her team with her— three recent college grads, two from Cornell and one from Harvard. All hardworking. All very smart. All insufferably annoying.

Everything seemed to be annoying her lately. Her emotions, normally muted at most, had pinwheeled wildly over the last week and a half or so. She'd cried at a freaking dog commercial. Not even a sad one! Just a normal dog commercial, advertising some vegan keto organic dairy-free gluten-free sugar-free pet chow or something similarly ridiculous. And she'd bawled like a baby. Prior to that, she could count on two hands the number of times she'd cried in her life at all.

So that was strange. Even stranger was how her stomach turned itself inside out when one of the Cornell grad associates, Digby—honest to God, that was his name; nouveau-riche Connecticuters had no taste whatsoever—brought in a steaming platter of chicken fajitas for the team to eat while they worked. Eliza had sprinted to the bathroom.

She'd vomited until there was nothing left in her stomach, including the yogurt she'd had with her coffee that morning. The same yogurt she always had, every morning. As she threw up, she relived the taste, and she made a solemn vow then and there to get rid of every single yogurt in her refrigerator as soon as she got home and never, ever buy them again.

As she threw up, she connected the dots.

By the time she was done, she knew with a sickening horror that she was pregnant.

That was why she was having this panic attack. That was why she was curled up in a little ball on the pristine, blue-tiled floor of the bathroom of the Goldman Sachs Leveraged Finance Capital Markets department, crying hysterically.

Time seemed to go slowly while she panicked. She had hours for every passing second, or so it felt to Eliza. Enough time to examine the grout in the tile and look at the light fixtures ensconced in the ceiling above. Enough time to see the gleam from the bronze faucets on the sink and from the thrice-daily-cleaned porcelain toilets.

She had enough time to remember when she first met Clay.

He'd come on board to GS after a stint as a consultant at McKinsey. He was whip-smart and knew how to dress. Hermès ties, always thin and sharp. Shoes shined one hundred percent of the time. Not a hair out of place, ever.

It *worked* for her. It *served* her.

He'd asked Eliza out at the company Christmas party that year, barely three months after starting. That took guts. Clay was unruffled. She'd said yes.

Dinner at Tao the following week ensued. Far flashier than anything she would choose for herself, but Clay seemed to like it. He relished picking up the bill, though both knew that they made more or less the exact same amount. They'd gone from there to a cocktail bar, one of the dark and red-lit ones that seemed to be popping up all over the city these days. All the bartenders had waxed mustaches and the drinks contained four times the normal amount of alcohol at nine times the price. The bar had lots of shady corners to make out in, which was what they did.

Everything after that had fallen into place like they had planned it all in advance. Five dates before they slept together. Nine months before they moved in together. A year and a half before they were engaged.

The engagement was extravagant, as Eliza had known it would be. Helicopter ride over the city, touching down on the Goldman Sachs helicopter pad; Clay had called in a favor from the CEO to get permission. Dinner on the rooftop. White tablecloths. Champagne. A ring. Some words were spoken; Eliza said yes. It was a very big ring, and Clay really did dress well.

"I love you," he'd said. His eyes were flat the whole time, like a shark's.

"I love you," she'd said. She squelched the voice in her head that asked her if she really meant that. Clay was right for her.

What they'd managed to avoid discussing during the whole courtship was the idea of children. The one time Eliza had sort-of-kind-of brought it up—she vaguely remembered showing Clay a picture of her nephew and niece, Holly's kids—Clay had laughed and said, "Good luck to her with the little rug rats," and changed the subject.

She knew then and there that it wasn't something he wanted her to bring up again.

But it was odd that he refused to explicitly say that he didn't want to have children. Was it because he didn't want kids in general, or because he didn't want kids with her? For every second she spent weighing that question, she spent at least two refusing to acknowledge it during her waking hours.

Only in her dreams did it come up. Eliza had always been a vivid dreamer, but not necessarily a logical one. Her dreams were chaotic and confusing and rarely made an ounce of sense. But when she woke up, she was always fairly certain what they had been about, and there was an image or two that stuck with her. The first time she had the kids-or-no-kids dream, it was an image of an empty bassinet at a yard sale. Not in a horror movie kind of way. Nothing creepy about it. Just the crib, unused, sitting there in a corner. An item that she wouldn't ever need to touch, gathering dust in someone's garage. Why would *she* need to buy it? She wouldn't be having any kids, would she?

And so, with that resolution in mind, she'd put it out of mind as often as possible. She kept taking her birth control. She and Clay kept having fast, punctual sex whenever their schedules allowed. They set a wedding date twenty-three months into the future and immediately hired a wedding planner to offload all the work onto. Neither of them had time to plan a wedding. They had work to do.

Which, coincidentally, was what Eliza tried to tell herself now, as she lay on the floor of the GS bathroom and struggled to breathe. *You have work to do. Get up.* That mantra had gotten her through plenty of stuff before. It had gotten her through the NYC Marathon three years ago. Through rehab for a torn ACL, suffered when her sparring partner in a kickboxing class misheard the instruction to "Strike!" It had gotten her through all of Sara's problems, during that stint when she'd been living in a crummy rent-controlled apartment in Queens and getting into far too much trouble and Eliza was the only family member around capable of helping her out. When she'd had to pick Sara up from jail or set a broken finger that she refused to go to the hospital for, Eliza didn't panic; she didn't freak out. She just signed the paper, paid the bail. And then she resumed her work. That was how Eliza operated.

But now, her mantra was failing her. The voices in her head were screaming at her to get off that disgusting floor—although it was not really so disgusting; God knows the cleaning staff were paid enough to keep it gleaming. But, clean or not, she could. Not. Move. Not a muscle in her body would budge. Not even her lungs, which were screaming for oxygen any way they could get it.

It was a five-alarm panic attack. *Red alert! Red alert!*

She needed something to break the spell. Anything. Anything at all. Her world was narrowing down to the grout on the floor she was staring at. Her exhales were steaming the tile. The grout was rigid and perforated with little dots ...

The baby.

Your baby needs air.

She breathed.

5

MAE

Where had the day gone?

Since the moment she finally built up the willpower to extricate herself from Henry's embrace and shoo him out of the house so she could start her chores and errands unmolested, Mae had been hustling nonstop. Sweep the foyer, vacuum the car, pop down to the Stop & Shop to scoop up a few things for dinner when Holly and the kids arrived that night. You could never be quite sure when folks were going to arrive on the island—the slow ferry only left every so often, and if you missed it, you'd just have to hold your horses and wait for the next one—so she opted to make a light salad with walnuts and cranberries that she could stash in the fridge until they got in, along with a roast that just needed maybe half an hour in the oven to be ready. She also snagged a box of frozen chicken nuggets, just in case Grady decided to put up a fuss. He'd been going through alternating phases of being a picky eater and devouring everything in sight, so Mae figured it was better to be safe than sorry. She was sure that Henry would have no problem wolfing down the nuggets if Grady was on one of his "good eater" kicks.

But at the store, she'd run into Mrs. O'Malley, who'd taught first grade to each of her three youngest children, and they'd spent almost half an hour in the bread aisle catching up. Mrs. O'Malley was a sweet old lady who could use the company. Her husband had passed away not too long ago. She seemed to be doing as well as could be expected under the circumstances.

"My son is staying at that inn of yours when he visits, you know!" Mrs. O'Malley had chirped.

Mae chuckled. "Oh, that inn isn't mine, thank goodness. That's my sister-in-law's business. I don't think I'd be quite able to handle that much chaos in my own home all the time!"

Toni Benson, Henry's older sister, ran the Sweet Island Inn, down on the other end of the island. She'd bought an old, rundown former bed-and-breakfast and poured her heart and soul into it for almost eighteen months of long, long days. She'd done nearly all the renovating and redoing herself, or with Henry's assistance, whenever she could coax him into lending a helping hand. She was a tough cookie, that much was certain. Finally, it had opened, about three years prior, and been an instant success. But even with all the praise and the steady flow of business the inn received, Mae just had no idea how Toni managed. She had seasonal help when bookings were heavy, but it was mostly just her, handling all the cooking, cleaning, map-making, and restaurant-recommending that the inn and its guests required. Not to mention the business end of things, which was a black box to Mae.

Once upon a time, she might've been up to the task. She'd formerly had a successful catering business, Mae's Marvels, and it seemed like there was a lot of promise in the concept. But if running it at first had been hard enough, then running it after having her eldest, Eliza, was difficult, and running it once Holly was born was darn impossible. She'd shuttered the operation and hadn't looked back once. She might have been sad about it, but being a mother was her pride and joy, her calling in life, and she didn't regret a single moment she'd spent with her four children.

"Oh my goodness, is that the time already?" she yelped when she happened to see a clock hanging on the wall of the grocery store. "Mrs. O'Malley, you'll have to excuse me. Holly and the kids are coming to stay with us for the weekend, and I am nowhere near ready!" She gave Mrs. O'Malley a kiss on the cheek—a flourish she'd learned from a distant French cousin and always been fond of—and hurried back home.

Now, Hurricane Mae was in full effect. She mopped the kitchen floor and each of the upstairs bathrooms, changed the linens in all three bedrooms, and dusted every single ledge and surface she could reach. She even fished her footstool out of the packed junk closet and did the top ledge of the mantel, the spot she always made Henry get because she wasn't quite tall enough to reach it on her own.

Finally, the place was starting to resemble a home rather than a pigsty. She was exhausted. She let herself sink into an armchair and close her eyes for a moment. One of the windows was open facing the water. It let in a warm ocean's breeze that tickled her nose with the sharp scent of salt. She let out a long sigh. Sixty-one years of age might not be quite too old to laugh around in bed with her husband on a lazy morning, but it sure felt too old to be running wild around her house like this. Her feet were aching already. She opened one eye and peeked at the wooden grandfather clock that stood on the far end of the room, catty-corner to the fireplace. It was almost three p.m. already. Holly and Pete were due in sometime around five, if all went according to plan on their drive up from Plymouth. A few more small things remained to tidy up and prepare, but the house was mostly in shape, thank goodness.

Mae bent over to pull her cell phone out of the side table drawer. She still didn't know how to work the thing all that well, but she'd managed to pin Brent down long enough to make him explain the core features, and she got by just fine with that much. When she had her reading glasses settled into place and the phone powered on, she frowned. No voice mails or text messages from Henry. That was unusual. He always texted her just before the boat left shore. It was another running joke between them, that she was like an eighteenth-century woman seeing her husband off on a whaling voyage. Sometimes, when he was taking the boat out to a spot on this side of the island, she'd clamber up to the widow's walk on the roof of their house and use binoculars to try and spot him. He'd mooned her once, and even from a mile away, she could make out the laughter when he turned back around and flashed a smile.

But today, radio silence. It would've been nice if he'd messaged her.

6

SARA

"Well, look at you all dolled up!" Gavin said. "You know, I don't think I've seen you in anything but work whites since our first interview."

Sara blushed. She was unwilling to admit even to herself how long she'd spent picking out her outfits for this trip, or how many friends she'd consulted via FaceTime on which heels to bring, which shirts were too low, whether rose gold or silver earrings sent the better message.

"Thanks," she mumbled. "You look great, as always."

As soon as the words were out of her mouth, she wanted to slap herself. Before, during, and after the wardrobe and packing processes, she'd given herself a long pep talk in the mirror, complete with finger pointing and lots of furious stares into her own eyes.

You will NOT act like a fool on this trip, Sara Benson. This is a professional trip and you will conduct yourself accordingly. You will not babble. You will not clam up. You will not behave like a high school teenager going to the movies with her crush. Got it? Kapisch?

She'd answered her own question with a firm "Yes!" that had echoed around her tiny East Village studio apartment. For a second or two, she even believed that she meant it.

Gavin's presence, of course, rendered that entire speech moot the second he strolled up to her at their terminal at JFK airport. He was wearing what she'd come to think of as the Gavin Uniform. She'd considered in idle moments whether Congress should pass a law banning anyone else from wearing the same. No one else could really do it justice like he could. Brown leather Clarks boots, left unlaced; dark denim jeans, slim enough to be flattering but not so skinny as to fall into hipster territory; and a plaid shirt with the sleeves rolled up to expose his forearms. It was casual, it was handsome, it was perfect.

The crowd around them buzzed and flowed. Sara ripped her eyes off her boss—her firmly forbidden, totally off-limits boss—and looked around them. She'd always loved airports. There was a sense of possibility that few other places could match. Like, if she was just one or two percent more spontaneous, she'd switch her ticket to somewhere unexpected and exciting and jet off on the adventure of a lifetime. She'd done something kind of like that, once, with a fun and reckless sort-of-boyfriend during her first year in the city. They'd shown up to LaGuardia with a backpack each. She was wearing a bikini under her sweater and had brought both mittens and sunscreen stashed away in various pockets. Ready for whatever. They ended up in Coeur d'Alene, Idaho, by dint of a random number draw, and spent three days jumping off rocks into the lake and eating potatoes in every form imaginable. That was a good memory.

This was a leap of faith of a whole different variety. More of an "out of the frying pan, into the fire" situation, actually. Because if being near Gavin at Lonesome Dove—a public establishment constantly buzzing with the cream of Manhattan's foodie elite crop—was already stressful, then flying solo with him on a quote-unquote "business trip" might be the straw that broke the Benson's back.

One step at a time, she counseled herself. *This will be over before you know it. Drama-free. Just a nice bonding trip with the boss. No sweat. No pressure.*

For a second, she even believed that, too.

Gavin smiled at her again. But, before she was forced to shove her foot even farther in her mouth than it already was, the airline employee announced boarding for their flight and they were promptly whisked onboard.

Sara had never flown first class before. It was a nice change of pace from her norm. Champagne before takeoff was a relief on her frayed nerves. It also was helpful in washing down the half of a Xanax that she'd bummed off Benny before leaving the restaurant yesterday. Between that and the roar of the airplane as they hurtled down the runway and took off, she dozed off before she could stop it.

She woke up with a start when they landed, a little bumpily.

"First-time pilot, I bet," Gavin grumbled. "Hack job on the landing."

"I'm sure he's trying his best," Sara said. She sounded just like her mother, jeez.

"Aren't we all?"

"Definitely. I'm trying my best not to look like an idiot on this trip," she blurted.

Gavin turned in his seat to look at her. Sara could do nothing but laugh. She might as well throw the rest of her caution to the wind, because they hadn't even landed in Boston yet and she was already breaking her self-promise not to act like a fool.

It was weird; she'd never been much of a lovestruck type before. She'd been the one to break up with every boyfriend she'd ever had.

She just got bored of them. People in general didn't intimidate her, ruffle her feathers, or throw her off the beat of the drummer that she marched to. Except for Gavin. But, somehow or another, he'd worked out the magic formula to get under her skin and throw a monkey wrench in her inner workings. She was curious what exactly that formula might consist of. There was the obvious, of course: the Gavin Uniform, those forearms, that mysterious cologne. She'd tried to find it once in a Macy's men's cosmetics section out of self-destructive curiosity, but she'd gone through thirty or forty different samples and couldn't find the right one. But underlying all those obvious attractors was just some ineffable Gavin-ness. She was too smart to believe that she was falling all over herself for him simply because he was both attractive and off-limits. She knew that was a deadly combo if ever there was one. But that timeless trap was for girls way ditzier than her. She—Sara Alexandra Benson—would never make such a foolish mistake.

Right?

"There's nothing to be nervous about, you know," Gavin reminded her. He'd said it a few times over the course of the week between him extending the invitation and their departure, but she'd laughed it off every time. Of course there was a lot to be nervous about! Three days! In Boston! With Gavin Crawford! The possibilities were endless, and each one was more horrific than the last. At best, this ended with a cordial handshake and a "See you on Monday!" At worst—well, she didn't want to imagine the worst-case scenario.

"Right. Not a worry in the world. That's me, Sara Benson. Notorious non-worrier."

Gavin chuckled as the seat-belt sign overhead dinged off and they stood up to retrieve their bags from overhead. "You're a funny one, Sara. Your boyfriend must love that."

"Boyfriend? Me? You're the funny one," she said.

"Really? No boyfriend? Well, how 'bout that. You're depriving the men of Manhattan of something really special."

Sara blushed again, harder than the first time. Since when was she a blusher? She was fair-complected, yeah—thanks a lot, Irish ancestry —but she couldn't recall the last time she'd spent so many consecutive minutes turning beet-red at the simplest stupid joke.

"Ah well, you know," she said, shooting for "casual." "Gotta make 'em work for it."

She wrestled her bag from the overhead bin to the ground without incident and hurried off the plane before she could find something else stupid to say.

They had a black car service waiting for them outside the terminal. The driver, a tall, skinny man wearing sunglasses and a peaked chauffeur's cap, was holding a placard with Gavin's name on it. It read "Gavin Crawford & Guest." Sara wasn't sure what to make of that. She decided not to think about it.

The driver insisted on taking the bags out of Sara's hands and stowing them in the trunk. Then he whisked them away to the Ritz-Carlton.

The banquet would be held that night in the ballroom, but they still had a few hours to kill before then. Gavin suggested they drop their bags in their rooms and go walk around downtown. They approached the concierge's desk.

"Good afternoon!" chirped the blonde woman. "Welcome to the Ritz-Carlton. May I have your name, please?" She had shoulder-length hair, pressed stick-straight, and a dark navy pantsuit on. She exuded a sense of competent, put-together professionalism that Sara was wildly jealous of at that moment. She'd trade a pinky toe for ten percent of that aura. She herself was feeling more like the cat from *Tom & Jerry*—she could never remember which one of them was Tom and which was Jerry—in that one episode where he's juggling eggs and the mouse keeps adding more and more eggs to the mix, until there are too many to manage and the cat starts missing them and they come falling down to break with a *splat* on his head, one by one by one.

"Good afternoon, darling," Gavin drawled. "Gavin Crawford."

She smiled. "Welcome, Mr. Crawford! If you'll give me just one moment, I'll pull up your reservation and do everything I can to make sure you enjoy your stay with us." Suddenly, Sara wasn't so sure that it was competent professionalism after all. The woman seemed to be smiling a little wider towards Gavin than she had when she'd first greeted Sara. Sara could almost swear that she'd undone the top button on her blouse and leaned forward a little more as she tapped away at the computer.

"Thanks, hon," Gavin replied.

Sara gave him a sidelong glance. For his part, he sure seemed to be pouring on the charm thick for this concierge lady. Now that she looked close, Sara thought the woman's hair was way too straight, and she had an awful lot of split ends.

"Here we ... Oh wait—oh, I'm so sorry, Mr. Crawford. It looks like we had a mix-up with the rooms ... Give me just one more second, please."

Sara's heart leaped up into her throat. This was it—the beginning of her undoing. The setup to a horrible romantic comedy scenario. The room wouldn't be ready, and every hotel in town would be full, and they'd have to share a single bed, and everything would explode into a nuclear-scale disaster because she just could possibly be left alone with Gavin Crawford behind closed doors ...

"There we go, all fixed!" the woman chimed. "Unfortunately, we will need just a few more minutes to finish preparing your room. The guest in the Presidential Suite before you overstayed, and our cleaning crew has not yet had a chance to prepare it for your stay. My sincerest apologies. I can offer you a complimentary drink from our downstairs bar to thank you for your patience. Oh—and your guest, as well." There was no mistaking the tone in the woman's voice at the end. It was either pity, as in "look what the cat dragged in," or maybe just straight-up jealousy. Either way, Sara didn't like it one bit. In a previous life, she might've had some choice words for this woman— her mom always joked that Sara must have some Viking blood in her, because she never backed down from a fight. Heck, even a few years ago, a younger and more temperamental Sara might've had some choice words. But she was old enough now to know better. Certainly old enough to just take a deep breath, smile, and say, "Thank you." Part of her almost meant it.

"We'll keep your bags secure in the bellhop's quarters until your rooms are ready. The bar is directly behind you. I'll call ahead and let the bartender know that you're coming, if you'd like?"

"Don't suppose we can say no to free alcohol, can we?" Gavin said. "Shall we?" He turned to Sara and offered his elbow like an old-timey Southern gentleman. Sara suppressed a giggle, jealousies forgotten, as she looped her arm through his. They sauntered off to the bar, leaving the flirty concierge to wrangle their luggage into the back room.

The bar inside was lit low and had soft music ushering through the speakers. The bartender greeted them. "Mr. and Mrs. Crawford?" The concierge must have called ahead like she'd said.

Sara started to correct the man, but before she could get the words out of her mouth, Gavin intervened.

"Something like that. Can I get a Crown Royal on the rocks? And a vodka gimlet for the lady, extra dry."

He remembered her go-to drink. That was weird. They'd been out on the town together as a staff at Lonesome Dove a couple of times. Once was after their soft opening for friends and family, and the other time was after the Michelin star was announced. But it was never just Gavin and Sara. It was always all the servers and line cooks and back-of-the-house crews mixed in together, getting wildly drunk like only restaurant workers know how to do. But somehow, amidst all that chaos, he remembered her drink. She decided not to think about that, either.

They took a seat near the unlit fireplace. Sara looked around. It was a moderate-sized bar, exquisitely decorated. Dark wooden and steel furniture was spread around most of the floor space in clusters of chairs, a few booths, a couple low couches. A massive fireplace took up one side of the room, done up in white marble and set into the wood-paneled walls. The atmosphere was sophisticated and cozy.

"How's the drink?" Gavin asked as they settled into their seats. She was perched at the end of a couch, and he was sprawled comfortably in the armchair next to her.

Sara took a sip of her vodka gimlet. "Yikes. Strong." The sleeping pill and champagne from the flight were mostly faded away now, but she was still wary of getting too drunk and making a fool of herself. This tasted like the bartender had mixed it with equal parts gasoline and moonshine. She resolved to sip as slowly as humanly possible.

"You're from up near the Cape, right?" he said.

Sara nodded. "Nantucket, actually."

"Ah, Nantucket. Beautiful place. I went up there a few years back, stayed in a nice little B&B. Sweet Island Inn, I think it was called. You ever heard of it?"

She almost choked on her drink in surprise. "Kind of. My aunt owns it, actually."

Gavin's eyes widened. He laughed and slapped a knee. "You're kidding! Well, that's crazy. Small world, I guess."

"Small island."

He nodded. "Yep, that too."

Sara heard a buzz. Her eyes strayed down to the table. There, next to his keys where he'd dropped them when they sat down, was Gavin's cell phone. He had a text lighting up his home screen.

The sender's name was saved in his contacts as *Melissa Babe <3*.

This time, Sara actually did choke.

"Whoa there!" Gavin said in alarm. He jumped up and pounded her on the back with a broad, flat hand. Despite the coughing fit, it wasn't lost on her that Gavin Crawford was actually touching her. Sara coughed until her eyes were studded with tears. Finally, she managed to catch her breath.

"I'm fine, I'm fine," she insisted weakly. "It's okay." She raised a hand to wave him back to his seat and accidentally brushed against his torso. It wasn't lost on her either that, beneath his plaid shirt, his body was very firm and muscular.

She'd been ignoring the Melissa Question since the moment Gavin popped the question of this Boston trip. And by "ignoring," she meant considering obsessively and then yelling at herself for doing just that.

Part of the issue was that the Melissa Question was really a bunch of questions all knotted up in one. *Who is she? Where is she? What are they? What does she think they are? What does Gavin think they are? Whose opinion matters more?* And on and on like that, leading nowhere productive but taking up all of Sara's available brain space anyway.

She hadn't seen what Melissa had texted Gavin, but the mere fact that she was texting him at all was enough to send her heart plummeting into her stomach acid. All of this was wrong. She shouldn't have said yes to this trip. She shouldn't be drinking a dangerously strong drink in this super nice bar with this ridiculously handsome man, who was utterly and completely off-limits to her.

And, beyond that, she should've said yes when Benny asked her out in her first week at the restaurant. She should've never gone to NYC in the first place. She should've stayed in Nantucket and kept working the line at the Club Car. She should've found a dark cave and become a hermit, maybe.

Any or all those choices could have prevented her from ending up in this exact circumstance. She wished she'd made one of them at the very least. Because she didn't want to be the other woman or just another notch on Gavin's belt. No, that wasn't appealing at all. But the worst part was that, if that particular opportunity arose, she didn't trust herself to say no.

"Excuse me?" said the bartender, approaching politely. "Your room is ready, if you'd like to go up now."

"Actually, we just—" Gavin started to say.

Sara cut him off. "Yes!" Way too loud, way too enthusiastic. She cleared her throat and moderated her tone a little bit. "Yes, that would be lovely, thank you. Lead the way." She put the way-too-strong drink on the table and left it in her rear-view mirror. That would only bring more trouble, and she was already up to her eyeballs in that.

7

BRENT

How had everything gone so wrong, so fast?

It had taken a bit to wait in line at the pumps and then get the boats gassed up, along with arranging all the rods and fishing tackle for the day's expedition. But soon, all those chores were behind them. The only thing left awaiting them was the gentle toss of the tide and some fish—hungry ones, hopefully. But forty-five minutes of motoring out to the first spot, and then an hour of casting and reeling had yielded … not a dang thing.

They'd gone from there to a second spot, and then to a third, but nothing was biting anywhere they looked. The ocean around them was calm and blue. Brent's boat, *Jenny Lee,* was anchored a few dozen yards away, so the pair of them were both manning Dad's *Pour Decisions.* His father was seated up top in the captain's chair with the long line that reached way off. Brent was perched down below on the stern with a few shorter lines set up in the rod-holders around him, gazing around into the bright sun.

"*Fish ain't going anywhere*, eh?" Brent grumbled sarcastically under his voice, repeating his father's line from earlier at the dock. He knew he was being cranky. Obviously, none of this was his dad's fault. But something in Brent was just a little bit sour at the prospect of a fruitless day.

He knew a trademark Henry-ism was coming. *Three, two, one ...*

"Life is meant to be enjoyed, isn't it?" Dad called from overhead. "The sun is shining, the birds are chirping, I'm out fishing with my son. I'd say things are A-okay, kiddo. Lighten up!"

Brent sighed. He knew his dad was right. He also didn't doubt that the six-pack of beers his dad had been nursing all morning wasn't hurting his mood at all. Brent eyed the beers wistfully. Eleven months of sobriety wasn't something he was willing to toss overboard in exchange for one lukewarm Bud Light, but he'd be lying if he said he didn't miss drinking. Still, some things were better left in the past, and he'd learned the hard way—and then learned it again and again —that alcohol and Brent Benson did not mix well.

"Oy!" shouted Dad from up top. "Got somethin'!"

Brent perked up, head on a swivel as he looked around to see which of the rods had gotten a hit. One of the ones stationed at the port side was bowed over. He raced towards it and plucked the rod out of the holder. The reel was whizzing yards and yards of line freely. Brent let it go for a moment longer before locking it in and yanking back as hard as he could in order to get the hook set.

"Something *big!*" Dad chortled gleefully. Despite himself, Brent laughed. He was dimly aware of his father scaling down the ladder and coming up behind him. But all his attention was focused on the fight with the fish. Dad was right; it was something big indeed. Brent was sweating already, and the muscles on his back were straining hard as he played the delicate game of tug and release, reel and relax, over and over.

Minutes passed, but inch by inch, he was gaining on the sucker.

"You got it, son!" Dad encouraged. "Get it in!"

Finally, a full twenty minutes of fighting later, the catch was almost close enough for Dad to use the net on it. One more yank and twist, a little more reeling, Pops swept down with the net in hand, and ...

Boom. The catch hit the deck hard.

It was a dead shark.

Brent always hated seeing stuff like this. Sure, he was a fisherman by trade, and this was par for the course in his line of work. But he had some of his father's softness at heart, and something about a dead animal that wouldn't get properly used just didn't sit right with him. He felt—well, not quite guilty, but something akin to guilt. Whether the animal had bled out on the hook or been chomped on by something else during the fight, Brent couldn't be sure. But either way, he'd had a hand in sending this creature to shark heaven.

"This day really does stink," Brent groaned. He fell into a seat at the back of the boat. A beer would've been especially nice right about now.

That had been an hour ago. After the shark debacle, all the wind went right out of Brent's sails. He'd hopped back onto *Jenny Lee* and followed his dad to the next spot, but there was just no more fight left in him. He was hungry, and tired, and the tug-of-war with the shark had sapped the last of his strength. He wanted to go back to his apartment, nest on the couch, and watch Red Sox baseball on television for the rest of the day.

Brent pulled up alongside *Pour Decisions*. "I'm done, Pops," he called over to his father, who was fiddling with one of the rods.

Dad looked up, surprised. "So soon?"

"Nothing's biting, I'm tired, I'm hungry, and if one more souped-up mega boat tries to come muscle in on our spot, I'm gonna lose it. Also, that looks like a nasty storm brewing off to the east. Let's just go home. Live to fight another day."

His father nodded slowly. Around them, the waves sloshed a little more angrily than they had when the men first set out that morning. Brent was right; that storm in the distance was dark, angry-looking, and picking up speed in this direction.

"You go ahead on in, son," his dad replied. "I'm gonna try one more spot. The Garden never fails, right?"

Brent shook his head. "No way, Dad. The Garden is at least twenty minutes to the east. Maybe more, if the chop picks up. You'd be heading straight for that storm. If you catch a cold getting soaked to the skin, Mom's gonna take my head off, not yours. Just come in with me and we'll go hang out at the house."

But his father was already standing and climbing up the ladder to the captain's seat. "No worries, Brent!" he called over his shoulder as he hauled himself up and took his place behind the wheel. "The Garden of Eden will have fish aplenty! We'll bring some home for your mama, and I'll even let you take partial credit for catching tonight's dinner."

Brent sighed for the umpteenth time that day. Fine. So be it. If his dad wanted to suffer through bone-chilling rain and a nausea-inducing ride out and back just to still come home empty-handed, that wasn't Brent's problem. Lord knows he had done similarly foolish things before and would do more in the future. And nobody on this planet could stop him when he had an idea like that in his head. Brent might be stubborn as a mule, but he'd learned everything he knew from his dad. He'd be better off saving his breath.

"You sure, Dad?" he asked. Might as well try one last time. If nothing else, he could say he gave it an honest effort.

But his father was already firing up the motors and didn't hear him.

Jenny Lee was washed down, loaded up on the trailer, and Brent had gone into the marina to chat with Roger. But *Pour Decisions* still hadn't returned home. Brent frowned. The storm in the distance wasn't so distant anymore. Up close and personal, it looked to be a particularly gruesome one, one of the fierce thunderstorms that sometimes came swooping down on Nantucket every now and then during the spring to drop four inches of rain and then disappear like a bad ex. It was rough enough being caught outdoors on the road during one of those suckers. Brent didn't like the idea of being caught on a boat during one of them.

He tried his dad's cell phone. He knew it was a long shot; cell service out at the fishing spot his dad had wanted to try, the Garden of Eden, was sketchy at best. Even if the call did go through, Henry wasn't exactly the world's greatest at keeping his cell on hand.

Buzz. Buzz. Buzz.

"Hello, this is Henry Benson. Leave a message, and I'll—"

Brent hung up. He resolved to give it one more try. *Buzz. Buzz. Buzz.*

"Hello, this is—"

Brent turned to the counter. Roger, the marina owner, was lounging behind it, smoking a cigarette and blowing the smoke out through a cracked window. He was in his mid-forties, with light brown hair, though balding enough to be the butt of jokes from some of the old-timers who came through the marina each day. A big anchor tattoo poked out from under his right shirtsleeve, like a Popeye caricature.

"Roger, when my dad gets back in, tell him to give me a call, will you?"

"No problem," Roger said. "He might need you to bring him a towel, at the rate that thing's cooking." He jutted his cigarette out through the window at the dark storm clouds.

"That he might," Brent replied, laughing.

8

ELIZA

When she'd pulled herself together, Eliza rinsed out her mouth in the bathroom sink and washed her hands. She was breathing fine now, but the sharp tang of fear that the panic attack left behind had not gone away. Maybe it never would.

She looked herself in the mirror and took stock of what she saw. Her hair was blonde, like everyone else in her family, though hers was a little thicker and more golden-hued than the others. She had some natural waves and curls in it. Most days, she wore it pinned up or pulled back in a bun. She'd decided to wear it down today, just in time to puke her guts out at work. Perfect timing. Back up it went. Her eyes were almond-shaped and a light greenish gray, set a little too narrow around a nose that she'd always thought went on just slightly too long. Below that, her lips were drawn in a thin line. If she didn't insist on the vanity of regular spray-tans, she'd be pale-skinned.

She looked like what she was: serious, driven, cold. *Had her eyes always looked so frigid?* she wondered. Truth be told, it had been some time since she'd really stared at herself in a mirror quite like this. She wasn't sure she liked it. In fact, she decided that she did not.

She took a deep breath and strode out of the bathroom, back towards the conference room where her team was assembled, cranking away on spreadsheets. The smell of fajitas was as nauseating as it was before. Eliza held her breath as best she could while she delivered her news.

"Something came up. I have to go. Send me the draft by midnight." She didn't stay to answer questions. Just pivoted on her Louboutin heel and went back out the way she'd come. She walked confidently, head held high, through the foyer and into the elevator. Down, out, through the atrium towards the big glass doors.

Only when she hit the street did she start to run.

There was a CVS situated a few blocks away. She got there as fast as she could, doing her best to ignore the pounding of her heart. Bursting through the doors of the pharmacy, she went straight back to the family planning section.

"Where, where, where ..." she muttered under her breath as she scanned the shelves. There. She grabbed three of the most expensive pregnancy tests and went immediately to the checkout counter. The kid behind the counter, a pimply teenager with unruly curls, asked her if she wanted to join the CVS Rewards program. She did not. She wanted to pay for these tests, confirm ASAP that her worst nightmare had come to life, and then figure out what on earth she was going to do about it.

Clay was not going to like this. Clay was going to hate this, actually. She knew that with a certainty that surprised her. After all, they hadn't talked about it much. They hadn't talked about *anything* much. They talked about work, of course, and they gossiped about the city, just like every New Yorker does. They swore up and down that they were going to leave just as soon as they made enough money. Each knew that the other was lying. They were bound to this city, by profession and temperament. Nowhere else gave the same adrenaline rush. Nowhere else was as fruitlessly addicting. They weren't going anywhere.

Good luck to her with the little rug rats.

She shivered. This was bad.

When she had swiped her credit card and snatched the plastic bag from the cashier's hands, she asked, "Bathroom?" The kid pointed towards the back. She nodded and strode off in that direction.

It took a lot of effort to make herself walk. But for some reason, she didn't want to embarrass herself any further in the eyes of the CVS employee. It was a silly thought—she was a powerful finance executive on Wall Street; why did she need the approval of an acne-scarred seventeen-year-old working a menial part-time job after school? The kid had enough to worry about trying to get a date to prom, and—she stopped herself. That was a rude thought. And unnecessary. Her own child might one day have pimples or messy hair. It was certainly plausible enough. What would she think if some stone-cold ice queen marched up on her child and made him or her feel small for no good reason at all? What gave her the right to be so condescending to this teenager? He'd done nothing wrong.

Her thoughts were pinwheeling all over the place as she barged into the single-occupancy bathroom and locked the door behind her. Ripping the first pregnancy test out of the box, she did her thing and set it on the counter. Then, the next. And the next. She closed her eyes and counted up to one hundred and then back down. Then she looked.

Positive.

Positive.

Positive.

This did not work for her. This did not serve her.

~

She decided to take the subway home. She normally took a black car service to and from work, since Goldman Sachs paid for it. But right now, she didn't want to be alone in that cold, sterile environment. She needed people around her. Sweaty people, bored people, weird people, normal people—just *people* of any variety. Living. Breathing. Doing normal people things.

Her life felt suddenly very much not normal. Why was that? Having a baby was a perfectly normal thing. Normal people got engaged to other normal people and procreated. They raised normal families and lived long, normal lives. Happy lives. Or something close enough to happy lives to pass the smell test.

So why did this feel like a death sentence?

Eliza laughed under her breath. It wasn't a happy laugh. More of a sarcastic, woe-is-me laugh. A gallows laugh. Of course this would happen to her. If birth control was 99.99 percent effective, then of course she would be the 0.01 percent exception to that rule.

She'd had a lucky enough life so far, that was for sure. She'd been born on Nantucket to parents who loved her. She was naturally good at softball and volleyball. She'd excelled academically. UPenn had given her a spot on the team to play softball, and she'd excelled there, too. Then, Goldman interviewed Eliza her senior year, and, as everyone in her universe expected, she excelled. She got the job. Moved to the city. She'd been the second-youngest female ever promoted to her position. Her fiancé was handsome and rich. That was a lot of blessings for one person.

Maybe now was just her turn to get screwed.

9

SARA

The elevator ride up to the room was as awkward as Sara could possibly have imagined. She didn't look at Gavin, not even once, for fear that he'd be able to see the battle raging in her eyes or the pounding of her heart against her rib cage. She was pretty sure that she could hear it herself. *Ba-bum. Ba-bum.* Like a warning signal that this was all one no-good, very bad, terrible idea from the get-go. What had she been thinking? Gavin was taken. The Melissa Question wasn't a question at all. It was a firm "Stay away." A no-fly zone if ever there was one.

And she'd ignored it.

When the bell dinged to let them know they'd arrived at their floor— the top one, naturally; Gavin never did anything halfway or substandard—she hustled off before he could.

"Sara."

She froze in place. She was already a half-dozen steps down the hallway ahead of him. But his voice halted her in her tracks. She was powerless to resist. Therein lay the problem.

"Yes?" she said, as innocently as she could muster.

"What's going on with you?"

She turned her head slightly, just enough to see his booted feet on the intricately woven carpet. She raked her gaze up, past the dark-stained jeans tucked into the boots, past the hem of his plaid shirt, past the arms crossed over his chest. She steeled herself and made eye contact. Gavin was looking at her, head tilted to one side like a curious puppy. His eyes were swimming with something unreadable.

"Nothing," she said. "Just a little drowsy from the flight and the drink."

"BS," he said right away. "Something's up. Talk to me."

Could it really be that easy? Could she just ask him the Melissa Question? No freaking way, right? That would be crossing so many lines as to be unthinkable. It would be like shoving all her chips into the middle of the table and laying her hand face-up for the world to see. It would be tantamount to saying, *I'm obsessed with you and I can't make it stop.*

Curse her genes. She blamed her dad. The inveterate whittler, the can't-stop-won't-stop man who raised her. Henry was like a dog with a bone when he found something he liked. He'd eaten Bill & Ted's Excellent Cereal every single morning she could remember, ever since that awful Hollywood-branded gruel had come out in the wake of the movie. When they stopped making it, he went around to every grocery store within a hundred-mile radius to buy up their surplus, and when that well went dry, he'd gone on eBay and hounded every seller he could find into giving up their stash to him, too. They used to have a closet full of Bill & Ted's Excellent Cereal at their house on Nantucket. She remembered asking him what was so good about it. He'd just shrugged and said, "It suits me."

Maybe that was part of the problem. Gavin suited her perfectly. He smelled like heaven and he was so funny when he chose to be. He was kind—she'd personally witnessed him peeling hundred-dollar bills out of his wallet when he'd overheard a dishwasher talking about being too broke to buy dinner for himself and the kid brother he was raising. He was bold and creative. The awards ceremony that evening in his honor was testament to that. It was like some mad scientist had gone digging through Sara's brain and picked out all the pieces that she'd liked in every boyfriend she'd ever had, and concocted the man who was standing behind her right now and—

Wait, no, he was coming around in front of her. He was circling to stand toe-to-toe with Sara, and then—what in the world?—he was pulling her towards him with a hand on each hip and kissing her.

Seeing how this was the culmination of over six months of near-daily fantasies, Sara expected to have a lot of thoughts running through her head at that moment. She guessed that she'd be thinking *Finally!* or *Oh no!* or something along those lines. But instead, her mind went completely and utterly blank. All she could think about was that he was every bit as good of a kisser as she anticipated. She could smell him filling her nostrils. The scruff of his five-o'clock shadow rasped against her own cheeks and lips as they kissed in the middle of the hotel hallway.

Didn't she deserve to be happy? Screw the rules. Screw the gossip. She did deserve this. She'd worked hard, hadn't she, over the years, to get in a position to—well, not to do this, exactly, but maybe something along these lines? She'd done everything Gavin had asked of her and more. She'd built up the kitchen into a team of all-stars. She'd served food that wowed critics and patrons alike. She'd arrived early and stayed late and done all the nitty-gritty dirty work in between. So yes, she deserved this. She'd finally found something worth really striving for, and now that that something was holding her in his arms and kissing her like a Disney prince come to life, she was going to let all her worries boil away and just enjoy it.

Until—

"What the hell?"

Gavin and Sara broke apart. Neither of them had heard the elevator ding or heard the footsteps of the person who exited it. And it was safe to say that neither of them expected Melissa to walk in at that moment.

Sara spun around. She'd never properly faced Melissa before. Seeing her in the past had always meant peering around a corner while she and Gavin sat together at a corner table or in his office or taking subtle glances at the framed pictures in Gavin's office. So, in this moment, looking at her face-to-face for the first time, was like seeing a movie star in person. A little smaller than she'd expected, a little less glamorous. The most notable thing about this moment was how non-notable it actually was. In all her dreaming about the various roads that might've led to a moment like this—kissing Gavin—she'd never pictured it unfolding in quite this way. Melissa hadn't ever been involved in those daydreams, except in an "I left her for you" sort of scenario.

She was just about Sara's height. She had dark brown hair with a little wave and volume to it. She was wearing it down right now. The ringlets at the very end lay on her collarbone, which was pale and adorned with a nice pearl necklace. She was wearing a navy blue dress that was flattering to her frame, along with a pair of nude pumps. It was clear as day to Sara that Melissa had dressed up for Gavin specifically.

"Babe!" gasped the man in question. Perhaps realizing how pathetic he sounded, he cleared his throat and tried again. "Melissa. What are you doing here?"

Melissa looked back and forth between Sara and Gavin. "I came to surprise you. The real question is, what is *she* doing here?"

"It's not what it looks like," Gavin said at once. "She came on to me. I was trying to push her off, but she wouldn't stop."

Sara's jaw dropped.

She whirled to face him. "I what?" she yelped.

Gavin's eyes never left Melissa's as he held up a hand in Sara's face to silence her. It made her so mad that she actually lost track of everything for a moment.

She had a bizarre flashback to a memory from—jeez, that must've been at least fifteen years ago, maybe more. Another fight with Mom, neither the first nor the worst nor the last. She couldn't even recall what this one was about. Probably something related to her bedtime curfew, or grades in school, or neglecting one or another of the various chores she was supposed to take care of around the house. She'd probably said some cruel things to her mother, because that's what Sara did at that point in her life. She and Mae had been standing at either end of the upstairs hallway. Sara had been screaming, she was pretty sure; her mom, on the other hand, had never been much of a screamer. Even when Sara got most worked up, Mae didn't really scream all that much. She was just too mellow by nature. Too kind. It had taken Sara a long time to realize that about Mae.

Eventually, after the worst of the screaming had passed them by, both women retreated to their respective corners to cry. Sara's father had knocked on her door.

"Sara," he'd said. She looked up at once because there was something in his voice that she didn't hear very often. *Happy Henry* was what her mom called him most mornings, as in, "Hello there, Happy Henry! Nice of you to join us!" But he didn't sound all that happy in that moment. He sounded somewhere north of serious and west of sad. *Somber* might be a good word for it. *Melancholy* might work, too.

"Come walk with me," he'd said then. Under 99.9 percent of normal circumstances, young Sara would've told him to stick his walk where the sun don't shine. She was feisty to a fault. It would take her a long time to learn how to temper her temper. But on this occasion, she didn't protest. She got silently to her feet from the beanbag in her bedroom and followed her dad out of the house.

They hadn't talked for a long time as they walked. She realized soon that he was headed for the beach. It had been cool but not cold outside. Must've been early fall—mid-September, or thereabouts. She'd just walked alongside him, head down, thoughts still swirling around whatever it was that her mom had fussed at her about.

Dad had walked her down to the water's edge and stopped there. He picked up a shell and skipped it across the moonlit waves. Then she did the same. They stayed there and threw shells for a while. There wasn't anybody else on the beach that night, so it was just the sound of the breeze in the dunes, the *shush-shush-shush* of the ebbing waves, and the tinny *plink* of the shells hitting the water when they threw them. It felt like she was throwing away little shards of her anger, piece by piece. She wasn't sure how many she threw or how long she stood there, but after a while, she realized she wasn't mad anymore.

Somehow, her dad knew that, too. He'd turned to her then. She could see it so vividly—the moon hit his eyes and bounced off his hair. It was still blond back then. He'd taken a knee so that he could look her right in the eyes—this was pre-growth-spurt Sara. "You're my little raging bull," he said with that somber half smile. "You go after what you want, always. And, contrary to what you might think, I don't ever want you to lose that part of yourself." He paused and looked out onto the horizon. Then he turned back to her. "But be nice to your mother. She loves you. She needs you. And she'll always be here when you need her, too."

She didn't remember crying in that moment, but maybe she did. If not then, then definitely back in her bedroom. Her dad's love felt so real then, on the moonlit beach. So tangible. So physical. Even now, separated by hundreds of miles and a dozen years, it almost felt like she could reach into her pocket and grab it again if she wanted to.

She looked up at Gavin's pointer finger, held in front of her face in a "Wait one sec" sign. Then she looked over to Melissa. It was obvious to Sara that Melissa was heartbroken. She wondered what the woman was going to choose.

It seemed pretty clear that there were two possible paths leading out of this point in time. Melissa could either elect to believe Sara that Gavin had been the one to kiss *her*, or she could choose to believe that Sara was a homewrecker and an employee who had brazenly crossed a very clear line.

Sara was not surprised when Melissa's eyes slid from Gavin to Sara herself, and the woman's face hardened. "You should go," she hissed. "Now."

Sara left. She called her mom on the way out.

10

BRENT

Brent was dead asleep when his phone started to buzz. His couch had been every bit as comfortable as he'd anticipated, the Red Sox playing a close one against the A's, and a much-deserved nap welcomed him with open arms.

But the sleep hadn't been as comforting as he wanted. That dead shark flopped around everywhere he looked in his dreams. Blood on the deck of the boat, scales flying, saltwater stinging his eyes.

Waking up with a start, Brent fumbled for his vibrating phone. He knocked it to the floor, then accidentally swept it under the couch. He groaned, got on all fours, and finally retrieved it. "Hello?" he answered wearily as he knuckled the sleep from his eyes.

"Brent, it's Roger."

"Roger?" That was unusual. Why would Roger be calling him? Brent checked his watch. It was 4:45. His sister Holly and her family were coming to Nantucket for the weekend. Their ferry was due in at 5:05, and then he was due at his parents' house in forty-five minutes to eat dinner with everybody.

"Yeah. Listen, buddy, you need to get down here right away." Roger sounded weirdly panicked. But leaving the warmth of his couch a single moment earlier than he had to was not in Brent's itinerary.

"Why? *Jenny Lee* okay?" He'd left his boat in her trailer at the marina just like he always did. He ran through the mental checklist in his head. He was pretty confident that he'd done everything right to make sure she was secure. That boat had cost him a pretty penny, and Brent was always conscientious about taking good care of his things. As far as he knew, she was in fine shape. A little rain wasn't gonna change that.

"Yeah, yeah, boat's fine, pal. Just come down."

"What's the rush, Rog? I got the ball game on, my couch is good, and if my boat's fine ..."

"I'd rather not say on the phone, but you should just—"

"Gotta do better than that, my man." Brent laughed. "Is Marshall messing with me?" Marshall Cook, Brent's best friend, was a notorious prankster. He could already picture Marshall laughing his tail off at the thought of Brent hauling his butt down to the marina and getting nothing but soaking wet for his troubles. Brent always joked that Marshall was thirty going on thirteen.

"No, no, nothing like that."

"Then what?"

"It's ..."

Brent started to get a bad feeling. Something wasn't right. Roger had served in the Navy, stationed in the Philippines, and then he'd worked commercial fishing vessels off the Cape for a long time. He wasn't easily rattled. But something right now had him shook. Brent could hear the fear in his voice.

"What is it, Roger?" he asked softly.

Roger sighed and hesitated. The phone crackled. *Storm must be messing with the cell towers*, Brent thought.

"It's your dad."

The scene at the marina was chaotic. Darkness overhead. Rain pouring. Red and blue lights flashing everywhere. Two Coast Guard boats and a Sea Tow were docked up front, and a handful of uniformed personnel were running back and forth between them.

Tied up behind the Sea Tow was *Pour Decisions*.

The boat looked horrendous. Sea salt dripped from every crack and crevice. Seaweed hung over the railings and from the seats. The vessel was sitting low in the water, and crooked, like it had had too much to drink and was forced to lean up against the dock for balance.

"No, no, no," Brent mumbled numbly. He left the keys in his truck and went sprinting towards the marina door. Halfway there, he saw a Coast Guard member and changed course. The rain was torrential now. Thunder boomed overhead like a massive gong. It was as dark as midnight outside.

Brent seized the man by the shoulders. "Where is he? Where is he?"

The Coast Guard looked surprised.

"Where's my dad?"

Recognition struck him like a bolt of lightning. The man stammered. "I, uh ... He—"

"Where's my dad?!" Brent roared. His hands were like vise grips on the man's shoulders. The whole world had narrowed down to just this man's face, and the knowledge that Brent knew lay in his head. This man knew what had happened to Brent's father, and if he wouldn't tell him voluntarily, then Brent would shake the truth out of him, no matter how long it took or how violent he had to get.

"There was an accident," the man in uniform said finally. "The boat capsized. The passenger was, uh ..."

No. No. No.

The man's mouth kept moving, but Brent didn't hear the rest. He didn't need to. He'd been on the water long enough to know what all the signs pointed to.

He was dimly aware of Roger and Marshall running up and pulling him away, guiding him to a bench under the awning of the marina and sitting him down.

But none of it felt real.

It didn't feel real when the ambulance pulled up.

It didn't feel real when the Coast Guard servicemen emerged from their craft with the black body bag.

It didn't feel real.

It couldn't be. It couldn't be. It couldn't be.

11

MAE

Mae had just finished tossing the chilled salad with her favorite raspberry vinaigrette. John Coltrane was playing on the stereo, the storm outside basked everything in the soft blanket of pitter-pattering rain, and her daughter, son-in-law, and grandchildren would be arriving at the ferry station in just a few minutes. She couldn't wait to see them.

The only blight on her mood was the fact that Henry hadn't come home or called yet. He was mostly pretty good about staying in touch —although, if he got to drinking beers at the bar after bringing the boat in, it wasn't unheard of for him to be a few hours late. She knew he was just as excited as she was to see Holly and the gang, and he wouldn't dare be late this time around, or else he'd risk Mae's spatula-wielding wrath. But she found herself getting irritated anyway.

She tucked the salad into the bottom shelf of the refrigerator and went over to the pantry. Digging through decades' worth of accumulated knick-knacks—she had enough Tupperware to store food for an army—she found what she was looking for: a wine bucket. She filled that with ice from the beat-down spare fridge they kept in the garage, then grabbed the bottle of Holly's favorite white wine she'd picked up from Stop & Shop and set it in there to cool down.

She'd just finished setting that on the counter when her phone started ringing. She'd left it on the side table in the living room. Wiping her hands on her apron, she strolled in to answer. She was sure it was going to be Henry, but to her surprise, Sara's name lit up the screen. She wrinkled her brow. This was unusual. Sara always called Henry's phone. She and her father had been close since the day she was born. Mae had had a harder time forming a close relationship with her youngest daughter. Thankfully, as Sara had aged and mellowed out some, things had gotten much better, but there was no hiding the fact that the first few decades of her life had been tough. She was a feisty baby who grew into a feisty toddler.

Mae could vividly recall Sara's screaming fits over bedtimes, timeouts, and various toys. Those things had changed in turn, too, until it was mother versus daughter in knock 'em down, drag 'em out arguments over whether Sara could take the car out for the night, or sleep over at a friend's house, and on and on like that. It just seemed like Sara zigged whenever Mae zagged. Mae was a patient person by nature, but Sara had a way of pushing her buttons repeatedly. She could hear Henry's voice even now, urging her to be calm, not to worry. "She'll grow," he would say. "And she'll realize how much you do for her. She'll see how much you love her. Don't worry, my little hummingbird. It'll all be A-okay." Then he'd tweak her nose and she'd smile despite her tears.

Yes, Sara was a tough girl, that was for sure. But Mae was beyond proud of the woman she'd become. She had taken a hard route off the island; culinary school was no joke. Nor was scrapping for jobs in the fine dining establishments of the Big Apple. Every time Mae would worry about Sara, though, Henry would tell her to remember how stubborn her daughter was. How darn tough she could be when she had her mind set on something. If Mae closed her eyes, it was easy to picture a young Sara, aged four or five, maybe, arm-wrestling Henry with full dedication to the cause. She had her tongue stuck out between her teeth and her brow furrowed in intense concentration. It was cute then. Now, it made Mae chuckle. She pitied any poor man who decided to underestimate Sara. And every time Sara called home—always Henry's phone, though, to talk to her daddy first—Mae would hear her daughter's voice, so fiery and fierce and stubborn as all get-out, and she would remember what Henry said: "It'll all be A-okay."

But for the first time in a long time, when Mae answered the phone, Sara didn't sound A-okay. She didn't sound okay at all.

"Hi, Mom," she mumbled.

"Sara, sweetie? What's wrong? You don't sound like yourself."

"It's a long story." The line buzzed and crackled for a moment. Mae could hear her daughter breathing, or maybe sighing was a better word. She sounded like the world was weighing heavily on her.

Mae picked her words carefully. "Do you want to tell me about it?"

Sara sighed again and said nothing.

"You don't have to if you don't want to, honey," Mae added. "But you know that you can tell me anything at any time, right?" Her stomach was up in knots. Something was wrong with her little girl, but Mae knew that she would have to wait. She couldn't pry anything out of Sara before she was ready. Patience was key.

"I know, Mom," she said. "I ... I just want to come home."

Mae nodded, even though Sara couldn't hear her. "Then you come home, baby. You'll always have a place to stay here. You know that."

"Yeah. I think I'm gonna. Can you tell Dad to pick me up from the first ferry tomorrow?"

"Of course, Sara. We'll be there."

"Thanks, Mom. I'll see you tomorrow. And Mom?"

Mae had been about to hang up, but she stopped. "Yes, sweetie?"

"I love you."

Mae was taken aback. Yes, their relationship had improved by leaps and bounds ever since Sara took off for culinary school at CIA, but their "I love yous" were still far and few in between. She decided to treasure this one, rather than look too deeply into it.

"I love you too, Sara." The line went dead.

Mae set the phone down and paused for a moment. What could possibly have upset her headstrong daughter so much that she was fleeing back to Nantucket? It didn't sound good, that was for certain. But part of Mae couldn't help but be pleased, too. With Brent already on the island, Holly and the grandkids coming to visit for the weekend, and Sara making an unexpected trip home, she'd have most of her family back under one roof. It was a happy thought. She considered calling Eliza to see if she'd be able to make a last-minute escape from the city, but then thought better of it. Eliza was devoted to her work, and Mae didn't want to guilt-trip her daughter into making the trek.

No, this should be a happy moment. The kids were coming home. Food was ready for dinner. The storm outside seemed to be wearing itself out at long last and the prospect of a warm, sunny, happy weekend loomed on the horizon. Mae smiled.

If only Henry would call. The lack of communication was starting to irk her now. She'd have to give him a spatula swat when he got home.

She heard a knock at the door and forced herself to smile. "That must be Henry," she said to herself. About time, too! He was forever testing her patience, only to surprise her with something sweet. She felt bad about her irritation. Shouldn't she give him the benefit of the doubt this evening? Why, just last week, on their anniversary, he'd dressed up in his wedding tux and knocked on the door. When she opened it, he'd sung her a song in a cheesy baritone—"The Way You Look Tonight" by Frank Sinatra; the same one they'd had their first dance to—given her a bouquet of roses, then swept her upstairs to canoodle the afternoon away. He'd said he was "courting her again," and then he'd kissed her neck in the spot that tickled and they'd laughed and laughed and laughed.

She fingered the wedding band on her left hand. Forty-one years of wearing it. Forty-one years of being Mrs. Henry Benson. Goodness, the man knew how to make her smile—and also how to tick her off when he wanted to. Now that he was home, she would give him a good needle or two, enough to make him grovel just a tiny little bit— *what, did cell phones stop working all of a sudden? Couldn't remember to call?*—and then she'd forgive him and banish him upstairs to handle the few chores that remained until he worked himself back into her good graces.

So when she went to the front door and pulled it open with a flourish, she wasn't ready for what stood on the other side.

Brent stood on the doorstep. He was soaked through to the bone and shivering from head to toe. The rain must be colder than she'd realized.

"Brent, honey, what on earth are you doing?"

It was only then that she looked up at his face and saw that his eyes were rimmed with red. His bottom lip was trembling and mixed in with the rain were tears. She hadn't seen Brent cry since he was seven years old and broke his ankle falling from the tree at Danny Carson's house. He was her tough boy, her go-getter, her soldier. He didn't cry.

"Brent, honey," she said again, ushering him inside hurriedly. "What happened?"

He wrung his hands in front of him. His lips moved like he was trying to talk, but no sound came out. He swallowed, wiped his face, and tried again. This time, his voice came out in a hollow croak.

"Dad's gone."

12

HOLLY

Holly was sick and tired of being tired and sick.

It had been one thing after another for weeks on end. First, Grady had developed a nauseating habit of sneezing directly into her face whenever the urge struck him. Say what you will about seven-year-old boys and their stereotypes, but it was unquestionably true that Grady seemed determined to make her life as gross as possible. He was a good kid, and she loved him with every fiber of her being, but that didn't mean she didn't sometimes want to lock him in a closet for a few hours.

Alice, her youngest, was an angel sent from the heavens above if ever there was one. But she'd taken to fighting her mother on small things, too. Getting dressed for school had become an ordeal to top all others. No outfit was satisfying to her daughter's budding fashion sense, but she refused to take the initiative and do things herself. She just turned up her nose and said, "Meh," to every combo Holly put together.

Then, a quick succession of homemaker mishaps conspired to take Holly's stress levels into new and uncharted territory. Unbeknownst to her, a raccoon had gotten stuck and died in the chimney, and it had taken Holly ages to find the source of the ungodly stench. The memories of getting the creature out of there were not anything she was interested in re-exploring anytime soon. Shortly thereafter, the oven decided it'd had enough and joined the afterlife. The part needed to bring it back to this realm was on six-week back order, so she'd been finagling dinners via a combination of creative microwaving and "screw it, we're ordering pizza."

She was already at wit's end when she got hit by yet another triple whammy. A broken window from Grady learning how *not* to throw a football, a screaming temper tantrum when Alice tried to do her own hair and cut lopsided bangs into her blonde locks, and the return of Holly's stress-induced eczema. It all came hurtling into her life like *bang-bang-bang.*

So she had ended up waking up early to dress Alice, staying up late to scrub the stank of dying raccoon out of her living room furniture, and not sleeping at night because she couldn't stop scratching at her hands and sniffling because of a runny nose that just would. Not. Quit.

Sick and tired of being tired and sick, indeed.

And then there was Pete.

What could one even say about Pete? The obvious, she supposed. You could say that he was handsome, and you'd be mostly right. He was tall enough, and muscular enough, and kind enough to qualify. He had a nice smile and soft hands and he was a very good kisser, when he worked up the spirit.

But something just was off lately. He'd been working a lot, and by a lot, Holly meant *a lot.* She had known when he was going into it that corporate law was a tough job if ever there was one. And, as the new guy at the firm, Pete got the crappy end of the stick more often than not. Not that thirty-three was that young, but Pete had gotten a little bit of a late jump on his law career, and he was already an old soul as it was, so to see him lumped in with all the twenty-four and twenty-five-year-olds in the firm's associate class was a little blow to his and Holly's egos—not that she'd ever admit that to him.

She was proud of her husband, of course. It had taken a massive stroke of willpower for him to wrench his life on track. He wasn't an especially bad student at Nantucket High School, but neither was he a particularly good one. Utterly forgettable, unless you happened to be young Holly Benson, a late bloomer in her sophomore year, walking past big bad senior Pete and his friends playing hacky-sack in the school hallway after lunch, in which case you didn't forget him at all. As a matter of fact, you fell so hard for him that you literally fell, and he came over to help you pick up your spilled lunch and mop the blood from your busted lip. You were so embarrassed that you wished you could die or disappear or just compress yourself into a tiny little mote of dust and float away on the wind. But Pete—well, Pete never got too embarrassed about anything at all, and he really truly didn't think any less of you for tripping—everybody trips sometimes, that's just how life goes, doesn't it?—so he didn't think you needed to be blushing quite so much, but he did think it was awfully cute, and he'd seen you around school before, and did you maybe want to go see a movie or something sometime?

It had been the start of the first truly significant thing to ever happen to Holly Marie Benson—the first thing that really felt like it was hers and hers alone. She was a middle child in mind, body, and soul, and God, it felt so good to have something that she didn't have to share with her siblings. She could look up at Pete and think, *Mine mine mine, you're all mine,* and she knew with absolute certainty that Pete, if he heard the train of thoughts running through her head, would've just smiled that soft smile at her and said, *Yup.*

Pete was great like that.

But corporate law as practiced at Zucker, Schultz, & Schultz was sucking the soul out of her husband. He still said and did all his Pete Things, the little peccadilloes about him that she loved because they made Pete Pete. He ate chocolate pudding first thing in the morning and last thing in the evening. He read newspaper articles about local politicians out loud to himself under his breath and exclaimed at the end, *Holly, can you believe this shmuck?!* and made her come read for herself. He called her his "beautiful, never-ending Hollyday" whenever the mood struck. She loved the Pete Things. But lately, they felt like empty rituals; calorie-free traditions. Like he was leaving the better part of himself in the basement cubicle he slaved away in each day.

And when it came to the kids, it felt like Pete was always a day late and a dollar short. He loved his kids—no one in Pete's orbit had even the slightest ounce of reason to doubt that. He had the fastest trigger finger in Plymouth County when it came to whipping out his phone and showing photos of Alice and Grady in all their splendor. Soccer practice, ballet recital, swim lessons—you name it, Pete had the picture to prove it, and no qualms about shoving it in your face so you could see just how great his kids were. It was cute. It was a Pete Thing. She loved it.

But the actual child care part of having children seemed to fall more and more on Holly these days.

To a large extent, that was fair and expected and totally fine, no worries at all. She'd chosen to be a stay-at-home mom, after all, hadn't she? She'd been fine with it. Hadn't her own mother been a stay-at-home mom? Hadn't Mae given up a catering business that really seemed to be getting some buzz around town—so the stories went—in order to raise the four Benson children? Hadn't they all turned out *mostly* fine? Yes, yes, and mostly yes. The point was that Holly had charged into stay-at-home-motherhood with fire in her heart and sanitizer in her hands, ready to take on all comers.

But didn't all mothers do that, to some extent or another? It was like being young and never believing you're going to get old. Every expectant mom hears the horror stories that come with the position —sleepless nights, thankless days, endless chores, then wake up and do it all again—and everyone fears it, of course. But there's also always that little inkling in the back of your head, like, *That won't happen to me.* She used to think, *I'll be more organized,* and *I'll have them help me with chores,* and *If I just stay on top of x, y, and z, then it won't pile up and it'll never become an issue. That won't happen to me.*

That wouldn't happen to her? Oh, how wrong she had been. She'd underestimated how hard it was to operate with no sleep, and she'd overestimated the ability of toddlers to do—well, anything for themselves. That wouldn't happen to her? Of course it had, and it'd been just a little bit worse for her having had the audacity to think that it wouldn't.

She loved her life. But it was tiring.

And this latest catastrophe was doing little to salvage her mood. They'd piled in the car that morning at eleven a.m. for the trip to Grandma and Grandpa's, all packed and ready to go. Up to that point, it had been relatively smooth sailing. Then, twenty minutes down the road, Grady revealed that he hadn't brought any shoes at all. Reverse course, grab shoes, try again. They made it thirty minutes this time before Pete remembered he didn't have his laptop, which he'd need in case anyone from his firm requested something from him. Reverse course, grab laptop, try again. Forty-five minutes down the road on take number three. The signs for Hyannis Port were in sight. Holly could taste the freedom. *A weekend at Grandma and Grandpa's. Let them spoil the kids rotten. Let me sleep.* She couldn't freaking wait. But, 1.3 miles from the port, Alice decided she had to pee, *RIGHT NOW.* Reverse course, find a gas station, help the five-year-old navigate one of the most revolting bathrooms Holly had ever encountered. Then and only then did they make it to the port, park, wrangle their luggage onto the heaving ferry, and settle in for the boat ride to Nantucket.

Then it started raining.

Now, they were standing huddled under cover at the ferry station, waiting for Grandma Mae to come pick them up. Nobody was happy, Holly least of all.

"Mom?" Grady whined, tugging on her hand. "I'm hungry. Can I get a snack?"

"No, baby," Holly replied. She was doing her best to mask her own irritation. "We're going to have dinner at Grandma's house as soon as we get there." She couldn't blame Grady too much for being hungry and whiny. She was pretty hungry and whiny herself. She checked her watch. It read 5:37. Her mother—the promptest individual ever to grace the face of Nantucket—was late. She said she was going to be at the ferry station at five sharp, and when Mae Benson said something like that, she followed through.

Except, not this time.

"Where do you think she is, hon?" Pete murmured.

Holly sighed and rubbed her temples. She had a massive migraine coming on, and the only thing that could forestall it was 3600 ccs of Chardonnay, *stat*. She knew her mom would have a bottle chilled and waiting for her at the house. Unpacking could wait. Holly needed that drink as soon as they walked in the door. "I don't know, Pete," she said.

"Have you tried calling her?"

Yes, of course she had tried calling her mom. Several times. Her dad, too, and Brent, but either the cell towers on the island were out or her whole family had decided to leave them stranded at the ferry station. "I'll try again."

She fished her phone out of her purse once more and dialed her mom's number.

Buzz. Buzz. Buzz. Her annoyance grew with every ring. She made a silent agreement with herself to wait for five more rings. Four more. Three more. Two more. One more—

"Hello?"

Hallelujah, Holly thought gratefully. "Mom, where are you? We've been waiting—"

"Sis, listen." It was Brent, not her mom. Why was Brent answering Mom's phone? "Something's happened."

As Brent explained, the color drained from Holly's face. Her mouth fell open. The shushing noise of waves against the docks behind them faded away. All she could hear was her brother's voice, saying something that couldn't possibly be true.

The phone slipped from her hand and hit the concrete floor with a thud. Grady went scrambling for it like it was a game. Pete and Alice looked at Holly in confusion.

"Babe?" Pete said. His eyebrows were wrinkled in concern. "Babe, what happened?"

Holly turned to face him. She was still holding Alice's hand. Pete's brown eyes were warm and worried.

"We need to get to the hospital," Holly said. "Right now."

13

BRENT

The call he was about to make was not going to be easy. He'd been staring at the phone in his hand for damn near twenty minutes now. Eliza's number was cued up already. He was about to press "Dial" when he noticed a little red notification bubble in the top bar of his phone screen. Frowning, he thumbed over to it. It was a text message. He must have missed it earlier in the day.

When he opened it, his heart sank.

Good day to be alive and on the water, ain't it, son? —Pops

Brent put his head in his hands and cried like a baby in the waiting room of the hospital.

His mother came out sometime later. Brent wasn't sure how long it had been. When he'd pulled himself together and stopped crying, he'd fallen into a weird and restless sleep, the kind of uncomfortable, pins-and-needles half sleep that seemed uniquely specific to hospital waiting rooms. It had been full of fleeting dreams that he didn't remember and didn't want to relive.

Mae had been in a small conference room down the hall with the Coast Guard crew who'd found *Pour Decisions* capsized. They'd been debriefing her on everything, and then the doctors had come in to deliver their final report and confirm what everyone already knew. Brent had stepped out of the meeting room to call his sister, but he'd utterly failed at that simple task. He'd failed his sisters, his mother, his father. It was a day of failure.

Brent woke up at the sound of his mother's footsteps. He straightened up in his chair and wiped the salty tear tracks from his face. He was shivering in the crisp air conditioning. His clothes were still damp to the touch from when he'd gotten soaked by the rain. It was night outside, now, and the downpour had ceased. All he could hear was the insect-like buzzing of the fluorescent lights overhead and the soft chirping of machines up and down the hospital hallway. That, and his mother's footsteps.

She was standing at the mouth of the hall. Standing still now, standing proud, standing dry-eyed. She was a strong woman. Brent knew that—he had been a handful. Between that and the way she butted heads with Sara constantly, Brent was aware that raising the Benson children had not been a task for the fainthearted. It took heart; it took a steel will. Mae had both in spades.

"Mom," Brent mumbled. He stood unsteadily.

She didn't say anything. She just strode over and took her youngest son into her arms. They held each other. Weirdly enough, neither of them cried. Brent had been sure, in the short seconds between her emerging from the conference room followed by the Coast Guard captain and the chief doctor, that he was going to bawl again as soon as his mother embraced him. He'd been dreading it. But to his surprise, he didn't cry anymore. And she didn't, either. He just hugged his mom, and she just hugged him, and that was that.

"I couldn't do it, Ma," he said when they finally pulled apart. "I couldn't call her."

She held him at arm's length and looked somberly into his face. "Brent Evan Benson," she said with a wavering voice, "you can and you will. You need your siblings here, and I need my children. Take a breath, get a cup of coffee, and call her."

She knew him inside and out. He'd never been the most complex of creatures, which was fine with him. Who had time for all the multifaceted layers of emotions that Holly and Sara both seemed to revel in? Brent took after Eliza and his father in that regard. Simple guy; an A-to-Z, soup-to-nuts kind of man. Straight-line fella. He took pride in that fact, or at least, he once did. He'd been wondering over the last couple hours, though, whether he was actually not stoic but emotionally stunted. Something less than the John Wayne-type gunslinger he'd spent his whole life picturing himself as. Maybe he just didn't have enough practice painting with the full set of emotional colors. Black and white worked great until you tried to paint a sunset.

He wondered, not for the first time, how his father would handle this situation if their roles had been reversed. The funny thing about people like Henry—people of strong and unique character—is that, even when they're not around, the people who know and love them know what they'd say and do if they did happen to be in the neighborhood. Brent could hear his dad's voice in his ear, as clear as if the man himself were standing just behind him out of sight.

"What's with the waterworks, kiddo?" he'd say. *"That sure ain't gonna help much."* Henry had been Nantucket-born and bred, but he'd picked up a Southern twang like he spent his whole life below the Mason-Dixon Line. Some folks around town used to call him the Nantucket Cowboy. Brent and Sara had chipped in to get him a pair of rattlesnake skin boots one Christmas—the flashiest, most ridiculous pair they could find online—and Mae had been straight-up mortified when Henry took to

wearing them around the island. Brent could still close his eyes and picture his dad stepping out of his beat-to-hell old pickup truck, the one with tools rattling around the bed and the radio permanently dialed in to 98.1 WCTK—the country music station. He could picture him hitting the ground, one rattlesnake skin boot at a time. He was pretty sure that Mae had thrown the boots out when Henry wasn't looking.

Should've never let you go to the Garden, Pops, Brent thought. He wondered if he was losing his mind. Maybe this whole imaginary conversation with a ghost was trauma-induced delirium. Maybe he oughta check himself into one of these hospital beds and hang out for a little while. Get the demons upstairs all sorted out. Lord knows they were flocking to the forefront of his mind right now, with the volume on their babbling cranked to ten.

You let him go.

You could've stopped him.

Why didn't you try harder?

Your fault.

Your fault.

Your fault.

"Brent?" Mae said, interrupting the chorus in his head. "I need you here with me right now, baby."

His mom was right. He didn't have time for this guilt trip. That would come later, probably, in his apartment with the lights off and the window blinds drawn. It would've been an awfully good time to have a drink on hand. This was a rainy-day emergency in every sense of the word.

"I'm gonna call Eliza now," he mumbled.

She nodded, studied his face one more time, then pulled him into another hug and raised herself up on tiptoe to kiss him on the cheek. "I love you, honey," she whispered in his ear.

"Love you too, Mom."

They let each other go again, and this time, when Brent went back to his rickety, uncomfortable little seat in the waiting room, he pulled up his phone screen, and dialed Eliza's number before he could think of an excuse not to.

14

ELIZA

The subway was chaotic. But that was how Eliza felt on the inside, so it was weirdly calming to see the outside world reflect her emotional state. It actually made her feel calmer. Like she was the center of the storm, holding the world together.

She rode the 2 train to the 96th Street station on the Upper West Side and walked the remaining four blocks home. On the subway and in the crowd that flowed off it, she felt like one little droplet in a big river. Her problems didn't seem so big or so pressing when she was surrounded by hundreds of people who had problems of their own. The people on her left and her right had bills to pay, sick parents, aching backs. They'd just gotten fired or married or caught the flu. They had leaking roofs and broken radiators and holes in the bottoms of their shoes. There were as many problems as there were people. So, in the midst of all that, a baby didn't seem like quite such a problem at all. In fact, it seemed like a blessing in comparison. A little baby for her to love, who would love her in return. Eliza wouldn't exactly say she was all of a sudden *excited* about the prospect of motherhood, but as she looked around and saw people begging and sweating and looking glum about life, she definitely felt a degree or two better than she had during her panic attack in the bathroom at work.

A sudden memory popped into her head. She'd been in the backyard one summer with her dad. She was eleven, maybe twelve years old. They were practicing for the upcoming softball season. Tryouts were a few weeks away. Eliza had begged her dad to come hit grounders to her. He'd pretended to protest when she asked, then laughed and got up from his reading armchair to rescue his old leather outfielder's glove from the junk closet. They'd played catch for a bit to warm up. It was evening, early enough for the sun to still be setting, but late enough for the fireflies to start exploring.

When she was ready, Dad had picked up the bat and started hitting grounders to her. Slow and easy at first. "Hit them harder, Dad!" she'd said. "Rachel McGregor hits grounders really hard every year. I want to be ready." Her dad had flashed a grin and acquiesced. Harder they came. And harder. And harder.

Until, *boom*, one caught a funky clump of grass at the last second. It popped up with a vengeance and cracked Eliza in the nose.

There was an odd gap in her memory there, like someone had snipped out a portion of the film reel in her head. When the memory resumed, she was lying on the ground on her back, looking up at the evening sky. It was streaked with orange and pink, the color of popsicles. Her dad was looking down at her. He helped her sit up and stanch the flow of blood from her nose.

"Don't think it's broken," he muttered. He looked so worried.

Eliza had looked up at him and smiled. "I asked for it, didn't I?"

Dad's eyes widened, then he laughed. He had such a warm laugh. "I guess you did, kiddo. Gotta watch out for that, though. Life throws a lot of screwballs at ya."

That was the truth for most people. Not for Eliza. Life had gone pretty much exactly as she'd planned it. But this pregnancy was a screwball of epic proportions. There was no doubt about that. It made Rachel McGregor's loping groundballs seem so simple and nonthreatening.

Eliza had a sudden pang of missing her father. Pulling her phone from her Gucci clutch, she dialed his number. It rang and rang, but no one answered. Dad was terrible at answering his phone. She'd try again later. He'd know just what to say to put this all in perspective.

She turned the corner and reached her apartment building. The doorman, Manny, gave her a nod and a hello as she walked in. She smiled at him and kept going towards the elevator.

From there, up to the twelfth floor, marked in the elevator button array with a "P" for "Penthouse." The doors opened and let her into the hallway. She walked down to her unit.

She was about to put her key in the lock when she noticed that it was open already. That was strange. She was a thousand percent sure that she'd locked it before leaving that morning. And Clay had gone out to that client site in Brooklyn, hadn't he? So he wouldn't be home yet. That left a few options, none of them good. Had the superintendent come in for something? But he wouldn't do that without telling them. He knew better than to cross a Type-A Wall Streeter tenant, much less a pair of them. Maybe an intruder, then?

Eliza took a deep breath and retrieved the pepper spray she kept on her key chain. She'd only had to use it once before, in her earliest months in the city, when a cracked-out mugger thought he had her cornered and frightened. It had done the job nicely that day. Since then, it had lain dormant. But she wasn't afraid to pull the trigger again if necessary.

She pushed the door open. It swung inward on silent hinges. Slipping out of her high heels, she set them aside in the entry hallway and crept deeper into the apartment. The foyer ended a few feet farther in and opened into an open-floor-concept living room/kitchen combo. The floors were a dark wood. Modern furniture was dotted sparsely around the space, all done in muted grays. The light fixture overhead looked like floating bubbles. It had cost a fortune.

She turned her gaze to the hallway that led towards the bedrooms. Art lined either wall, mostly expensive abstract pieces devoid of color. But Eliza's eyes were rooted straight ahead. She definitely heard noises now. A shuffling, a sniffling. The scrape of a chair. Who on earth was in her apartment?

She paused outside the guest bedroom door. Solid oak, imported— Italian, if she remembered correctly. Or was it Brazilian? She wasn't sure. The doorknob was bronze and gleaming; they'd had cleaners in here a day or two ago, the best in the city. From within, the shuffling noises continued. It was definitely a person. Sniffling for sure. Snorting? Inhaling?

Oh no.

Eliza let her hand holding the pepper spray drop to her side. She pushed the door open, defeated even before she saw what lay in wait within the room. She knew already, before the door opened and revealed the ugly truth.

She didn't even blink when she saw Clay seated at the desk pushed up against one wall. She didn't cry out when she saw white powder lined up in neat little rails on the wooden desktop and caked under his nostrils. She just sighed as she took in the straw in his hand, and the wide, red-rimmed eyes he was looking at her with.

"El-Eliza, you ... what? I mean ..."

What could she say? Clay's drug use had been a blip on the course of her otherwise perfect life. She'd assumed at the time it was the one and only blip she would have to deal with for a while. That was what —fourteen months ago? Maybe longer. She was suddenly having difficulty keeping track of time. Not usually a problem for a businesswoman like Eliza Benson. But dates and times were swimming around her head, refusing to lie down in order.

However long ago it had been, the facts of the scenario were still relatively straightforward. Clay liked using drugs. Cocaine, to be specific. Was it uncommon in their line of work? No, of course not. Half the young kids applying for associates jobs were only in it because they'd seen *The Wolf of Wall Street*, starring Leonardo DiCaprio, and surmised that the financial industry was basically a reckless bacchanalia of drugs and partying. Plenty of bankers operated at a relatively high level while—well, high.

Clay was not one of them.

He was a schmoozer in everything but title. Meaning that his job was to wine and dine clients, to court new ones and maintain strong relationships with the bank's current roster of tech CEOs and hedge-fund stars. Meaning that he spent a lot of time at expensive dinners and on expensive yachts. That was why he had such a close link to the firm's CEO, and why he'd had sufficient gravitas to call in the helicopter pad favor for their engagement. Meaning, also, that he spent a lot of time around temptations of various ilks. Powerful men liked powerful distractions, it seemed. Clay didn't have the backbone to say no to drugs. Eliza had picked Clay up from the back exit of a club one night, drugged out of his mind. She'd distributed hundred-dollar bills to everyone in sight to keep things on the down-low. When he'd woken up the next day, he'd apologized profusely and sworn it would never happen again.

When, of course, it did happen again, he'd actually been the first to suggest rehab. She'd said okay to that. Two weeks in the Arizona desert and he came home with a fresh somberness in his eye. At the time, it seemed like that was that. Competent Clay was back, and Cocaine Clay was a thing of the past.

Now, she saw that that was a lie.

Her fiancé was an addict. Correction—the *father of her baby* was an addict. He loved drugs more than he loved her, and even if he knew about their baby, Eliza was fairly certain that Clay would love drugs more than him or her, too. So she didn't bother giving him the choice.

She threw four things at him. The first was her engagement ring. It was a good throw—she didn't make All-American and All-Academic softball teams for each of her four years at Penn for no reason. The ring hit him in the chest with a *plink*. Clay just blinked and looked down at it where it landed in his lap.

The second, third, and fourth things that Eliza threw at her now-ex fiancé were each of the handful of pregnancy tests she'd stuffed in her purse. Since the moment in the Goldman Sachs bathroom when she'd known—just *known*, as clear as day, long before she'd hustled to CVS and confirmed it as a cold, hard fact—that she was pregnant, she'd harbored a stupid, never-gonna-happen fantasy that she would come home and show Clay the tests, and that everything would change. She'd imagined that he would see that little plus sign and the shell of his emotionless exterior would crack, revealing the Prince Charming in an Hermès tie who had been hiding within him all along. He would love her with a warmth that she knew she needed. Like a husband loved his wife, not like a shark loved blood. A chorus of angels would sing and rainbows would beam through the window.

She knew that wasn't actually going to happen, even though a part of her really earnestly wanted to believe it. But she'd never anticipated that reality would burst her bubble quite so viciously.

"I am leaving, Clay," she said calmly and simply. "Our engagement is off. Do not call me. Do not text me." She didn't know where she was going, but she was going somewhere for sure. Anywhere but here.

He looked down at the pregnancy tests and the engagement ring in his lap and his face settled into something alien and unrecognizable.

"Okay," he said meekly. He didn't sound that sad at all.

On her way out of the apartment, with a hastily packed weekend bag in hand, her phone buzzed. She answered at once. It was Brent. He told her the news.

"Okay," she said through a throat that felt tight. She didn't know what else to say, though "Okay" seemed like a terrible reply. Outwardly, she knew she sounded like a robot, like a heartless monster—like Clay, even. But inside, she felt far more than she knew how to put into words. So she just said, "Okay," and nothing else. The world outside looked far colder and grayer than it had on her way to work this morning.

She knew where she was going now, at least.

She was going home to Nantucket.

15

MAE

"Eliza's coming home," Brent said.

"What?" Mae hadn't heard him. She was lost in thought. They were still sitting in the hospital, though there wasn't really any reason for them to be there anymore.

He repeated what he said.

"Oh," said Mae. "That's good." Her voice was vague and distant. She knew that Brent needed her, but it was just so hard to focus. She'd used up the last reserve of strength she had when she'd told him to call Eliza. That had been an uphill struggle, just getting the words out of her mouth. But Brent was her baby boy, her little one, and even though he was a trooper and not really such a baby or so little anymore—when had he gotten so old and weary?—she still knew him. He needed her. As her children arrived one by one, they would all need her, too.

This wasn't how she pictured this weekend going. It wasn't so long ago that she'd been buzzing around the kitchen, doing her little hummingbird tasks—oh no, oh no, that word hurt too much now.

She'd be quite happy if she never saw a hummingbird again. That was Henry's word for her. She didn't want to hear it anymore.

Her sadness was weird. She'd never spent much time wringing her hands over unpleasant futures. Mae Benson, neé Warner, was not a worrier by nature. So she just didn't have the mental infrastructure to really take all of this in at once. As far as she was concerned, that was just fine. There'd be lots of time to take it all in later. Lots of lonely moments, quiet ones that Henry had once filled and wouldn't be filling any longer. Oh my. The house would be so quiet. She'd been looking forward to stepping back into her own home, but now the thought filled her with a gray sense of foreboding. His clothes would still be in the closet. And she knew for certain that he'd left his coffee cup in the sink before he left the house that morning. She was forever yelling at him not to do that, but he was forever forgetting. She wouldn't have to yell at him about it anymore.

Oh my.

"Mom?" Brent said. She looked over to him. They were seated side by side in the waiting room chairs. Goodness gracious, were these things uncomfortable. They certainly were not designed to bear the weight of a grieving old woman. Mae felt so gosh darn *old* all of a sudden. Just a few hours ago, she would've replied to anyone who asked that she was a spring chicken with a second wind. "Look at me!" she would've said, laughing, spreading her arms wide. "All the pep is still in my step!" Now, though, the mere thought of getting out of this chair seemed impossibly exhausting.

"Did you say something, dear?"

Brent nodded. "I said, Holly's here." He pointed towards the hallway. Holly was standing there. She was holding both Alice's and Grady's hands. Pete was standing a couple feet apart from them. Mae thought that was a little odd. Pete was such a sweet man, and he so loved her Holly. Holly was biting her lower lip. She'd done that ever since she was a kid whenever she was worried or sad. Mae had a flashback to

Holly as a little girl, playing house with her dolls, pigtails flopping side to side as she ran around and made mud pies at the beach. What a sweet thing she'd been. Still was.

"Hi, Mom," Holly said. She rushed over, kids in tow. Alice and Grady looked confused. Mae reached out and stroked each of their cheeks in turn. Brent helped Mae to her feet so she could hug her daughter.

"Hello, honey," Mae murmured. That took so much effort to say.

"I'm so sorry, Mom," Holly cried. She buried her face in her mother's shoulder. Mae patted the back of her head absentmindedly. She stared out the window on the far wall as she held her middle daughter and let her whimper for a few moments longer. The rain had stopped now. It was just another quiet Nantucket night in April.

Eventually, Holly let go and stepped back, holding Mae at arm's length. "Are you okay? Have you eaten? Did you have any water today? You never remember to drink water."

Mae chuckled softly. It felt strange coming out of her mouth. "You are me, aren't you? Always mothering the rest of the world." Holly blushed, and Mae chuckled again, though she didn't really feel like laughing. It was true; Holly had always been the most domestic of her children. It didn't surprise anyone in the Benson clan when she married Pete, her high school sweetheart. Nor did it surprise them when she had two beautiful children in quick succession. Holly had been ready for motherhood practically from the day she was born. Mae smoothed down one of Holly's flyaway hairs. "Don't worry about me, darling."

"Of course I'm worried about you, Mom!" Holly cried. Pete stood off a few feet away, wringing his hands and looking down. Mae could still remember when he'd asked Henry for permission to marry Holly. She'd been peeking around a corner—guiltily, but she just couldn't help herself sometimes; she was so curious by nature—and remembered just how humble and honest Pete had been. He'd sworn to work hard and provide and be a good husband and son-in-law.

He'd kept those promises as far as Mae knew, so the sense of awkward distance she could feel between him and Holly was strange. She made a mental note to ask about it later.

"Mom, I'm hungry," Grady whined. He tugged at Holly's shirt. Mae and Holly looked down at him. His shirt was disheveled and his face was drawn with exhaustion.

"Grady, not the time!" Holly hissed.

"No, no, it's okay," Mae cut in. "Let's go home and get you some food." It felt good to be able to focus on a little task like that. Her own version of *one step at a time*. First—get home. Then—feed Grady. She had chicken nuggets in the freezer for him. That was easy. It was straightforward, and heaven knew she needed a straightforward path to walk down right now. She'd zapped her battery dry while talking to the doctors and the Coast Guard and then Brent. Putting chicken nuggets in the oven would be restorative in the strangest way. It would feel like normal, on a day where nothing else had been.

Pete led the way down the hall. Mae followed. Alice held her hand as Grady scampered along ahead of them. She heard Brent and Holly whispering behind them as they wound their way outdoors.

The sky overhead was studded with stars. The parking lot was mostly silent. Mae could just barely hear the waves crashing on the beach. "I'm parked this way, Ma," Brent said. His head was bowed, like he couldn't bear to look at her. He reached out and pulled her into a hug. If Mae closed her eyes, for a brief second it felt like she was hugging Henry. Brent had the same build as her husband, the same broad shoulders and big barrel chest.

But when she opened her eyes, she saw Brent's green eyes, the same as her own, rather than Henry's baby blues. "Okay, darling," Mae said. She didn't have the strength to say much else. Brent looked down for a moment longer, then turned and walked over to his pickup. She watched as he clambered in, pulled out quickly, and drove off.

"This way, Grandma," Alice said. Mae took her granddaughter's hand again and went off towards where Pete had pulled the SUV around. She climbed in and they went back to Mae's house.

It was a short drive, fifteen minutes or so. When they pulled into the driveway and Pete killed the engine, the silence felt very heavy, like a knit blanket. Mae didn't like it very much. She waited as Grady leaped out of the car and held the door open for her. For all his energy, he was a good boy. Holly and Pete had done a good job raising him thus far. He had the same twinkle in his eyes as Henry.

Mae smiled and patted her grandson's cheek gently. "Thank you, Grady," she said as she stepped down. She walked up to the door, unlocked it, and let them all inside. The house was still, and the silence in here was even heavier than it had been in the car. The smells were the same though, and home was still home, so she did what she always did when she returned. She put her keys on the seashell-shaped key hook that hung by the door, slipped off her shoes on the "Welcome to Nantucket – Make Yourself at Home!" mat that had always lain just inside, and went to flip on the kitchen lights.

The kitchen wasn't that big, but it was homey and it was hers. The fluorescent lights overhead flickered to life. She could hear the buzz of the refrigerator running. She knew there was a chilled salad inside, and a bottle of wine with Holly's name written all over it. Plus apple juice and chicken nuggets for the kids, and a six-pack of Coors for Pete. Mae started to explain all that to Holly, but her daughter just shushed her. "It's okay, Mama," she said. "I'll handle it all. What can I get you?"

There were an awful lot of answers to that question. *A time machine* would top the list, but Mae wasn't quite ready to offer such a quippy answer yet. *Get me my husband back* was far too morbid, and Mae had never been morbid. What to say, then? What did she want?

"I think I'll just go upstairs and freshen up," she said finally. That seemed reasonable, and it seemed straightforward, too. Go upstairs, splash some water on her face, touch up the tiny bit of makeup her vanity insisted upon every day. Perhaps change clothes; the dress she was wearing stank of hospital disinfectant. Belatedly, she noticed, she was still wearing an apron, for crying out loud. Those nice Coast Guard men must have thought she looked so silly.

"Okay, sure thing. I'm gonna pour some wine for you too, okay?" Holly said. Her brow was furrowed as she searched Mae's face. Mae knew that her daughter was holding back plenty of tears of her own, for her sake. She touched her face just like she'd touched Grady's. She tried to say with her fingertips what she was having a hard time saying with her words: *Thank you, I love you, I'm hurting too, we'll make it through this together.* Any and all that stuff. She couldn't say for sure whether Holly got the message. She hoped she did. A grieving child required nothing more than her mother's love.

But, for right now, Mae needed just a moment of stillness away from everyone else. She'd been surrounded by people since Brent had first knocked on her door. It would be nice to just step inside her bedroom and shut the world out for a moment.

She turned and left the kitchen. She mounted the stairs one by one. Her knee creaked. Had it always done that, or was that recent? Mae wasn't quite sure. She supposed it didn't really matter. She gripped the handrail carefully as she made her way up, past her children's old bedrooms, and down to the master at the end of the hall. Stepping inside, she shut the door behind her.

Only then did she cry.

Her tears surprised her. It felt like they came out of nowhere. But they weren't the blubbery, wailing tears she might've expected. They were more like movie starlet, dab-at-her-eyes-with-a-handkerchief kind of tears. Mae almost laughed. If Henry was here now, he'd be making fun of her for crying so melodramatically. *Where are my big, fat tears?* he would've joked, probably. *Can't even let loose one "Why, God?!" on my behalf? Jeez Louise, Mae, it's the least ya could do for me.* He would've winked then, and pulled her into a Happy Henry hug, and kissed the top of her head and made it all feel just a little less heavy.

She walked over to the edge of the bed and sat down. The thought of Henry had dried up the tears, mostly. Just a sniffle here and there left in their wake. She surveyed the room around her, the one she'd shared with her husband for so many, many years. The closet was open. His plaid shirts hung in there. His work boots were on the floor, one keeled over, the other standing tall and upright. He'd left his watch on the nightstand.

Mae stood up and went over to the closet. Taking one of his shirts in her hand, she pressed it against her nose and inhaled deeply. Ah, that Henry scent, that cologne and man-musk and woodsy, fragrant saltiness that was so utterly and completely him. She had always had a sharp nose and she could tell when Henry had just vacated a room by the lingering scent of him alone. This, now, was like aloe on a burn. To smell him was to have him here with her. It felt like he was about to walk right back in the door and keep right on loving her.

She would've really liked that.

16

MAE

THREE DAYS LATER

Henry Howard Benson was buried on a Sunday.

The whole day was a blur to Mae. The pews at First Congregational Church in Nantucket were full to bursting. People of all ages, creeds, and colors came streaming in to pay their respects and bid farewell to the Nantucket Cowboy. Never before had it been so clear that Henry was as lovable a man as had ever graced the earth.

In fact, the words spoken at the service and reception were gushing almost to the point of ridiculousness. Mae wanted to grab the microphone from the preacher and let everyone know that, for all that he was warm and generous and quick to lend a shoulder to cry on to just about anyone who'd ever needed it, Henry Benson was far from perfect. He sometimes used an online bookie service in the Cayman Islands to place illegal bets on football games. He ran red lights if there was no one else on the road late at night. Once, she'd caught him painting Brent's toenails while he was sleeping as a prank, and when Brent had woken up and cried, her husband had framed his own daughters for the crime.

But those memories just made her laugh and tear up instead. Maybe it was better that she kept them to herself, actually. Those were the things that made Henry *her* Henry. If she was the only one who had those little treasures tucked away in the back of her mind, so much the better. She felt intensely selfish that Sunday, in a way she never could have predicted. She'd heard all the usual things from well-wishers—"Mourn in your own way," "Take all the time you need," "Let me know if there's anything I can do to help." Little of it was helpful, though all of it was offered with good intentions.

Mae had spent the better part of a century living by the Golden Rule. Her father and her grandfather before him had always harped on the value of being a good neighbor in a time of need, and Mae had done her best to be the best neighbor she knew how to be. She made marshmallow fudge for Lola, she helped Cindy MacMillan down the street clean out her attic, she volunteered alongside Trisha Brady knitting hats for the overseas troops down at Purls Before Swine, the sewing club that met at her house on the first and third Tuesday of every month. She'd done all those things for years and years because it was the right thing to do. Besides, she liked staying busy and she liked being helpful.

Perhaps that was why she was having such a hard time being on the receiving end of her neighbors' graces. Her kitchen was full to bursting with casseroles and lasagnas wrapped in tinfoil. She had wine bottles stacked in the garage fridge and fruit baskets arriving daily. Everyone meant well; Mae knew that. But she wouldn't be too upset if it all stopped.

And yet, it didn't stop. It was a never-ending day, seemingly. The service lasted an eternity, or so she thought, though her wristwatch said it was only twenty-three minutes long. That, too, was a blur. If she was being honest, she couldn't remember a single word that anyone had said. She'd requested the most expedited service possible, and the preacher was agreeable to that. She wanted to remember her Henry. Let the others remember who Henry had been to them; that was all well and good. But let her keep some parts of him to herself. That seemed so very important.

Afterwards, the burial was to take place in the church graveyard. The members of the crowd who hadn't been invited to that filed past Mae to touch her hand and offer teary-eyed condolences. Mae's eyes had remained dry so far—how exactly that happened was a miracle, but it did make things somewhat easier.

Mae noticed Toni, Henry's sister, lingering at the back of the church. "Excuse me," she said to Mr. Arthur Fleming, an elderly man who volunteered as the organist at the church sometimes. He didn't hear so well anymore, so Mae had spent the last five minutes having the same conversation several times over. Mr. Arthur tottered along, nodding and mumbling somberly under his breath. Mae went over to Toni and touched her on the shoulder.

"Hi, love," she said. Toni turned to her. Mae had always thought that Toni was a striking woman. She was tall, like her brother, though much more petite. She had the same blonde hair, similarly turned to gray with the passing of the years, and the same blue eyes that had such depth to them. It warmed Mae's heart to see Henry's eyes in another person. It felt like she was looking at him again.

"Come here," Toni murmured. The two women embraced and stayed there for longer than Mae could ever remember hugging anyone before. Nothing needed to be said. They each had lost a version of Henry that only they knew best, and so it felt good to just hold each other and let the obvious truths hang around. That all could wait until later. There would be plenty of time for "I miss him" and "He was a good man." They both knew that. This, right here and right now, was about slowing down this blur of the day and finding little memories to hold onto, like breadcrumbs that would lead them through this mourning period and back towards something that resembled normality.

Finally, they pulled apart, though they stayed close. Mae started to ask, "How are you?" and then thought better of it. It seemed like a silly question, given the circumstances. She settled instead on, "I've never felt quite so useless."

Toni laughed at that. She dabbed at her eyes. "You can say that again, sister."

"What are we going to do with ourselves, Toni?"

Her sister-in-law sighed. Both women were dressed similarly, in black felt dresses with high collars. Mae had decided against a veil. It felt too stiff and formal. Henry would've poked fun at her for wearing it. *My old whaling wife!* He would've cackled. *Gone to see me off to sea!*

"I can't stay here," Toni said finally. "I need some time away, I think."

Mae nodded. That certainly made sense, and she couldn't fault her for it. "Where will you go?"

"A cruise, maybe, if I can tolerate all the old fogies. Then again, I guess I could count myself as one of them these days."

They chuckled together. "You and me both," Mae joked. "But what will you do with the inn?"

Toni opened her mouth to answer, then hesitated and fell quiet again. She rubbed her chin between thumb and forefinger—just like Henry—*no, stop it, woman!* Mae scolded herself. "That's funny you should ask," she said. "I thought I might ask you a favor."

"Uh-oh. Should I be worried?" Mae grinned through her sadness. Toni was a schemer, just like her brother. She clearly had something cooked up.

"Well, I just know how busy you like to stay. And I can't imagine wanting to be in that house right now. So I thought that perhaps you'd be interested in running the inn for a bit while I'm gone."

Running the inn. Now there was a proposition. It seemed like an idea out of left field, and yet the more Mae thought about it, the more attractive it became. Sure, she'd be busy, but wasn't that a good thing, all things considered? Idleness was the enemy she was staring it in the eye right now. She hadn't been idle in nearly fifty years, and if she started now, she'd be tearing her hair out within the week. She had the skills, didn't she? Mae's Marvels had prepped her for that. She could cook and clean, and she knew this island like the back of her hand.

"I'll run all the business end of things while I'm gone. The ads and the bookings and all that, you won't have to worry about it at all. The power of the internet, you know?"

Mae nodded slowly, letting the whole idea sink in.

Toni went on, "So you'd be my woman on the ground. Handle the guests and the rooms, do the cooking—all the stuff you're so talented at. To be honest, I'm kicking myself for not trying to lure you into my trap earlier. You're a natural fit, Mae."

Mae had never been one to toot her own horn, but she had to agree with Toni. She'd been groomed for this role by her children and husband and her own love for all things food, wine, and Nantucket. This could be perfect. It was like the chicken nuggets for Grady had been on the night of the accident—something simple and straightforward and uncomplicated that she could focus on. Her own version of one step at a time, leading away from this sadness and into —well, she didn't know quite where this would take her, but it was somewhere different than where she was currently, and from where she was standing, that seemed like the only thing that mattered.

"Let me think about it," she decided. "It's a lot to take in. But I think it could be just the right thing. And you do deserve a break. You just have to promise to send me a postcard or two, okay? I've always loved the way the French Riviera looks in pictures."

Toni smiled warmly and squeezed Mae's hand again. "You're a good woman, Mae," she said. "Henry loved you with all his heart."

Mae bit back tears as the two women hugged once more.

"Excuse me, Mrs. Benson?" came a timid voice. Mae pulled away from the hug to see the preacher standing at the end of the aisle with his hands folded. He was looking down respectfully. "As soon as you're ready, we can perform the final piece of the service."

Mae swallowed and nodded. Toni held onto her hand as they followed the preacher out of the church.

The burial was quick. The casket went into the earth. Mae stood next to Sara, Eliza, and Holly as the first bits of dirt were shoveled on top. Her daughters held her close while she cried.

Brent was nowhere to be found.

PART II
SUMMER

17

BRENT
FOUR MONTHS LATER

It had been four months since ... since what happened. It had been a hard four months. Maybe the hardest of Brent's life. What else would count? What else would even be in the running for such a hard, horrible stretch of sleepless nights and drunken days? Brent had had his fair share of troubles. The alcoholism had beaten him down for a while, but just when it seemed like he'd shaken that monkey off his back, *this* happened.

Life had been good for a little while, hadn't it? It had been fulfilling. Working alongside his father in the sun, ending up tired enough to sleep soundly through the night with nary a nightmare to bother him ... Yeah, that was the good life.

But not anymore. Now, the nightmares had returned with a vengeance. He and his sisters had always been vivid dreamers. The whole Benson family was like that. He remembered days—younger days, better days—when they used to sit around the breakfast table and swap dream stories. Mom, Holly, and Sara's dreams always made perfect sense. Henry, Brent, and Eliza were at the opposite end of the spectrum. They were more of what he called "slideshow dreamers."

Their dreams were a series of disconnected images, or at least, that's all he remembered of them.

So, when he shot up in bed on the morning of August 1st, panting like he'd just run a marathon or hauled in a sailfish as big as a house, all he had to point to as the source of his panic was a single image: *Pour Decisions,* tied to the dock, dripping seaweed like a bad hair day, and spewing saltwater from places it ought not to be spewing from.

He didn't linger in bed. Grumbling and groaning—his head hurt terribly—he thumped his way over to the bathroom of his crummy apartment and flicked the light on. It took a second to get going. But when it finally shimmied to life and decided to stick around for a while, Brent reconsidered whether turning the light on was a good idea at all.

He looked like something the cat dragged in. No—he looked like something the cat had decided was far too gross to drag in. There was a purple lump on the left side of his forehead, and the fading shiner on his eye to match. His bottom lip was split and twisted with something scabby. The bags under his eyes would keep the Stop & Shop grocery store stocked for weeks. And the eyes themselves were bloodshot. Panicked. Glazed.

He was hungover; that much was beyond doubt. He briefly considered trying to make himself throw up just to rid his body of all the poison he'd consumed last night, then decided against it. Better just to brush his teeth real quick and crack open a cold beer. Treat last night's damage with the hair of the dog.

He'd doubled down on the drinking, big-time. He was worse than he'd ever been. He knew that. He sure didn't need anyone telling him, least of all the wide variety of people who'd tried telling him that in some form or another over the last four months. Roger, Sara, Eliza, Holly, Marshall, random people he'd never met or never remembered meeting.

Whoa, slow down, buddy!

Take it easy there, pal.

Why don't you have some water—throttle back for a bit?

No, I won't, and *no thank you,* were his responses in order. In Brent's eyes, it wasn't the drinking that was the real issue at hand. It was what the drinking brought out of him—a mean, aggressive drunk he never remembered being before. Since when did he, Brent Benson, fight strangers? Since when did he get ornery if some out-of-towner eyeballed him the wrong way down at the bar? He could recount on two hands the number of times he'd been in a real fight in twenty-two years, and half of those were with Marshall, meaning it had been over just as soon as it began and ended with their arms slung around each other's shoulders, saying stuff like, "You caught me with a good one there, amigo."

But these days, he was ready to throw fists at the drop of a hat. A doubled-up song at the jukebox, someone cutting in when the bar was busy, a spilled drink—he'd brawled for all of that and more over the last days and weeks. If he could remember correctly—and that was a fuzzy proposition at best—last night's brawl had begun when someone elbowed him in the back on accident while passing by. A few choice words later, and he was out in the parking lot, getting his face ground into the cement by someone bigger and angrier than he was.

It never felt good to fight. It sure as heck didn't feel good to get beat up. But Brent was losing these ruffle-ups at least as often as he was winning them, and that didn't seem to slow him down at all. Winning wasn't the purpose. Maybe he just needed to feel something knocked into that thick skull of his.

Hardheaded. Husky dog. Gotta make him see the purpose, or he won't change anything at all. All the things his dad had seen in him and said over and over throughout his childhood turned out to be truer than either of them had realized. He was fighting and he wasn't gonna stop, because there didn't seem to be any reason. Same went for the drinking. As far as he was concerned, he could live out the rest of his days like this. Just another angry drunk on this godforsaken island.

Brent heard a buzzing that interrupted his thoughts. He thought about ignoring his vibrating cell phone, but decided he'd be generous enough to the caller to answer and tell them to leave him alone. He was just about done looking in the mirror, anyway. There was nothing in there he wanted to see.

He jammed a dry toothbrush in his mouth, killed the light, and stomped over to his bedside table. He grabbed the cell phone off the charger. "Yeah?" he grumbled around the toothbrush.

"Brent. Get dressed." It was Eliza. She had her no-BS voice on. She'd been good at that tone practically since the cradle. She was a no-BS kind of woman; Brent knew that. She had her own fair share of problems these days, too—a baby on the way with no man in sight, life all turned upside down—but Brent didn't have time for anyone else's troubles but his own. Sometimes not even that.

"What for?"

"We're going out. You, me, and Sara. Gonna go down to the bar. If you're gonna be drinking, you might as well drink with family." Her tone was firm.

"To the bar? Little early for that, sis."

She laughed hollowly. "Early? It's almost six in the evening, Brent."

Brent furrowed his brow and held the phone away from his ear to check the time. "Well, I'll be damned." She was right. He'd slept the whole day away. He didn't feel rested at all. Felt like death warmed over, actually, but that was mostly par for the course this summer. No better or worse than normal. He'd pretty much gotten used to it.

Well, if Eliza insisted, he'd be amenable to getting a dinnertime beer. Maybe he'd be able to scarf down some wings or oysters to get a little substance in his stomach before returning home to down another twelve-pack or two on the couch alone.

"All right," he said, pulling the toothbrush out. His voice cracked when he spoke. "Meet you there."

Eliza hung up without saying anything.

"You look awful, bro," was the first thing Sara said to him when she and Eliza strolled into the bar to meet him.

"Good to see you, too, my lovely siblings," Brent said. He raised his glass in a mock toast. He hadn't waited for them to arrive before ordering. Eliza was pregnant, and he wasn't sure if Sara was still doing her nunnery thing where she abstained from vices of all stripes. She'd kept it up for a bit since Dad's ... thing, but it had been a few weeks now since he'd checked in with either of them, despite them all once again living on the same island.

The girls had both pretty much stayed put on Nantucket since the funeral. They'd made one trip back to NYC together to gather their things, but since then, they'd just been hanging around, living at home and helping Mom run the Sweet Island Inn whenever they had time. Eliza was doing some business thing to help increase bookings, and Sara was cooking dinners for the guests here and there. Neither one seemed concerned about money at the moment. Must be nice.

For his part, Brent was broke as a joke with little prospect of changing it and even less interest in doing so. He'd been picking up odd handyman jobs here and there, and Marshall had been harassing him to be a crew member on one of his charter fishing trips, but he wanted to do the bare minimum necessary to skate by. If he could keep the fridge stocked with cold beer and scrounge up sufficient cash for rent, he figured that was good enough.

"What've you been doing, Brent?" Eliza asked. She settled down onto the stool on one side of him and ordered a seltzer from the bartender. Sara came around to the other side and asked for a glass of chardonnay. Guess she wasn't teetotaling anymore, then.

"You're lookin' at it."

"Charming."

"Nothing like the love of a sister to brighten your day."

Sara butted in. "Jeez, you are really a black hole tonight."

Brent raised his glass. "I'll drink to that." He knew both Eliza and Sara were rolling their eyes, but he didn't care. He was long past caring at this point. His dad was gone and it was his fault, so what else was there to do but drink? Amen. Bottoms up. Rinse and repeat.

What was worse than self-pity was the pity of others. Yeah, Brent knew that his life had gone from not much to nothing at all, but that was his problem, not theirs. Why wouldn't they get off his back? Every time he thought he'd convinced them that he would be just fine sooner or later if they would just leave him be, they came storming back, knocking on his door with platters of food or insisting that he come join them on some outing or another. He tried to refuse —he didn't want to walk downtown, or go to the beach, and he sure as heck did *not* want to take a boat out on the water. He couldn't possibly state that last one firmly enough. His mom was the only one who didn't push him, and even then, he knew that she was worried to death about him.

He felt worst of all about that. Lord knew his mom had been dealt an awful hand this spring. He was well aware that he was doing not a darn thing to make it any easier, either. Still, he was glad that she was busy with the inn. What had Dad always called her? That silly pet name. His ... *hummingbird*, that was it. It suited her. Mae Benson loathed idleness. She was the little engine that could, and if she ever ran out of steam or train track, Brent had no idea how she would operate. Aunt Toni's offer had come at the right time for Mom's sanity, that was for sure. Thank God for small blessings, he supposed.

Brent, on the other hand, didn't want to do anything. He just wanted to sit in a quiet corner and drink his beer unbothered. Eliza and Sara didn't seem to have gotten that memo.

"When did you last take a shower? You smell god-awful," Sara said. She wrinkled her nose. Never too subtle, that one.

"Have you been working?" Eliza asked.

He straightened up and raised his hands to both of them. "Look," he began, "I'm gonna say this one time and one time only: I'm fine. I don't want your help, money, or pity. I just want to drink my beer in peace. Is that so much to ask?" He could sense Eliza and Sara making eye contact and doing their sisterly telepathy thing he'd always hated so much. He used to pitch a fit whenever they did it around him when they were young. *Dad! They're doing it again! Make them stop!* He wished Pops was around to cajole his sisters into using words around him. Then again, maybe it was for the best that Brent couldn't hear what they were saying. It would only piss him off further.

Sighing, Eliza and Sara settled into the bar and nursed their drinks for a while. They chitchatted about people they'd seen around town, about Holly, who was back home in Plymouth with Pete and the kids, about guests at the inn. Stuff seemed like it was going well, relatively speaking. Brent chimed in often enough to keep them off his back, but for the most part he just kept his thoughts to himself. He was an extrovert by nature, but he hadn't felt like much social interaction lately.

After an hour or so had passed, Brent decided that he'd had his fill of sibling bonding. He made his excuses, said his goodbyes to Eliza, Sara, and Big Mack behind the bar, then strolled out. He could feel everyone's eyes on his back as he left, but he didn't much care.

He'd held himself to a pair of beers, so he felt plenty confident in getting behind the wheel of his truck again. He fired her up and started home, but when he got to the third intersection, he had a sudden change of heart and went right instead of left. A few more minutes brought him to the marina. The sun had set maybe forty-five minutes ago, so the place was mostly empty and the boat ramp was chained up, with the CLOSED 'TIL TOMORROW sign hanging from its post. But the night was clear and the moon was full, so he could see well enough to hitch up his trailer and back *Jenny Lee* into the water. From there, it was only a few short minutes until he was out on the ocean.

He knew where he was going, even though he hadn't ever consciously decided to go there. But it was no surprise to him that he ended up at the Garden of Eden, the little spot out by the underwater drop-off where his dad had wanted to go on that fateful day.

It was only the second or third time Brent had been out on the boat in the last four months. The first couple times he'd tried it, he'd been a nervous wreck. Every bump of an unexpected wave sent tremors racing down his spine, and he'd wanted to turn back just as soon as he'd left.

But tonight, he felt none of that. He didn't feel much of anything as he surveyed the dark, rocking waters. The stars were out, and he could see for miles out here. There was little to see. Just water and Nantucket night sky. He killed the engine and sat down with a heavy sigh. Reaching into one of the side hatches, he pulled out a cooler in which he kept an emergency twelve-pack.

"This one's for you, Dad," he said, cracking open a can and raising it to the heavens.

What in the world was he doing out here? There were no answers forthcoming; he knew that. He'd never been much of a believer in anything he couldn't lay his hands on. It had taken his third-grade teacher, Mrs. Reese, several days and a number of apples dropped on his head to convince stubborn Brent Benson about the existence of gravity. All of which was to say that he knew darn well his dad's ghost wasn't about to speak to him out of the clouds or anything like that. No one was gonna answer any of the questions he'd spent four months running from. But for some reason, he felt like asking them anyway.

"Why'd this happen to us, Dad?" he called out to nobody. He took a sip of his beer and continued. "Why didn't I try harder to stop you? You shouldn't have gone out there, I knew that. You'd been drinking and you were frustrated and I was being a crab. But I knew that storm wasn't good. I should've tried harder to stop you. It's my fault you're gone."

Silence. Waves slapped the side of the boat, but there was no rhythm or meaning to it. It was just noise, nothing more than that.

He wasn't sure how long he went on like that, hollering nonsense to no one, before he got tired and lay down, but he'd been yelling for long enough that his throat was sore and it was good to be quiet for a while. He hadn't gotten a single answer to any of his questions, but that was fine. He felt a little more settled anyway. Like something that had been shaken up in his chest had clicked back into place and everything around it could ease up now. Like he could finally take a real, deep breath.

Oddly enough, he felt somewhat at peace for the first time in months.

He fell asleep like that, under the stars.

18

SARA

Eliza and Sara turned to each other as soon as Brent left the bar. They each had the same worried expression on their face. He was getting worse and worse every day. If something didn't change, and soon, they knew their baby brother was headed for a brutal crash landing at rock bottom.

"What are we going to do?" Sara asked. Eliza would know the answer. That was how she'd been for their whole lives. Big sister, know-it-all, control freak. Things usually turned out well when Eliza was in charge. Well, not so much lately, what with the baby and the breakup. But, up until now, her track record had been pretty good.

Which was why Sara's worry ticked a notch higher when Eliza sighed, rubbed her temples, and said, "I honestly do not know."

Sara took a sip of her wine. She thought clearing her head of all externally induced demons would be good, but she hadn't felt better after a few months of abstaining from all vices, so she'd figured she'd at least enjoy a little buzz if she was going to be worried and sad. "He looks awful."

"Horrible."

"Terrible."

"Train wreck."

"Dumpster fire."

Eliza chuckled and swatted Sara. "Hey now, that's my brother you're talking about."

Sara raised her wrists towards Eliza. "Guilty as charged. Lock me up, officer."

The girls laughed together and took another sip of their drinks. But the laughter felt forced. The truth was that Brent really was in a bad way. Not to say that either of their lives was going much better. Sara hadn't been back to Lonesome Dove since the Melissa Question was answered with sickening finality. She'd had Benny empty out her locker and relay a message to the head chef, Carlo, that she was going to be taking a break for a while. It wasn't such a big deal—the restaurant industry was full of flighty people who took off at a moment's notice—but Sara didn't like being unreliable. Still, faced with a choice between putting a dent in her career trajectory and facing Gavin again, she'd take the hit ten times out of ten.

She'd done her best not to think about him in the days and weeks since returning to the island. It had been a mostly successful effort. He'd texted a few half-hearted things, which she ignored. She knew he didn't really mean them. He'd been interested in her as a little weekend fling, nothing more. He didn't deserve her attention. Melissa didn't deserve her jealousy. Sara felt bad for Melissa, actually. It must be hard to live with that cognitive dissonance of hitching her wagon to a man who'd shown her his true colors in gruesome fashion. Still, everyone had to make tough choices sometimes in life. It wasn't a black-and-white kind of world.

"Maybe Brent needs a wife," Eliza mused.

Sara cackled at that. "Baby Brent? Married?! That'll be the day. There's not a single woman in Nantucket that would shack up with that one right now. Not until he cleans himself up, at least."

"Yeah, you're probably right. What about a dog?"

"To own or to marry?"

"Oh jeez, that's dark," Eliza said, rolling her eyes and burying her head in her forearms.

"He can barely take care of himself," Sara went on. "The last thing he needs is another living creature to feed and shelter."

"Two strikes. Should he become a monk, then?" Eliza smiled wryly.

Sara laughed again. She had noticed her sister becoming a little— well, looser wasn't quite the right word, but more relaxed, maybe? Like someone had eased the tension on the guy wires that propped up Eliza Benson. She wasn't sure whether to chalk it up to the wreckage of her sister's life plans, the magic in the Nantucket air, or a little bit of both. But no matter what the cause, Eliza definitely seemed a little less *Eliza*-ish since they'd both returned home. It was an odd change, to be sure, but not necessarily an unwelcome one.

"Only if he's one of those monks who makes beer. He might actually fit in there." It was Sara's turn to sigh. "The Benson family fortunes have really taken a downturn, haven't they?"

Eliza smiled thinly. "I knew I never should've made that deal with the devil. Stupid monkey's paw."

"I hope you got something good out of it, at least." Sara laughed.

"Definitely. The associate on my team with the bad breath got shipped off to London."

"That's a dark joke, too, Lizzy," Sara replied, shaking her head.

Eliza shrugged. "Such is life these days."

She wasn't wrong. The Benson family was indeed struggling a bit. Between Brent's downward spiral, Sara finding herself out of a job, Eliza somehow winding up pregnant and single, and Holly getting frustrated with the domestic life she'd chosen for herself, Mae was the only one who was actually coping with their trauma in anything that resembled a healthy manner. Their mother was sad, of course, but she responded to her grief by staying busy and being helpful. The Benson children had taken the opposite tack.

Sara shivered. It was freezing in here all of a sudden. Trust a Nantucket bar to keep the A/C on an absolutely frigid setting during the summer. "I'm gonna go outside and get a breath of fresh air," she told her sister.

"I'll be here."

Sara nodded and wove her way through the dinnertime patrons and outside. Over the last four months, she had been getting weirdly claustrophobic at the randomest times. Like, she'd just be sitting around, perfectly fine—or at least, whatever passed for perfectly fine lately—and then *boom,* it would feel like the walls were bulging inwards and the roof was about to collapse right on her head. She'd be possessed by an overwhelming need to be outside immediately, and nothing else could calm her down.

She stepped through the doors and was hit at once with the smell of ocean salt on the breeze. There wasn't much of that smell in NYC, which seemed to specialize more in eau de sewage. She hadn't realized how much she missed the sea scent. It had a calming effect on her. She was home here. At peace. She closed her eyes and let it drift over and through her. Her hair trailed in the breeze. She'd been growing it out a little longer than she did normally, and keeping it down. It was almost to her mid-back now. It felt nice not to have to put it up in a severe bun every night so she didn't fry it off over an open flame at work.

"Nothing like that smell, am I right?" came a voice from her right.

Sara nearly jumped out of her skin. She'd thought she was alone. But there was a man sitting on the bench next to her, smoking a cigarette. She whirled around, eyes wide, only to realize that she recognized him.

"Russell Bridges?"

"Oh wow!" he said, looking back at her with the same astonishment on his face. "Sara Benson! Ain't that something."

The decade since high school had treated Russell well. He'd lost the baby fat on his cheeks—the beard helped with that—and his face had a lean, angular look. His hair had the faintest dusting of salt in it now, but mostly the thick black locks were the same as she remembered. He must've picked up exercise or some outdoor hobby, too, because his Nantucket red button-down shirt clung tightly to his chest and biceps.

"You look great," she gushed. She wasn't even fawning; it was just the truth.

"You, too," he said with a grin. "I thought you were in New York, though? I saw your name in an article a little while back."

"I was," Sara replied, waving a hand behind her as if to say, *That's all in the past now.* "Back home for a bit, though."

"Oh. Oh right." Russell's eyes widened and he looked sad all of a sudden. "I forgot. I heard that news, too. I'm so sorry about your dad. He was a great guy."

"Yeah." Sara's gaze fell to her feet. She nudged a leaf with the toe of her shoe awkwardly. She was still so bad at this, no matter how many times she'd had an identical conversation over the last four months. What was she even supposed to say? *Thanks? Yeah, he was? I miss him more than life itself?* Those answers were all equally terrible for one reason or another. Eliza and Mae were much more adept than her at navigating these small-talk waters, so she usually deferred to them whenever possible. When it was just her, she retreated inwards like a turtle until the moment passed.

A beat or two went by before Sara looked up again. "I didn't know you smoked."

Russell blushed. "Bad habit. Trying to quit."

Sara tilted her head to the side and smiled devilishly. "Let me bum one."

He cocked an eyebrow, but said nothing as he fished out the pack from his breast pocket and extended it to her. She pulled a cigarette out and held it between her pursed lips. He stood up and cupped one hand over hers as he lit it for her. When he removed his hand, the slightest warm tingle lingered, like static electricity.

"How's life?" she asked him after she'd taken a drag. It rushed into her lungs. She had to suppress a cough. She hadn't smoked since she first moved to New York. She'd given it a shot then, in a *Maybe I'm one of those cool chef chicks who smokes and curses like one of the guys* kind of moments. But she had quickly discarded it and hadn't looked back. Now, though, it felt weirdly good. She liked having something to do with her hands.

"How's life? Jeez, tough question. Not that swell, to be perfectly honest." Russell ran a hand through his hair. Sara remembered that nervous tic of his. They'd dated, once upon a time, way back when. He was a senior when she was a sophomore. It had started as a stupid kiss in a drunken game of Truth or Dare and emerged into one of those tender high school relationships that kept her sane during years when her hormones threatened to make her run screaming for the hills. He was a good guy, she remembered. Caring. They'd broken up amicably when he left for college and she hadn't seen or heard much of him since, outside of a few random Facebook posts.

"Wait, didn't you get married?" she asked quizzically as she took another drag on her cigarette.

He nodded solemnly. "I did. Then unmarried. Well, been separated for a few months now. But made the split official today, actually." He raised his left hand and waggled the fingers. Sara could make out a faint tan line where his wedding band must have once been.

She winced. "I'm sorry."

He shook his head. "Don't be. I'm sorry enough for both of us. Wasn't exactly a clean split."

"Irreconcilable differences?"

"Sure, as in, she wanted to be with someone different, and I wasn't able to reconcile with that." He chuckled and shook his head again.

"Yikes. If it's any consolation, my life isn't exactly all that grand at the moment."

"Divorce?" he asked cautiously, looking at her left hand where she held the cigarette at her side.

"Nah. Didn't even get that far. Boss, employee, other woman. You can connect the dots. It was pretty ugly, too."

He let out a low whistle. "That's a raw deal right there. What're you doing now?"

She laughed. "You're full of questions."

He blanched at once. "You're right, I'm so sorry. I don't know why I'm prying. Not very polite of me at all." He turned to leave, but Sara caught his forearm.

"I'm just teasing. It's fine. You show me yours and I'll show you mine, you know?"

He hesitated, looking into her eyes to see if she was serious. When he realized that she was, he relaxed a little. "If you're sure. Really, though, I don't mind leaving. You just came out here for a breath of fresh air, not the Spanish Inquisition."

She waved him away. "Nonsense. I want to catch up. Let's sit." They settled down onto the bench. "You asked what I was doing. Not much, is the answer. I had some savings built up, so I've been all right since my dad's funeral. Living at home helps. But I'm running low, and I can't go back to New York. Gavin—that's the guy—he's a big shot down there. Anyone who'd hire me would want his okay first, and to be honest, I'm terrified to find out what he'd say."

Russell nodded. He hadn't taken his eyes off her since they sat down. Not in a creepy way, but just an intense listening expression. His eyes were a light gray. "Makes sense. I heard your mom was running the Sweet Island Inn now. How's that?"

Sara ran a hand through her hair and took the final puff on her cigarette before stubbing it out in the ash tray at her side. "Great. She needs to be busy. The inn is perfect for her. Work never stops there."

"I figured. I know the feeling."

"You're still living here, right? What're you doing for work?"

"Yep, still on the island. Doing some internet marketing. It's gone fairly well, not to be a braggart, but it keeps me busy all hours of the day."

Sara smiled suspiciously as she looked at him. "Vague 'internet marketing,' lots of money, and a weird schedule? Russell Bridges, are you a drug dealer?"

He threw his head back and laughed for a good long while at that. He had a nice laugh. It reminded her of her dad's. He really committed to it—tearing up, slapping a knee, a full guffaw from deep within. It was the kind of laugh that made you want to laugh with him. Warm, inviting. Finally, he simmered down.

"I forgot you laughed like that," Sara said with a smile.

He grinned sheepishly. "MaryAnne hated it. Said I laughed like a buffoon."

"Well, you don't have to worry about that anymore, I guess. If you're looking for an upside." Sara thought maybe she'd gone too far when Russell winced, but his smile quickly returned.

"I suppose you're right," he said. "Maybe it is time to start looking for the good stuff yet to come. Speaking of which," he continued, "I'm starving, and I've been craving a slice of pizza since we sat down. Any interest in joining me?"

Sara thought about it and then nodded. "That sounds great. Let me go tell my sister I'm leaving."

"You got it. I'll be here."

After sticking her head back in the bar and telling Eliza she was going to get pizza with an old friend, she and Russell went and sat outside the pizza parlor for a while. They had a couple beers each and more slices of pizza than Sara cared to admit. It felt good to catch up with him. He really did have a nice laugh, and this older Russell was handsome. He was such a good listener, too. He looked like he immersed himself in whatever she was saying, as if there was nothing else in the world more important than the words coming out of her lips. After months of pining after someone who didn't seem to give a darn what she did or said, it felt nice to be attended to like that.

Plus, he was funny. He had her howling more than once during the couple of hours they sat together, wiping tears from her eyes and the whole nine yards. Making fun of people they both knew from high school, of his ex-wife and Gavin. For all that he seemed weighed down by his own worries, Russell was a lighthearted person. In his presence, Sara felt her own burdens ease up somewhat.

"Oh, shoot!" she blurted after a while. "It's almost nine! I promised my niece I'd call to tuck her in." Sara and Alice had a standing agreement to video chat on Friday nights so that Sara could "tuck her in" virtually. She would've just done it here, but her phone was dead and she'd left her charger at the house on Howard Street.

"Well, all good things must come to an end, I guess," Russell said with mock-mournfulness.

"Afraid so."

"Maybe we can do it again sometime?" he asked. He didn't quite look at her as he said it, and he didn't voice it outright, but Sara knew what he was getting at.

"If you're gonna ask me on a date, you better do it properly. I am a lady, after all."

"You curse like a sailor, so I wasn't quite sure."

She smacked him on the shoulder. "Watch it!"

Russell laughed. Then, he pretended to doff an imaginary cap and said, "M'lady, would you do me the pleasure of sharing your company again on some other fine evening?"

Sara groaned and rolled her eyes. "I changed my mind. I prefer the first method."

They chuckled together again. "For real, though," Russell said after an awkward pause. "I'd love to take you out sometime. Like on a real date. If you're interested."

She gave him a wide smile. "Yeah. I think I'd like that a lot."

"Perfect," he said. "Then it's a date. I'll see you soon, Sara Benson."

"Good night, Russell Bridges." She kissed him on the cheek and then left before he could say anything else.

19

ELIZA

Brent gone. Sara gone. Just Eliza left by herself. Life had been doing that to her far too often lately. She'd been weirdly nervous about it, too. Anxious, in a way she never used to be. She had spent more or less the entirety of her life as a lone wolf. Introverted, yes, but more in an "I don't need other people" way than anything resembling shyness. She'd done just fine on her own. She'd come this far.

So why did she suddenly need people around her?

Since the day she found out she was pregnant, she'd been victim to a constant need to be surrounded by others. Her family was the best salve for her anxieties. Having Mom or Brent or Sara or Holly around —though each of them was currently messed up in their own way— was the closest thing to a cure for the heart-racing, sweaty-palmed fear that overtook her whenever she had a quiet moment to herself. Even now, in a bar full of people on the island where she'd grown up, she felt uncomfortable. She kept shuffling around in her seat. The seltzer seemed flat all of a sudden. The music was overly loud. Was that guy looking at her?

"Get it together," she mumbled to herself under her breath. Sara had left what, five minutes ago? Stuck her head in the door and said she'd run into an old friend and was going to get pizza. The thought of pizza turned Eliza's stomach. This pregnancy was doing strange things to her body. She was hypersensitive to smell, though she'd never been one to have a strong nose for fragrances before. Now, if she closed her eyes and focused, she could sense the sweat hiding beneath the heavy-handed cologne worn by the man four stools down at the bar. She could smell the limes in the garnish caddy a few feet away.

"Need something, Liz?" asked Big Mack from behind the bar. Her eyes flew open. She knew him vaguely—a friend of her brother's in some form or another. Always seemed like a nice enough man. He looked like a grizzly bear, large and hairy and tattooed. But nice. Warm.

Eliza smiled at him. "I'm good, thanks."

"You got it. Lemme know if you want a refresher on that thing," he said, nodding towards the seltzer she'd been babysitting since she first arrived.

"Will do."

He turned away to help someone else who was calling for his attention from the far end of the bar. Eliza let out a long sigh. She was far too deep inside her own head these days. Four months of quivering whenever she was left alone and smelling stuff from dozens of yards away, like she fancied herself a superhero, was really doing a number on her psyche. She used to be strong. Fearless. She batted leadoff her entire life because the pressure never got to her. First up to bat, no idea what kind of heat the opposing pitcher would be bringing, it didn't matter. She knew how to execute. She knew how to do the work.

But what did she know about anything that was happening now? She knew nothing about death, or babies, or breakups. The only thing she knew for certain was that she didn't know what to do next. She'd left so much in her wake: Clay, work, the city, her safe and richly decorated life. It had seemed so easy to rid herself of those accoutrements. She'd ended things with Clay with four neat pitches into his chest: engagement ring, pregnancy test, pregnancy test, pregnancy test. Then goodbye forever. She'd left Goldman Sachs— temporarily—with a blunt email to Marty Fleishman, also CC'ing Janine, the head of HR.

I need some time off. I have vacation days accrued. Please consider this an indefinite leave of absence.

Best, Eliza.

She knew Marty wouldn't like it, but she also knew that she'd already hit her revenue goals for the year, she was his best employee, and Marty could just figure out how to pick up the slack in her absence. She'd be back when she got her head screwed on correctly. When she had a plan.

It was easy to leave New York behind. Easier than she might've expected. She'd always told herself she loved the city. Didn't everybody tell themselves that? "Oh, it's just so lively! There's always something happening! It's the capital of the world!" Blah, blah, blah. Everybody said the same garbage. Few, if any of them, believed it, or took the time to see it for themselves. In Eliza's experience, most people moved to New York with starlit dreams of galivanting down Fifth Avenue and attending rock 'n roll shows in East Village. But— down to a person—they always ended up building a nest in some overpriced apartment and leaving it as rarely as they could manage. She was no different and no better than the rest. She'd done exactly that.

But she didn't miss her nest. Not one piece of art or furniture. Not a single aspect of the decor she'd slaved over. She didn't care what happened to any of it. Let Clay keep it or sell it or give it to a homeless man in the Bowery. As a matter of fact, she didn't want to see any of it ever again.

She sighed and took another sip of her seltzer. Nantucket was a different world than New York. She could smell the ocean no matter where she went, super-powered nose or not. People here looked her in the eye and smiled when she passed them on the street. She knew all the street corners and the shop owners. It was nice to feel like a living, breathing person and not another rodent in the rat race.

It also compounded her anxiety tenfold. People around here knew her. They expected her to do well. She always had done well, hadn't she? Yes. Of course. Eliza Benson succeeded. That was what people knew. That was the promise she had spent a lifetime delivering on. Dad had always introduced her to his friends and clients as "Eliza, my rock-star eldest." It used to make her proud. She'd smile and shake hands like an adult, with a fire in her eyes that said, "*Yes, that is what I am.*"

Now, though, she was faking the heck out of that.

She looked around the bar. The sun had set not too long ago, so it was almost dark out. Brent liked this bar because Big Mack served him doubles and only charged for singles. Sara liked it because there was live music a few nights a week. Eliza liked it because it was the least likely spot to run into someone she knew, and the open windows kept the smell of sticky beer from getting too nauseating.

The crowd looked like a mix of regulars and tourists, weighted towards the latter. A few tanned fishermen were knocking back pitchers in the corners. Some old ladies were chitchatting over their chardonnays. And then there was Eliza, smack-dab in the middle all by her lonesome, with a room-temp seltzer and the threat of a migraine looming on the horizon.

That, plus the wet spot on her back when someone suddenly jostled into her from behind and poured half their beer down her side.

"Oh man, I'm so sorry!" came the voice from behind her. She came to her senses and turned around. The guilty party was a tall man she didn't recognize. He had dark hair, long and unruly, with high cheekbones and bright green eyes. His skin was pale—he must not be from here—and the hand that he offered to help her up from her suddenly soaking wet stool was soft and supple. "Someone bumped into me, and—ay, I got you good."

Eliza looked down and grimaced. She was wearing blue jeans and a white blouse. Both were drenched down her right side with a Nantucket craft beer. The smell was overwhelming. She got a little dizzy for a second and had to reach out to grab the stranger by his outstretched hand to stop herself from falling.

"Whoa. You okay?" the man asked, his eyes narrowing in concern.

"Yeah. Yes. Fine," Eliza murmured. She blinked a few times to clear her head, then looked up at him. He was handsome, in an artistic sort of way. Sad, expressive eyes, and very full lips. He looked like a runway model, the ones she'd seen a few times in Manhattan, usually prowling down the sidewalks on the Lower East Side with cigarettes dangling from their mouths.

"What's your name?" he asked her. His voice had changed a little bit. Dropped in tone, a little softer, enough to make her lean in just slightly. He had a dark, swirling scent radiating from him. Eliza couldn't place it.

"Eliza Benson."

"Eliza Benson," he echoed. "I don't think I've seen you around here before."

"Was I supposed to check in with you?" she snapped.

He held up his hands in mock defense. "No insult intended," he said. "I'm just the bar pianist. I see most of these people all the time. But not you. You, I would remember."

She winced and felt bad immediately. Why was she being so confrontational? It wasn't his fault that she had a migraine coming on and a bevy of personal and familial tragedies on her plate. She made a conscious decision to lower her defenses a little bit. This was Nantucket, not New York. She didn't need to be so on guard against everyone.

"Sorry. Didn't mean to snap. Just had … a rough day, let's call it. A few of them in a row, actually."

He nodded solemnly. "I can see it on your face."

She laughed at that. "Oh? Are you the bar fortune-teller, too?"

The man chuckled. "No. I just have a knack for reading people. Nothing supernatural about it. You have sad eyes."

Eliza blushed and looked down at the man's feet. He was wearing dark leather boots, despite the heat, and slim-fit jeans tucked into them. "Sad eyes, huh?" she murmured half-heartedly. She wasn't sure what she was really supposed to say to a statement like that. She felt dumb immediately. She couldn't remember the last time she'd felt so thick-lipped and slow-witted.

"Yes, sad eyes," the man repeated. She risked a glance up. He was frowning—not in a mean way, more studiously, like he was really *looking* at her, with a degree of intensity that was honestly a little bit unnerving. "But a proud face. Anyway," he said, shaking his head like he was coming out of a trance, "I'm sorry I spilled my drink on you. Can I get your next round to make up for it?"

Eliza raised her seltzer to show him. "Good with this, thanks. Pregnant." Apparently, she'd forgotten how to use nouns and verbs in her sentences. Why was she fumbling over her words all of a sudden? It was strange. The man had an aura to him, which—before this moment—was something that Eliza would have found utterly ridiculous for anyone else to say about another human being. Eliza

Benson was not the kind of person who believed in energy or vibes or auras. But there was something distinct about this man that was messing with her head a little bit.

Probably wasn't the man, actually. Just the stress of the last few months piling up. The death of her father, pregnancy hormones, and a sudden breakup, all compounding into a weird misfiring of her once rock-solid mental circuitry. Yes, that made way more sense. This man was just a catalyst for all that. Nothing more.

He nodded again. His eyes hadn't left hers since the moment they'd first met. *Intense* was exactly the right word for him. He didn't blink. Just stared at her with those piercing green eyes.

"May I sit?" he asked, pointing at the stool next to hers. "I'm done for the night."

She hesitated, then nodded. "Sure. Make yourself at home." The man settled down next to her. "You know," she said, turning to him, "I didn't catch your name."

"Oliver," he replied.

"Oliver what?"

"Patterson. Want a business card?"

That, she knew, was sarcasm. She blushed again. She'd never been much of a blusher—until tonight. "Sorry. Just wondering if I knew your family. Are you from Nantucket?"

He shook his head and grinned sheepishly. "Now it's my turn to apologize for being aggressive. To answer your question—no, I am not from Nantucket. Tennessee, originally. Been kind of floating around the East Coast for a while now. Got sick of the snowbirds in Florida, so here I am." He spread his arms wide. "King of the Bar."

Eliza hid her laughter behind a drink from her glass. Big Mack came by and refilled it, giving her a subtle wink on his way over. "Quite the kingdom you've got here, Your Majesty," she teased.

"Oh, you don't know the half of it," Oliver said with a shimmer in his eye. "Everything from the Coors Light taps to the men's restroom is my domain. My loyal subjects worship at my feet."

"Watch it, bud," Big Mack warned with a chuckle from behind the bar.

Oliver waited until he strolled away, then stage-whispered to Eliza, "Insolence will not be tolerated."

"I heard that!" Big Mack called.

They all laughed.

"So, Eliza Benson," Oliver continued, turning to her and steepling his fingers, "you must be from around here, then. What's your story?"

Eliza opened her mouth, then swallowed her words. For a wild moment, she'd been about to launch into the whole thing. Not just the recent stuff, but also the way-back stuff. The growing-up-here, golden-child stuff. The sprint-to-the-city stuff. The GS-and-Clay-and-unexpected-pregnancy stuff.

Why on earth would she spill her heart out like that to this man?

"Cat got your tongue?" he asked with an arched eyebrow.

"No, it's just—I don't know you, and I was about to tell you my whole life story."

Oliver smiled. His eyes stayed locked on hers. "Give it to me, Eliza. I'd love to hear it."

He looked sincere. So she did.

By the time she caught up to the present, two hours had passed, and some of the patrons were starting to filter out of the bar to go home. Oliver had scarcely blinked for the whole time she was talking. The craziest thing was that, once she started, she couldn't have stopped if she wanted to. It was like she'd been dying to unload her burdens on a stranger, though she hadn't felt any such impulse even once in her entire life before now.

Well, no—the *actual* craziest thing was that Oliver had listened to the whole thing, start-to-finish, with a full-body intensity that unsettled Eliza. She'd never felt so *seen* before. Oliver was straddling his stool to face her, and he nodded and laughed and looked heartbroken in all the right places. It was like he was feeling her life *through* her, feeling it *with* her. It was, to put a word on it, really freaking weird. But not necessarily weird in a bad way. More like weird in a way as if she'd relived every moment of the last few years and realized that she'd had a ghostly presence alongside her the whole time. Once she got used to it, it was actually kind of comforting.

"... And so, here I am, nursing a lukewarm seltzer water and contemplating what my life has become, when some smart aleck who thinks I have sad eyes comes along and spills his beer on me."

Oliver nodded. "Guilty as charged. I am your rock bottom."

"Cheers to that," Eliza said, tapping her glass against his in a mock toast.

"A very handsome rock bottom though, wouldn't you say?" he pressed with a smile.

"Let's not get ahead of ourselves." She hadn't stopped smiling since Oliver first bumped into her, and her cheeks were starting to hurt. But their banter was infectious. It felt natural. They'd fallen right into it without any hesitation or confusion. No stepping on each other's feet. She'd never felt anything like that with Clay. Or with anybody, really. Her dad, maybe, but that was a whole different kind of relationship. This was like fencing, which she'd dabbled in at a roommate's insistence back at Penn. Shanti was the daughter of a telecom executive in Mumbai. She went to a prep school somewhere in the UK before coming to Philadelphia for undergrad. She was a sweet girl with a mischievous streak. She'd dragged Eliza to an open call for the fencing team one summer when Eliza had run out of excuses to avoid it. Eliza had picked it up quickly—she was a good athlete, after all—and found that the rhythm of it, the back and forth and advance and retreat—was pleasing to her. The best fencing matches had a beautiful cadence to them. This, now, felt like that had felt back then. Lunge, parry, riposte, retreat. A place for everything and everything in its place. It was oddly satisfying.

"What's on your agenda tonight then? First day of the rest of your life, you know. Since I'm your rock bottom and everything. Can only improve from here."

"Lord, I hope so," she muttered. Oliver pretended to let his jaw fall open like she'd mortally wounded his ego. She blushed immediately. "Not like that! Not like that. Honestly, you're the best thing that's happened to me in months. My dad is gone, my brother might as well be, and my sisters are ... well, they've got their own stuff to deal with. I've always been a little more independent than them, anyway. It's nice to just sit and talk with such a good listener."

Oliver smiled, nodded, and smoothed away the loose bangs that had fallen over his forehead. "It sounds like you need to have some fun."

Eliza nodded. "Yeah. Like a hot date. Know anybody?"

He sat up straight, serious as a heart attack, and looked around the bar. "What about him?" He pointed at an old man slumped in a corner with a half-empty whiskey dangling from his hand.

"About forty years too old, I think," Eliza retorted, playing along.

"Him?"

"Too bald."

"That one?"

"Too old *and* too bald."

He shrugged. "Guess you're stuck with me, then."

Eliza laughed. "It would appear so."

"So how 'bout it? A hot date with the king of the bar?"

"I'll have to check my calendar."

Oliver stood up, nearly knocking over his stool. "Nonsense. You look free to me. Come on."

"Now?"

He nodded with the utmost seriousness. "Right now. You've been sitting in that chair way too long and depriving the dance floor of a beautiful woman's presence. Plus, I love this song, and I'm one hell of a dancer. So, take my hand, and let's go cut it up."

Eliza gnawed at her lip again. She thought about saying no. Flirting with this handsome stranger was one thing. He was funny and charming and also smart and perceptive. He had a presence that seemed bigger than himself, like it could wrap her up in him. And the dimple in his chin was very, very cute.

But on the other hand, she'd just ended an engagement not too long ago. She had the smoldering ruins of her happily-ever-after still looming in the rear-view mirror, and it didn't feel right to turn her back on that quite so soon. After all, what would Clay think?

That was the thought that made her stand up and take Oliver's hand. *What would Clay think?* More to the point was, who cared what Clay would think? Clay was no longer a part of Eliza's life. As far as she was concerned, this baby was the product of immaculate conception, and whatever relationship she once had with the man in the Hermès tie was now dissolved by mutual accord. She was leaving behind helicopter engagements and dinners at Tao and expensive abstract art.

That sounded lovely to Eliza.

She took Oliver's hand, and they went dancing.

20

HOLLY

Holly Benson was about to rip her hair out by the roots. Her house looked like a war zone. Decapitated G.I. Joes and Barbies were strewn across the living room floor. Holly and Pete thought they were connecting their kids to their own childhoods when she'd given each of them the toys they'd grown up with, instead of the fancy new gadgets that every kid on the block seemed to crave these days. But that had backfired, clearly, because Grady loved nothing more than performing gruesome surgery on the figures—transplanting heads, trading out arms for guns, and on and on like that. And Alice—her sweet, gentle Alice—thought that it was the funniest thing in the world, to Holly's surprise. So, between the action figure debacle, snack time that had devolved into a food fight despite Holly's best efforts and sternest Mom Voice, and the housework that seemed to pile up and never, ever end, she was this close to losing it.

Summertime was always tough, with the kids home from school. But this summer was especially hard. She'd been having—well, calling it "PTSD" felt wrong to her; that was for soldiers, not housewives—but it felt something like that. She wasn't sleeping well. Pete either rolled around or he didn't move at all and she wasn't sure which option was worse. Most nights, she woke up from what little sleep she could find to check his breathing and make sure he was still with her. When the kids weren't looking, she'd had a half-dozen "episodes," as she called them, when she would find herself getting short of breath and dizzy and having to grip the kitchen counter just to make sure she didn't fall over. She jumped at unexpected noises and lost her temper far more easily than ever before.

She was always the mild-mannered middle child. Easygoing, pleasant, upbeat.

Not so much these days. Not so much at all.

And Pete ... where even to begin with the problem of Pete? He had tried to do what he could in the wake of her family's tragedy. He'd said the right things and held her at the right times. He was a good guy at heart, after all. But even while holding her tight and kissing her forehead and wiping her tears away, he still felt ... distant? Absent? She wasn't quite sure what the correct word was, but it was obvious that, even when he was with her, he was never fully present.

He had his own things to handle. It was clear that he was just as frustrated as Holly with the kids' newfound chaotic tendencies. Beyond that, he was continuing to drown in work. The firm had taken on a bevy of new clients, which was ostensibly a good thing, but as far as Holly could tell, thus far it meant only more hours for Pete and no concordant bump in pay. He left the house early and came home late or not at all. Spending multiple nights per week at the office wasn't something a thirty-three-year-old husband and father should be doing, in her opinion. But the partners at the firm couldn't seem to care less. Work needed doing, and Pete was apparently the one who had to do it.

They hadn't had a date or a night alone together in God knows how long. Even on those rare nights when all the stars aligned and both Grady and Alice had sleepovers at friends' houses, she and Pete just sat on opposite couches and watched TV until one or both of them fell asleep. They'd almost made it through a whole half-hour sitcom without snoring, once. But for the most part, they were like two ships passing in the harbor. Some muted greetings in the morning, a quick kiss goodbye, and then off into their own worlds.

Holly missed *Pete*. Not Pete as he was currently constructed, but the old Pete. The goofy, dorky Pete who loved her like he loved breathing. The Pete Things had all but disappeared. In their place was the behavior of a soulless automaton. He left the best parts of himself at the office each day and either couldn't or wouldn't bring his heart home to her like he always had before.

She'd understood, at first. She'd been supportive. But it was weighing on her now like the sky itself had settled on her shoulders. When she wasn't anxious, she was sad, and when she wasn't sad, she was exhausted.

This was no way to live.

She looked up at the clock. It was seven forty-three p.m. That meant she could hustle the kids through the bath and into bed in seventeen minutes. That wasn't such a long time span on paper, but it seemed like a daunting eternity with how dog-tired she was from chasing after her children all day. Grady thought it was funny recently to yank on his sister's pigtails, and Alice had learned a few curse words from a bad kid at school, so it had been tête-à-tête between them since the moment they opened their eyes.

Who on earth invented summer vacation? It was the bane of Holly's existence at the moment. Sure, she enrolled her kids in various camps and daily activities like any good mom would do. But those weren't every day, and the weekends still loomed like a bear in the back of a cave. Thankfully, Grady and Alice would both be going to a five-week summer camp in the Green Mountain National Forest, starting tomorrow. Holly had had the date circled on her calendar for months. She felt guilty for being so giddy about it. A good mom would be sad about her kids going away for five weeks. Did looking forward to it make her a bad mother? She wrung her hands and decided not to think about it. She loved her children, but being a stay-at-home mom felt like a thankless job from hell some days.

She spent the next seventeen minutes making herself a cup of tea and keeping an eye through the window on Alice and Grady running around in the backyard. The fireflies were out in the dim light of the setting sun. It looked like the kids were having a contest to see how many they could catch.

The tea helped calm her nerves. She checked her cell phone. There was a text from Pete. *Not super late tonight. Be home in an hour, give or take.*

She texted back, *Love you,* but he didn't respond.

An hour later, the kids were bathed and bedded. They'd both been reasonably good throughout the process. Running around outside must have worn them out, because they were both asleep pretty much as soon as their heads hit the pillow. Thank the Lord for small favors.

Holly pulled the door of their shared bedroom closed behind her as silently as she could. Tiptoeing down the hallway—avoiding the creaky spots in the hardwood floors, as always—she went into her bedroom and let out a long sigh.

Her heart hurt. She missed her dad. He was always so good at cheering her up on the rare occasions she got down. She wondered what he'd say right now. Something cheesy, no doubt. *Keep your chin up,* or *Don't let the rug rats drive you too crazy!* It was the *way* he said things more than what he said. She still had a voice mail he'd left her almost eight months ago. She listened to it sometimes when she felt really sad. It was just him rambling about Christmas plans, but she loved hearing the timbre of his voice again. Little mementos like that were the last things she had left of her father. She treasured them all.

She took a quick shower and then wrapped herself in the fluffy white bathrobe that Pete had gotten her for their wedding anniversary two years ago. It had "Mom" embroidered on the breast pocket. The big master bathroom was steamy from the hot shower. She swiped away a patch of fog and eyed herself in the reflection.

She was pale and worn, that much was obvious. Bags under her eyes and red-rimmed irises stared back at her balefully. She pinched and tugged at the skin of her face. She felt *thin*—not thin as in skinny, but thin like a sheet of dough that had been rolled out too much. Like one good poke from something unexpected would do irreversible damage.

She heard Pete arrive home. First, the car pulling into the driveway and the engine cutting off. The jangle of his keys as he opened the front door, then the clomp of his feet down the hallway towards their bedroom. She winced. He never avoided the squeaky spots, and he was such a heavy walker. She'd read him the riot act if he woke up either one of their little hellions. She held her breath and listened for the telltale "Moooom!" that would erupt from their room if that happened. But, thankfully, it didn't. He pushed into their bedroom.

"Holly?" he called softly.

"In here."

She heard the thump of his briefcase hitting the ground, followed by one shoe, then the other. "Christ almighty, I'm beat."

"Long day?" she asked.

"Relative to my other days? No. Relative to the normal limits of human exhaustion? It went above and beyond."

She waited for him to ask her, *And how was your day?* Pete always asked her that. She had an answer ready. *It was long. I needed you here.*

The kids were terrible and the house is a disaster and I'm at my wit's end. If I knew you were by my side, maybe it wouldn't be so bad. But I feel like you're nowhere to be found when I need you the most, and even when you're here, you might as well not be.

But the question never came.

She sighed, pivoted, and pushed open the bathroom door. Pete was already snoring softly on the bed, still wearing his suit and tie. She looked at him for a long moment. Should she say what she had been contemplating for weeks now? It was on the tip of her tongue and she wanted to say it so badly. But once it was said, it couldn't be unsaid, so she had to be very, very sure.

She loved Pete. That much was never ever in question. But her dad had always told her, on those occasions when Brent consented to let one of his sisters join him and Henry out on a fishing expedition, that a good fisherman knew when to cut bait.

She wanted so badly to raise a family and be a good wife to her husband. But she wasn't getting anything out of what she was putting in. She couldn't keep trying so hard with no return.

"Pete," she said, nudging his foot. "Pete, honey, wake up."

"Mmf?" he mumbled.

"Pete, we need to talk."

He cracked an eye open. "Can it wait 'til morning?"

She shook her head. "No, we need to talk now."

Sighing, he opened the other eye and propped himself up on an elbow. "What's up?"

She steeled herself, closed her eyes, and said the words she'd been practicing in the mirror for almost two months: "Pete, I want to take a break."

~

The next day was the strangest one Holly could remember in a long time. Pete had called in sick and taken the morning off work to help her pack up the kids for their sleepaway camp. He hadn't said much, which was unusual for him, but he'd been extra helpful. Loading the bags into the car, feeding the kids breakfast, the works.

It only served to make things that harder when he asked her if she was sure about the plan she'd laid out last night. She could barely hold back her tears when she nodded and said, "Yes, I'm sure."

He'd looked her in the eyes, one at a time, as if to double-check. He must have seen something in there, because he just nodded and handed her a thermos full of hot coffee. "Drive safe then. Let me know when you get there."

"I will," she said.

She'd gotten into the car, with the kids buckled into their seats in the back, already absorbed in whatever movie or TV show or video game was currently in vogue. She'd driven the four hours into Vermont and dropped the kids off at camp, doing all the chitchatting with other parents and the kids' counselors in the process. She'd made Alice and Grady's bunk beds in their cabins, she'd kissed them goodbye, and she'd told them to be good. Then she'd gotten back in the car and turned around to head home.

Not home as in the house she shared with Pete, but *home* as in Nantucket. She needed somewhere she could go to clear her head for a while. She needed her family.

21

MAE

Where had all the time gone? Four months had vanished in the blink of an eye, whooshing past like cars headed the other direction on the interstate. Mae had stayed busy—she'd made darn sure of that. If there was one thing her parents had taught her not to be, it was a lazybones. Mae Benson was a sled dog—at her happiest when she was working.

Which wasn't to say that she was happy, exactly. How could she be? Life had given her a whole bushel of some very sour lemons lately. If she dwelled on it too long or too fiercely, it was liable to overwhelm her. Parts of her ached that she'd never known could ache before. Her heart hurt physically most days, this throb in her chest that stayed constant no matter what else was going on around her. She knew without even having to ask that she was going to feel that ache for the rest of her life.

But, ache or no ache, she was a hummingbird down to her core, and she couldn't just sit still. Toni's offer had been a blessing in disguise. Because the Sweet Island Inn was endless work. Every morning, she'd start early, before the sun. Better that way than to dawdle in bed and let thoughts of coulda, woulda, shoulda drag her down into their depths. She'd wake up and, before she could think to do anything else, toss off the covers, stick her feet in her house shoes, and get moving. A quick brush of the teeth and fixing of her hair, slight dab of makeup, and the day began.

It had taken her some time to get used to this new home. She'd spent so long at 114 Howard Street. She knew that house inside and out. Every squeak and loose floorboard, every drafty spot. But the inn wasn't hers, not truly, and so she and it were taking some time to get to know each other.

Thankfully, Toni was as responsible and orderly a woman as there was on this planet. Everything in the inn had a place, a pattern. Breakfast came first. That meant grinding up coffee beans and setting hot water to boil. While that was getting going, Mae started heating up the skillet and putting bacon on so it could fry up in time for the early-bird guests to fill their bellies. Mr. and Mrs. Hansen, a stylish older couple from Boston, had been the first ones downstairs each morning since they arrived for their summer vacation four days ago. Mae knew that Mr. Hansen liked his bacon extra crispy, while his wife used so much creamer in her coffee that it was like she was starting her day with dessert. They were pleasant and polite as could be. Mae had enjoyed getting to know them.

With bacon sizzling and the hot water now poured over the coffee grounds in the French press, the kitchen began to smell delicious. Mae got out the big glass mixing bowl and cracked in a half-dozen eggs to make omelets from. Alongside that, she chopped up a few fistfuls of vegetables—tomatoes, onions, and peppers from Lola's garden—along with cracking open a new jar of Puckermouth Jalapeños, a local brand. Donnie Alvarez, a Californian man staying in Room 3, liked his breakfast spicy. Lastly, she set the buffet up with cutlery and plates for everybody to grab at their leisure. Breakfast was technically open from seven a.m. to nine thirty every morning, though Mae had been known to relax the rules a bit for guests who she'd taken a shine to.

No one was up yet, though, so Mae tucked the bacon on a tray in the hot drawer and stashed the omelet ingredients in the fridge while she went about her other errands.

Spare linens were kept in the downstairs closet on the left-hand side. She pulled out a set of bedsheets and bustled down to Room 1 to prepare the bed for a guest who would be arriving that afternoon. The booking he'd made was unusually sparse on details. The Sweet Island Inn's website asked guests to provide a little blurb about who they were and what they wanted to do while they were visiting Nantucket, so Mae usually had some idea of how she could best accommodate her guests during their stay. But this one had only a name—Dominic O'Kelley—and an open-ended booking duration, nothing more. Odd, but not something to get too worked up over.

She dusted his room a bit once the bed was made and checked in the bathroom. She made a mental note to come back and bring fresh towels, since there were none in there at the moment. After that, she watered the plants in the main areas and mopped the foyer where the Davidsons, a cute little family of four, had tracked in sand after their beach visit yesterday.

The rest of the morning went on and on like that. It was busy work, exactly what she wanted, and exactly what had filled up every one of her days that summer. It was good to be out of her home. There were far too many memories there, lingering around every corner. Even the most innocuous things had threatened to bring a tear from her eye during the few days after her husband's funeral. Like the mantelpiece above the fireplace, where Henry had bumped his head hard once while trying to sneak up on Mae reading a book in her favorite overstuffed armchair. Or the doorframe in the kitchen, notched with her children's heights over the years. The whole home was brimming with things that she couldn't bear to remember right now. Staying at the inn was much less difficult.

She'd done a good job of staying active and social, even when she just wanted to retreat into her bedroom and mourn. She still went on her weekly Sunday evening walks with Lola and Debra, her lifelong friends. She still attended town council meetings on the first Thursday night of every month, so as to be an informed citizen of the island. She knew that people expected her to dissolve into a puddle of tears, but she was determined not to. Chin up, smile plastered on —that was how Mae Benson liked to live her life, even when it felt awfully hard to stick to those principles. When it was hardest, that's when she stuck to it most. "Fake it 'til you make it," as Henry would've said, and, even when some days still weighed more heavily on her than others, she was making it, slowly but surely. Little by little, the fog was lifting, though the ache in her chest never shifted.

She'd just finished tucking some dirty bedsheets into the washing machine to start a batch of laundry when she heard some footsteps thumping down the stairs. She hit the ON button on the machine and went into the kitchen.

"Good morning!" she chirped brightly. Mr. Davidson was filling up a cup of coffee. He'd told her upon arrival that he was an engineer of some sort, and he certainly looked the part. He was a tall man, with thinning hair. Mae thought he was in his late forties or early fifties.

"Good morning, Miss Mae!" he said back to her with a kind smile. "Miss Mae" was how she introduced herself to everybody who stayed at the inn. It set a little string in her heart thrumming sadly every time, but the truth was that she was no longer a Mrs., and she didn't much want to delve into that topic besides.

"What are we off to do today?" she asked him. "Can I make you some breakfast? Omelets this morning!"

He held up a hand. "None for me, thank you. We're headed downtown to walk around the shops. Then the beach this afternoon, I believe. Say, I was wondering if you had any recommendations for a good brunch spot out that way?"

Mae smiled. "Why, of course! Let me grab you a map and I'll give you a few to pick from." She went searching through the drawer in the foyer and retrieved one of the Nantucket map brochures that Toni kept piled up for just such an occasion. Brandishing a highlighter pen, she gave Mr. Davidson directions to a few of her favorite breakfast restaurants on the island, along with a little bonus of a hidden beach not too far off the main road.

"Thanks so much," he said warmly when she was finished. "You've been an amazing hostess. I'm so sad our vacation is almost over."

"Well, I'll be here whenever you folks decide to come back. You have a beautiful family, and you are all welcome here anytime!"

He stuck out a hand to shake, but Mae pulled him into a gentle hug. "I'm a hugger!" she said by way of explanation and/or apology. Mr. Davidson looked sheepish, but he laughed and hugged her back.

"Gonna go wrangle Diane and the kids, and then we'll be off to breakfast, then."

"Enjoy!" Mae called back as they parted ways.

Mr. and Mrs. Hansen came down shortly thereafter, headed to the beach again to laze the day away pleasantly. Mae gave them a little picnic basket she'd prepared the night before. It had a few snacks and some water bottles in it to help them along their way.

Donnie wasn't far behind, but he was on the island for business, so he just grabbed a thermos for the road and bid Mae goodbye for the day.

And with that, suddenly the inn was empty. Mae checked her phone. She hadn't heard from any of her children yet that day. Eliza and Sara usually came over to help out around dinnertime. Sara had taken to testing out new recipes on the guests, all of whom were continually amazed by her finesse in the kitchen. Mae always smiled when Sara made sure to let them know that her mother had taught her everything she knew. After years of butting heads, it sure was nice to be in a good place in her relationship with her youngest daughter.

Eliza was more of a complex case. She'd always been so self-sufficient that Mae to this day wasn't quite sure about the inner workings of her eldest's mind. But she'd been volunteering her time, too, mostly on the business end of things, helping Toni manage bookings and the inn's advertisements on Google and Facebook.

Holly had gone back home to Plymouth after the funeral, but she and Mae still talked on the phone a few times a week. Compared to Eliza, Holly had always been an open book. She wore her emotions plainly —not quite to Sara's heart-on-her-sleeve extent, but still enough that Mae could tell just from the tone of her voice that not all was right in her middle daughter's world. She'd have to find some time soon to suss out just what was the matter.

And then Brent ... well, that was a heartache in and of itself. She needed to check in on him today, but he likely wouldn't be awake until the early afternoon, so she'd text him then. Best not to think of that until she must.

All in all, it had been a horribly hard summer for the Benson family. It seemed like all of them were suffering from blow after blow. Mae offered up a silent wish that their luck would start turning soon. With nothing pressing to do, she walked into the living room and eased down into the rocking chair by the window. She just wanted a moment to take the load off her feet. She'd been scurrying around since before dawn, so it was nice to close her eyes and just breathe for a moment.

But no sooner had she sat down than someone knocked at the door. She opened her eyes and frowned. Who could that be? All her current guests were gone and the mysterious Mr. O'Kelley wasn't due in until the afternoon. She was wary of unexpected knocks at her door these days, not that anyone could blame her after what had happened last time around.

She exhaled a heavy sigh and took to her feet again. Going over to the door, she guiltily peered out through the peephole before opening it.

Not very innkeeperly of her to do, but oh well. She didn't recognize the man waiting on the other side of the door. He was dark-haired with bushy eyebrows and a thick beard, offset by delightfully vibrant hazel eyes. His curly hair was tamed and neatly parted along one side. He was standing politely with his hands crossed in front of him and a well-worn leather duffel bag looped over one shoulder. There was no denying that he was very handsome indeed, though it had been a long time since Mae's thoughts had strayed anywhere in that direction.

She unlocked the door and opened it. She suddenly felt a little silly, in her apron and house slippers, and she wrung her hands in front of her anxiously. "Welcome!" she said with a cheer that she didn't quite feel. "What can I do for you?"

The man looked at her and smiled. "I'm Dominic O'Kelley," he offered. "I believe I have a reservation at the Sweet Island Inn. Am I in the correct location? Please forgive me if I've strayed off the beaten path."

He had a lilting Irish brogue in his voice. All his Os were long and open, and the burble of his voice went up and down, reminding her of nothing so much as a river running over mossy stones. She normally didn't get quite so poetically minded, but the man's accent alone seemed to bring a little bit out of her. It took her a second to snap back to reality. "No, of course, of course! Come in!" She stepped out of the way and ushered the man inside. "I'm so sorry. It's just that I wasn't expecting you until this afternoon. You caught me off-guard, that's all."

Dominic smiled and gave her a slight little bow. He seemed to be full of charming affectations like that, and Mae found herself smiling in return. "I beg your forgiveness then. It wasn't my intention to catch you unawares."

"Nonsense, no apology necessary," she said. "Can I take your bag?"

"Oh, that's quite all right. I travel light, so it isn't much for me to manage. Actually, I—" Mae wasn't sure what he was going to say, because before he could get the words out, his stomach rumbled loudly. Dominic bowed his head at once, color rushing to his cheeks.

But Mae just laughed. "You must be hungry! I'm sure you've had a long journey. Here, set your bag down there then, if you're stubborn enough to not let me help you, and come into the kitchen so I can fix you some breakfast."

Dominic looked like he was about to protest, then relented. "I suppose my stomach has given me away. I am quite famished, actually. Breakfast would be excellent." He smiled again, broad and toothy.

He followed her into the kitchen and she set to work at once, whipping up an omelet in record time while Dominic sat at the kitchen table with his hands folded in front of him, watching her cook. When she set the plate down in front of him, he looked up and smiled once more. "I hope I'm not being too forthright, but would you care to join me? I've always hated eating alone. Product of growing up with seven brothers and sisters, I suppose."

Mae hesitated. She'd done most of her chores around the inn already, sure, but there was always something else that needed doing. Best to stay busy, no? But something told her to take a seat, so that's what she did, settling down into the chair across from Mr. O'Kelley.

"Well, thank you for the invitation," she said carefully. "Did you say seven siblings? I thought my four children were a handful, but that's hardly the half of it. Your mother must have been a regular Wonder Woman. How did she manage?"

Dominic laughed. Even his laugh sounded Irish, which caught Mae by surprise. "Oh, not for too long," he said pleasantly. "My father was never in the picture and my mother passed away when I was young. It was a bit of everybody raising everybody, really."

Mae went white as a ghost. "I'm so sorry, Mr. O'Kelley. I didn't mean to—"

He held up a hand to cut her off. "Please, don't be. It was a very long time ago. She had a good life. And also, Mr. O'Kelley is far more than is necessary. I'd much prefer to just be Dominic."

She folded her fingers in her lap and nodded. "Understood. Dominic it is, then." She felt terribly awkward, but he seemed to be at ease, so she made a conscious decision to let the faux pas go and settle back in her chair. "Can I ask what you do for a living, Mr. O—Dominic, I mean?"

"I'm a novelist," he said. "I'm here researching my next book." He took a bite of eggs and exclaimed through a mouthful of food, "Why, this is delicious! Thank you very much for cooking for me. This is perfect."

"A novelist?" Mae asked, intrigued. "Well, that's a new one for me. We've had engineers and doctors and lawyers aplenty, but I believe you are my first novelist guest. How did you get into that?"

He took a sip of coffee before explaining. "I was the oldest, so it always fell to me to put my siblings to bed at night. Everybody always wanted bedtime stories, so I started making them up. Turns out I had a bit of a knack for it. I've had some lucky breaks since then that let me keep dreaming up stories for a living."

Mae tilted her head and looked at him again. Now that he mentioned it, there was a kind of dreamy sheen to his emerald eyes, like he was capable of seeing things that most other people weren't.

They went on talking for a while as she learned about his home country and his current project. Sitting at the kitchen table and talking to this nice man made her long for her husband. The two men were different in just about every way they could be. Dominic was a dreamer; Henry was a man of the earth. Dominic was dark-haired and pale-skinned, while Henry had bright blonde hair and a deep tan from all his years on the water. Dominic was an Irishman;

Henry was the Nantucket Cowboy. But they were both kind, handsome, and looked at her with a warm, indescribable quality to their gaze.

She wasn't sure what it meant, that she thought of Henry when Dominic looked at her. But, for just a moment, her heart ached a little bit less.

22

BRENT

The morning sun was stabbing ice picks into Brent's eyes. Lord have mercy, it was a bright and a hot one today. Wait—today? Sun? Morning? It took his beer-addled brain an embarrassingly long time to put all the pieces together.

He'd fallen asleep on *Jenny Lee* out at the Garden of Eden fishing spot. He must have slept the night away. How long had it been since he'd done that? Heck, he hadn't gotten more than two hours of consecutive restful sleep in the last four months. And now he'd gone and slumbered until maybe an hour after dawn, by the looks of it. Where had that come from?

He hadn't thought there was much solace to be found out here, but the fact of his sleep begged to differ. He took a deep breath and opened his eyes again to take stock of himself and his surroundings.

Sleep or no, however, any peace he'd found last night was long gone. Now, the only sensation he was aware of was a god-awful hangover. His mouth was bone-dry, his eyes were crusted and throbbing, and his head felt like someone had gone to town on the inside of his skull with a drill bit. Oof, and the nausea! He'd never been one to get seasick, not since he first set foot on a boat. But right now, the rocking was too much to bear. He leaned over the side and hurled his guts up once, twice, three times. When he had nothing left to retch, he leaned back and rinsed his mouth out with the only thing he had available. Unfortunately, that was a warm beer. He almost puked again at the acrid taste, but he managed to hold it back.

He used the heel of his hand to grind some wakefulness into his eyes, but it didn't do much good. He just felt terrible, plain and simple. What was he thinking coming out here? He should've gone home. At least then he would've woken up hungover on his couch instead of eight miles out at sea. He felt like an idiot.

Pulling himself together, he got the boat in motion and headed back into shore. It took every ounce of willpower to keep his eyes on his destination and his hands on the wheel. Stuff the cat dragged in, death warmed over—he was starting to run out of metaphors to describe how bad he felt each morning.

His mood was not improved when he got into the marina area and saw some tourist who was bungling the process of putting his own boat in the water. It wasn't such an uncommon scene. Half the guys who came down here to launch boats had never done it before. High-flying finance types from Connecticut or Jersey or wherever who'd made some money doing Lord knows what and decided to splash it all on a big, expensive toy. Problem was, they didn't know the first thing about watercraft. More often than not, they made a huge mess of things. It ended up being guys like Brent, who actually knew their way around a boat, who had to pitch in to get things straightened out.

But Brent didn't much feel like straightening anything out today. He just wanted to go home and shower, then soak in his own misery for a little while. The salt clung to him like a second skin, and he stunk to high heaven of beer and body odor. He idled for almost fifteen minutes, watching this portly, sunburned man move his truck back and forth, back and forth, with the boat still firmly planted on the trailer. He wasn't any closer to getting things lined up correctly than he had been when Brent first pulled up.

"Gonna make up your mind?" Brent called over to the man.

The guy turned to him. "You talking to me?"

Brent looked around. "I don't see anyone else holding everybody up!"

Brent could see the store tags still on the man's never-before-worn fishing shirt as he marched around the front of his truck and over to the dock near which Brent had pulled up. "Watch your tone, boy," he warned.

Brent didn't like that at all. "I'm nobody's boy. And watch my tone? Tell you what—you get out of my way, and you won't have to worry about my tone at all. Think you can manage that?" He knew he was being rude, but he'd left his cares back at the Garden. Heck, he'd actually left them by Dad's grave, when he'd snuck over there one night a few days after the funeral. This man needed to move his dang boat and let Brent go back to his miserable little life. Was that so much to ask?

"You've got a smart mouth, son."

That did it. Brent liked that even less than the first comment. He threw a quick rope to tether *Jenny Lee* to the little spit of a dock, then hauled himself up on it and went chest-to-chest with the out-of-towner.

"I think you're the one who needs to watch his tone, pal," Brent snarled.

He was dimly aware of Roger coming running down the dock steps towards them, but he paid him no mind, because the fat man cursed at Brent and gave him a hard shove. Brent gave back as good as he got, shoving the man to the ground and landing on top of him. They rolled around on the dock, ripping at each other's shirts, growling, and cursing up a storm. Brent felt Roger's hands trying to tug him off.

"Brent! C'mon, man, cut it out! Get off him!"

Brent had no interest in getting off the guy. In fact, he wanted very much to keep swinging his fists until one of them connected with the man's wobbly chins. But the presence of a new pair of hands and a new, more authoritative voice was finally enough to wrench him away from the fight.

"Gosh darn it, Benson!" roared Mike Dunleavy. He was the local sheriff and a longtime friend of Brent's father. He must've been nearby—he liked to stop and chat with Roger over a cup of coffee most mornings—and seen the fight unfolding.

Together, Officer Mike and Roger got the two men separated. Mike dragged Brent a few yards away and threw him up against a dock piling. Brent was panting, chest heaving. His head was one giant ache, and his throat was rubbed raw from the brawl. He eyed Mike, who was crouched in front of where Brent was sitting.

"He called me boy, Mike."

Mike sighed and took off his sunglasses to rub the bridge of his nose tiredly. "I don't care what he called you, Brent. You can't just go swinging on someone like that. Especially not a rich tourist with money to blow. Did you see that guy's boat? He's got four 450-hp engines on there that have never so much as tasted saltwater. You think he won't pay out the nose to get you drawn and quartered on all charges? Like hell he won't."

Brent was still heated, but he had to concede Mike's point. Mike had always had a way of putting things that got through clear as day to Brent. Even back when he was a little hellion running around Nantucket causing all sorts of minor mischief, Mike had been able to keep Brent mostly in line. And he was as right now as he ever was.

Brent looked over where Roger was talking to the guy. They were seated on the dock steps, with the man holding an ice pack over his blackening eye and scowling in Brent's direction.

"Listen," Mike said, "Roger and I are gonna talk to him and get everything straightened out. I want you to sit here—don't move a muscle—and cool your heels while we do that. Got it?"

"Got it," Brent mumbled.

"Didn't hear you."

"I said I got it."

"Alrighty, that's the ticket. Stay put."

Half an hour later, Brent was riding shotgun in Sheriff Mike's patrol car, getting taken home. He hadn't taken any kind of a serious knock in the fight, but he was sore from the night on the boat and still hungover as all get-out.

They pulled to a stop at a four-way intersection. Brent could sense Mike looking over at him. "You know, I was real sorry about your pops," he said.

Brent sighed. He didn't have any interest in talking about his dad. But he knew that Mike was just as stubborn as Henry had been, and he was going to say his piece regardless. The least Brent could do was pay him the respect of listening. His dad had raised him well enough to know that that was the right thing to do.

"Real sorry," he went on. "He was a good man, and a good friend to me. A good father to you, too. I know it wouldn't make him happy seeing how you've been going lately. Don't you agree?"

"S'pose so," Brent admitted.

Mike was right, of course, and Brent would be the first person on earth to tell you he was in terrible shape. It just didn't feel good to hear someone he respected saying those words out loud.

"I think so too. You're a good man, just like him. I know you are. Everybody on Nantucket knows you are. Which is why I'm telling you this now, man to man, with all the love I got in my heart for ya: you gotta pull yourself together."

Brent looked over. Mike was looking at him, sunglasses pushed up on his head. He had gentle brown eyes, the kind that said, *I'll let you get away with it just this once.* Brent felt dangerously close to crying. He wasn't going to do that, of course—he would never—but still, the urge was there. He didn't trust himself to talk.

Mike must have sensed that, because he slowly accelerated through the stop sign and kept trundling down the road nice and easy. He kept talking, too. "You and I both know you've had some troubles these last few months. I've helped you out as much as I can, but there's a point where you just run out of rope, kid. And once you get there, I'm gonna have to do what I have to do. Do you understand me?"

Brent nodded. He was no dummy, despite what his recent behavior might indicate.

"I gotta hear some verbal confirmation from ya, Brent. Let me know you're listening to me."

"I understand," Brent croaked. His throat was parched.

"Good," Mike said, nodding contentedly. "That's real good." He cleared his throat. "You're down this way, correct?" He pointed towards where a fork in the road veered off to the right. Brent followed his finger. That way would take him back to his dark, stale apartment. The only things waiting for him there were beer in the fridge and silence yawning in every room. Suddenly, he felt violently opposed to ever going back there.

"Think you could take me to the inn instead?" he asked.

"Sure can. That'll be this way, then."

Yeah, the inn was where he wanted to go. His mom was there. He sure could use a hug.

23

HOLLY

Holly woke up to an empty house. That alone was enough to freak her out utterly and completely. When was the last time she'd woken up to pure silence? Grady was seven, so at least that many years. But even before then, Pete was a notoriously noisy morning person, forever blending coffee and whistling some radio jingle and emptying the dishwasher in what he thought was a sneaky, ninja-like fashion but actually could probably wake up the neighbors if he really put his mind to it. She'd grown used to it and she loved it in its own bizarre way—another Pete Thing—enough so that waking up and hearing silence so all-consuming that it made her ears ring was unsettling in the extreme.

Compounding the weirdness of the silence was the guilt that had been steadily consuming her ever since she pulled out of the driveway of their house in Plymouth. All the way from Plymouth to Vermont to drop the kids off at their sleepaway camp, she'd been racked by it. It felt like a physical thing, nestled up in her chest between her love for Pete, her grief for her father's loss, and her sheer soul-deep exhaustion. She felt guilty for leaving Pete alone, even when she rationalized to herself that now he wouldn't have to worry about her or the kids, at least for the few weeks of their trial separation. He wouldn't have to bother taking his shoes off at the door like she always nagged him to do. He'd be able to eat in front of the TV—wasn't he always talking about how much he missed eating in front of the TV, which Holly refused to allow?—and watch whatever the heck he wanted to watch. Usually a back-to-back-to-back Pete special of *Jeopardy!*, some boring NBA basketball game, and then whatever late-night black-and-white cowboy flick TMC was showing. He could do all that and more, because, for at least five weeks, he had the house to himself.

But she knew darn well that it wouldn't be good. Coming from work to an empty home would be a frying-pan-into-the-fryer situation. Sadness compounding sadness. Pete was—well, mopey was the wrong word, but when he got down, he really burrowed inside of himself. Like Eeyore from Winnie the Pooh.

Groaning, she made herself get up and splash some water on her face. It was surreal to be back in the home where she grew up. 114 Howard Street had changed, but not too much. It still had the same smell that she always associated with it, some combo of flowers and cleaning supplies and, oddly enough, cigar smoke, though as far as she knew, none of her family had ever smoked cigars. It should've been comforting, but Holly figured that maybe she just wasn't ready to be comforted yet.

Once she'd brushed her teeth, pulled her hair into a bun, and thrown on a blue sundress, she went downstairs and made coffee. Neither of her sisters were awake yet. Holly had arrived at the house last night to a key under the welcome mat and a note on the door from Eliza. It said that she and Sara had gone to the bar with Brent and would be home later. Holly had meant to wait up for them, but she found herself falling asleep on the couch, so she dragged herself up to bed and slept the sleep of the dead. She hadn't heard Eliza and Sara come home, so she couldn't even be sure that they were home at all, though it would be strange for either of them to stay out all night.

She hadn't told her mother that she was coming home yet. She knew Mae would want to know the reason why, and she wanted to give her that whole story in person. She figured she'd surprise her mom at the inn in a little while. First, she was going to do her best to enjoy the silence.

With some coffee and a bagel in her system, she was starting to feel a little more alive. All the things she'd spent the last few months telling herself seemed more plausible in the light of day. *Pete is going to cut back on his hours at work and rejoin the family. The kids are going to rediscover their respect for me and get back on good behavior. Life is going to be one sunny stroll in the park for the rest of eternity.* Believable, semi-believable, and—well, maybe not so much. But fighting the same stresses day in and day out had worn down on her so much. She was surprised that, even without an absent husband to long for and wild children to chase after, she still wasn't feeling Zen at all. In fact, she was agitated. She tried to blame the coffee—she was never a regular coffee drinker—but she knew that it was a deeper issue.

"Shake it off, girl," she mumbled to herself. What she needed was a little adventure. Interact with some people, see some old places, do something to keep her mind off everything she'd left behind in Plymouth. She decided to go for a bike ride downtown and then maybe go sit at the beach and read for a while. She'd had a novel sitting on her nightstand at home for ages that she'd been itching to dive into, and this was the perfect opportunity. Holly put a bathing suit on under her dress, then packed a tote bag with a towel, sunscreen, and her book. With the bag slung over her shoulder, she jammed a sunhat on her head and slipped out of the house before Eliza and Sara woke up.

The old beach cruisers were in the back shed where they'd always been stowed. Holly plucked hers out of the bunch—it had purple and pink tassels—and tested it out. The tires were a touch on the flat side, but they ought to hold up for the journey. The chains groaned as she put her foot to the pedal, and a shower of rust went *poof*ing up into the air. Slowly but surely, though, the bike got moving and took Holly along with it.

It was a quiet Saturday morning on Nantucket. The sky was just losing the last of its violet hues, giving way to a clear blue with just a few fat clouds on the horizon, looking like lost sheep. She passed a few folks out on her way downtown and gave them all a friendly wave, but she didn't stop to talk to anyone.

Downtown was as cute and intimate as she remembered. She passed the candy store and the pizza spot and the bars. Most of it was closed, since it was still early, but people were just starting to move and groove and get the day going. It was going to be a hot one, that was for sure. The air was already sticky with salty humidity, and Holly felt herself starting to sweat a bit. Maybe she'd take a refreshing dip at the beach to cool off. *Pete would hate this,* she thought, and then immediately squelched the thought. Pete hated humidity and sweating. He preferred the winter months, which Holly thought was utterly insane. Who liked snow and blistering cold? Pete Goodwin, her crazy husband, that's who. The word "husband" floating through her head made her shiver. Was he still a husband to her? Of course he was; it wasn't like they were divorced or anything. *Yet.* Holly squelched that thought, too.

She kept going through downtown and came out the other side. There was a hidden beach not too far from here, a little off-the-beaten path that the tourists stuck to. She decided to head for that.

Fifteen minutes later, she found herself alone on the sand, with the roar of waves filling her ears. She lay on her back for a while, then her side, then her belly, then the other side. It was like she couldn't get comfortable. She cracked open the book, read a page, lost her spot, started over. Around and around she went in mental circles.

Just relax.

I can't.

Just try!

I AM trying!

And on and on like that, fighting with herself like she was losing her mind. Eventually, she succumbed to what she'd been dying to do since the moment she woke up. She pulled her cell phone out of the tote bag and flipped through her apps to find the one that controlled the security cameras in her Plymouth home. Pete had proudly installed them the year before, though he didn't have a handy bone in his body. She smiled, remembering how he'd beamed when he insisted she download the app and check out what he'd put together.

Opening the camera app, she kept her expectations low. Yes, it was a Saturday, but Lord knew Pete had spent plenty of Saturdays at the office since he started working there. It wouldn't be so strange to look onto an empty house.

Front yard—empty.

Back yard—empty.

Kitchen—empty.

Dining room—empty ...

Wait. No, it wasn't. To her surprise, Pete was there. He was seated at the dining room table with the newspaper spread out in front of him and a cup of coffee off to one side. But Holly knew right away that he wasn't reading it. He had his chin resting on his hands and he was looking off into the distance vacantly. The quality of the footage wasn't the best, but it was enough to see the sadness in his face.

Her heart broke a little bit. She loved him; all she wanted was for him to love her and be with her the way she needed him to be. If he couldn't do that, then she would have to find her own path in this world. The guilt reared its ugly head again. Holly felt a tear sliding down her cheek before she hurriedly closed the app and tossed her phone back in the bag.

She wanted so badly to reach out to him and kiss the sadness off his face. He was a good man; he didn't deserve to be so sad. But she'd made a promise to herself to try this separation out, and she knew deep down that it was necessary. She needed time to reevaluate everything. This was a careful decision, and no matter where they landed on things at the end of it, she needed to stick to her guns.

24

MAE

Mae woke up on Saturday morning with a dry mouth and a little bit of a headache. She knew what was to blame—one too many glasses of Pinot Noir the night before. But it had been necessary. Medicine, in its own way. The wine and the friends who'd brought it over, Lola and Debra, had gone a long way towards making her feel a whole lot better than she had before they'd arrived.

It had been a bad night. Quite possibly the toughest night she'd had since losing Henry. After sharing breakfast with Dominic at the inn, she'd busied herself with a long-overdue deep clean of a section of the basement she'd had her eye on since moving in. That had taken up most of the afternoon. By the time she was finished, guests were starting to return home from their daytime excursions. They all needed her for one thing or another—extra towels, restaurant recommendations for dinner, and so on and so forth. She was more than happy to accommodate. After all, that was her job now. But, little by little, she'd felt some rain clouds moving in over her heart. She wasn't quite sure where they came from. All she knew was that, once they were there, she was in for a sad night indeed.

It seemed like Henry was waiting for her around every corner. Each time she bustled into an empty room, she half expected to find him in there, fixing something or other.

She'd stepped outside for a breath of fresh air just as Debra happened to be passing by on an evening stroll. Debra had noticed Mae's sadness right away. That was what good friends were for, she thought. They could tell at the drop of a hat when she was down. And Debra was certainly a good friend. They'd known each other for almost three decades now and had shared plenty of laughs and tears along the way. Mae had been there for Debra when her brother was in a tragic car accident down in Boston. He'd made it, fortunately, but it was touch-and-go for a long time, and Debra had needed the support. Now, it seemed, it was Debra's turn to repay the favor.

"Oh, darling, come here," she'd said, pulling Mae into a hug.

Mae had dabbed at the tears threatening to spill from the corners of her eyes. "I've been keeping myself so busy," she murmured, "but sometimes that's not enough."

"You're as busy as they come, Mae Benson," Debra had said confidently. "But sometimes, you need to do the exact opposite. I know just the trick. I'll be back in half an hour. Clear your calendar!"

Mae had smiled through her tears as Debra set off towards home with a purpose. Sure enough, she'd come back exactly thirty minutes later, with Lola in tow and two bottles of Pinot Noir between them. The ladies had sat out on the front porch of the inn. After one glass of wine, Mae felt her sadness start to lose its edge. After two, she could smile again and really mean it. She wasn't going to have a third, but Debra was an insistent pourer, and so Mae had reluctantly obliged and eventually found herself hooting and hollering with her friends as Lola told a story about chasing after her house cat while still on crutches after her ankle injury. Tears were streaming down her face, but these were happy tears now. She hadn't realized before how much she needed her friends. Debra was right: being busy was all well and good, but sometimes, the cure for sadness was a bottle of wine shared between friends.

Long after the sun had set, Lola said her goodbyes and walked back home. Debra did the same a few minutes after that. That left Mae by herself, which was fine. It felt good to sit and look out at the night sky. It was a clear, pretty night, and she could hear the waves even from her seat on the porch. She was halfway to dozing off when she heard someone opening the door behind her.

She sat bolt upright and twisted around in her seat. Dominic was standing there with a guilty smile on his face. "I'm sorry for interrupting you," he said. "It seems I have a knack for catching you when you're not expecting it."

"That you do," Mae said, grinning back.

"I just got back from a long walk on the beach and thought I heard someone out here. Would it be rude if I joined you?"

"Oh, of course not!" Mae said. "Please, have a seat. There's even a little wine here, if you're keen on that."

Dominic settled himself into the rocking chair across from Mae with a pleasant sigh. "How could I say no to the lady of the house?" He grabbed one of the empty glasses that Mae had brought out earlier and handed it to her. She filled it for him and passed it back. They sat in a comfortable silence together as Dominic sampled the wine and let out a long, pleased *Mmm.* "You have a beautiful home here," he said, gesturing with his hand to encompass the whole island. "Quite different from the home I know."

"I can only imagine," Mae sighed. "What is Ireland like?"

"Damp," Dominic answered at once.

She giggled. "Oh come on. There's gotta be more to it than that."

"Yes, of course," Dominic said with a roguish grin. "It's as green as everyone says it is. Quite beautiful when it's not frigid. Beautiful hills with lush grass and breezes flowing through them."

"I can see why you're a novelist!" she exclaimed. "You've got such a way with words."

"I might just be showing off for you."

He winked, and she giggled again. Was she drunk? No, of course not. Tipsy at the most. Mae Benson would *never* get drunk.

She looked down at the wineglass she was fiddling with in her lap. "I would love to visit someday," she said softly.

"Have you ever been to Europe?"

"No, never. Henry didn't want—" She fell silent at once. She hadn't said his name out loud in quite some time now. It felt strange on her lips. Like a favorite word in a language she once knew well but had long since forgotten.

Dominic tilted his head. "Who is Henry?"

Mae stammered, "Henry is … or rather, was … um …" Her tongue didn't seem to want to cooperate with her brain.

Dominic turned white. "I'm dreadfully sorry. I've said something wrong. Please forgive me; I'll go now." He made to stand and leave, but Mae put a hand on his forearm and urged him back to his seat.

"No, please don't. I enjoy your company, and you haven't said anything wrong," she insisted. Dominic settled back down, but warily, like he was ready to spring away at any moment if she showed any signs that he should do so. "Henry was my husband," she continued with a little more resolve now. "He passed away four months ago in a boating accident."

Dominic bowed his head solemnly. "I am very sorry to hear of your loss," he said in that rolling brogue that prickled her skin like a cool breeze. "The death of a loved one is a difficult thing to bear."

"Yes, it is," Mae said. "But don't you go getting all dark on me. I've had a sad night, yes, but my friends came over and put a smile on my face, and I'd like to keep that going, if you'd be so kind as to indulge me."

Dominic looked up at her and smiled cautiously. "I can arrange that."

"Tell me about this book you're dreaming up," she said when she saw that he'd finally relaxed into his chair.

Dominic spent the rest of the evening telling her about the world he was envisioning and the characters he foresaw walking through it. They wandered from there to other topics, like favorite books they'd read, movies they'd seen, trips they'd taken.

Only when she saw him futilely try to hide a yawn did she call it a night and usher him up to bed. She did the same herself, still buzzing pleasantly from the wine. Dominic was a good man, she decided as she lay under the covers falling asleep. She liked that he was solemn and very respectful of her, but not overly grim. She found his manner somehow reassuring. And she liked his smile a lot.

The warm glow that the alcohol had given her was still lingering when she woke up in the morning, despite the mild hangover. She got ready and went downstairs to brew some coffee and pop a couple aspirin. But before she could take the pills, she heard a knocking on the front door of the inn. Again? At such an early hour?

The first unexpected knocking of late had been terrible.

The second had been unexpectedly nice.

What would this third one bring?

When she opened the door, she got her answer. It was Brent on her doorstep again. This time, he was with a police officer.

25

ELIZA

Eliza woke up late on Saturday morning. She had never been much for sleeping in, but it felt good to take advantage of the opportunity. Nowhere to be and nothing to do? Might as well snooze the morning away. Besides, she'd been up later than usual last night. Oliver had kept her dancing until well past midnight. He was a good dancer, graceful and dominant. Eliza liked that. She wasn't much of a dancer in her own right, but she was an athlete through and through, so she just relaxed and followed his lead. His smell had been driving her wild the whole time she was pressed up close against it. It was infuriating that she couldn't place it. Not quite cologne and not quite musk. Something in between, but intoxicating nonetheless. She shook her head. Pregnancy hormones were really doing a number on her thoughts these days.

She looked down at her belly. At four months in, she was really starting to show now. Not huge, but very clearly pregnant. She laid a hand on her abdomen. For some bizarre reason, she was afraid to talk to her child. It was like speaking words out loud would make it real. Despite all the doctors' appointments and things of that nature that had more than sufficiently confirmed that she was in fact pregnant, the baby still didn't feel wholly *real* yet. She'd read in one of the waiting room brochures that, at twenty weeks, babies were about the length of bananas. She must definitely be a little sleep-addled, because before she knew what was happening, she was talking to her baby. "My little banana," she began, then stopped to giggle. What on earth ... Who was she? *Giggling?* Making corny little mom-brain jokes like that? Maybe she wasn't as prepared for this whole ordeal as she spent most of her daylight hours convincing herself that she was.

My little banana. Jeez. She cut herself off and made herself get up out of bed at once. She padded down the hall to the bathroom and took a quick shower. Not that quick, actually. With her morning looming wide and unencumbered by things to do, she might as well take her time. Like sleeping in, she had never made much time for long showers. She could probably blame years of frigid locker room showers for that, or maybe it was just her businesslike nature. A little bit of both, most likely.

When she was done, she blow-dried her hair and braided it. She'd left off from her normal monthly highlights and let her hair fade to its natural platinum blonde. She didn't like being thought of as a ditz, so she'd taken to darkening it a bit. But between the Benson family blonde genes and the beaming Nantucket sun, it was longer and lighter than usual. She didn't mind the look. It felt summery.

She started to leave the bathroom, then turned back. Lately, she hadn't been bothering with makeup, either. Who did she have to impress? Nobody on Nantucket, that was for sure. But Oliver wasn't a nobody, was he? She halted *that* train of thought before it could leave the station. Even at close to eleven a.m., it was still too early in the morning to be daydreaming about a nice guy who'd listened to her babble about her tragic life all night long. Save that for later in the day. Or never. Never might be better.

She compromised with a quick blot of foundation and a swipe of mascara, then ran downstairs before she could second-guess herself. Downstairs, she put a pot on to boil to make tea. After some initial withdrawal symptoms from cutting off her daily coffee infusion, she was starting to level out. There was something meditative about starting her morning—or, at this rate, her afternoon—with a cup of hot tea anyway. She set out a tea bag and her favorite mug; it said "You Wish You Could Throw Like a Girl," with a silhouette of a softball pitcher in motion on the side, then wandered into the hallway while the water heated up.

Holly always used to complain that the hallway was the Eliza Hall of Fame. That wasn't truly fair—only the first part was dedicated to Eliza. There she was with a high school state champ trophy, Dad smiling at her side. Walking across the stage at her Penn graduation ceremony. With Brent and Dad, holding up a big sailfish they'd spent a whole morning wrestling in.

Moving farther down the hallway, she got to the Holly section. It was all Holly in dresses—First Communion dress, prom dress, wedding dress. Eliza chuckled and rolled her eyes. The middle Benson daughter was a girly-girl if ever there was one.

Past Holly Street was Sara Avenue. There was a distinct tone change between the two. From frilly dresses to chef's regalia. Sara in the full outfit, white hat and everything, holding an eggbeater in one tattooed hand and a knife in the other. Eliza remembered that picture being taken. The whole family had gone to visit Sara at the Culinary Institute of America down in Poughkeepsie. Mae had insisted that Sara pose for a picture holding some kitchen implements. Sara had argued that no chef in their right mind would ever be holding an eggbeater and a knife at the same time. They'd ended up bickering about it and spoiled the mood for everybody else for the rest of the visit. Her mother and sister were just too alike, in Eliza's opinion. Not on the surface—Mae was a regular Suzy Homemaker, while Sara had always been dead-set on testing the limits of the rules and doing things her own way. But, once you got past those things, they were both emotional—bleeding hearts, really—though neither one liked to show it too much.

At the very far end of the hallway was Brent Island. It was almost exclusively fishing pictures out this way, almost all of them featuring Dad with his arm slung around Brent proudly as they brandished some monstrous fish for the camera. There were the other normal boyish pics, too—Brent in his Pee Wee tackle football uniform; Brent getting his yellow belt in karate at age eight—but Eliza found her gaze wandering back to the pictures of Dad and Brent out on the boat together. They both looked so happy. In their element.

Eliza's thoughts were interrupted by the sound of Sara stirring upstairs. It was a little odd being back in their childhood home, but with Mae staying at the inn while she was running it, it made sense to have people at 114 Howard Street to keep things clean and orderly. "You finally getting up, Sleeping Beauty?" Eliza called up the stairs to her sister.

"Look who's talking, Rip Van Winkle!" Sara hollered back. "You just got up a few minutes ago!"

Eliza laughed and went back to the kitchen. Her teapot had just started steaming, so she poured it in her mug to steep the tea as her sister came bumbling down the stairs.

"Well, you look lovely," Eliza commented.

"Bite me," Sara shot back. She was still in pajamas and her bed head was a mess, but she couldn't care less. Classic Sara. "Where's the coffee?"

"Gotta make it yourself. I'm on tea these days, remember?"

Sara rolled her eyes. "Little sucker isn't even born yet and he's already making demands of you. You're in for it."

"Or she," corrected Eliza. "We don't know yet." Eliza had been determined to keep the sex of the baby under wraps until the birth. She didn't know and she didn't want to know. It was better that way. One more thing to let her pretend that her little banana was still not all the way real yet.

Sara was getting the coffee ground up and set to brewing. When she'd turned the machine on, she spun back around and leaned against the counter to scowl at Eliza. "Something's different about you," she said with narrowed, suspicious eyes.

"Different?"

"Yeah. Different. Different aura."

"I cannot possibly roll my eyes any harder."

Eliza and Sara were on opposite ends of the "aura question." Sara was a firm *yes* on all things woo-woo and spiritual like that. Eliza was constitutionally unsuited to believe in anything that couldn't be measured.

"Well, roll away, because I'm not wrong. Who'd you talk to last night?"

Eliza was stunned to find herself blushing. "No one." She turned away and went to take a seat at the kitchen island.

Sara lit up and stalked after her with a beaming smile. "Liar! I knew it! Who was he?"

"I said no one," Eliza grumbled, but she knew she'd been called out already.

"If you don't tell me, I'm gonna do something drastic."

"You're always on the verge of doing something drastic."

"Yeah, well, it's who I am. Are you gonna tell me or not?"

Eliza sighed and admitted defeat. "His name is Oliver. He's a pianist at the bar."

Sara cooed and leaned on her elbows on the opposite side of the island. "Ooh, tell me more. Tall, dark, and handsome?"

"Something like that. We danced."

"Tall, dark, and handsome, and he can dance?! Lizzy, where do you find guys like this? You're out here waltzing around with an artistic Prince Charming, and I'm stuck plumbing the scarily shallow depths of my past relationships for love? Unfair."

That perked her ears up. Now, it was Eliza's turn to do the interrogating. "Past relationships? Who are you talking about?"

"I ran into Russell last night outside the bar," Sara admitted. "That's who I got pizza with."

Eliza's jaw fell open. "Russell Bridges?! From high school? You're joking."

Sara shook her head and chuckled. "No, not joking. He's had a rough go of it. His wife was cheating on him. They just got divorced."

"Sara ..." Eliza began in a warning tone. She and her sister had touched on the Gavin Issue a few times over the course of the summer, but Sara had been highly reluctant to dive too deeply into it. She just kept saying that it was a mistake, but it was over, and that was that. Eliza wasn't so sure she agreed, but she respected her sister's wishes and didn't press the topic too hard. Still, she could sense that her sister's heart had taken a beating. She didn't want her to make the same mistake twice.

"I know, I know," Sara said. She held up her hands as if to say, *Don't lecture me.* "But it's okay, I promise. Besides, we didn't do anything. Just got pizza and caught up."

"And then what?" Eliza always knew when her sister was holding back information.

Sara hid her face in her hands. "And then ... he asked to take me out."

"Like on a date?"

"Exactly like that."

"And you said ..."

"I said yes! What do you want from me? He's cute and single and a nice guy. Very few qualities in common with Gavin. You'd like him. One date isn't going to hurt anyway. It'll be good to have some company. I've been living like a cloistered nun for months now. I'm itching to have fun again."

"If you say so." Eliza sighed. Like any big sister, she was protective of her younger siblings' feelings. She remembered Russell from when he and Sara used to date way back when. He had been good to her. She just hoped he hadn't left that aspect of himself in his past.

"Anyway," Sara said, changing subjects as the coffee machine beeped to let her know the brew was finished. "Have you talked to Holly?"

"No," replied Eliza. "I figured we'd just see her in the morning, but it looks like she left already. I'll text her." Eliza grabbed her cell phone from where she'd left it charging on the counter the night before and texted Holly to see where she was. The reply back was instant.

Went for a bike ride. At the cove by downtown. Bfast?

"Wanna get breakfast with Holly?" Eliza asked Sara.

"Sounds good to me. I'd do horrible things for some eggs Benny and a Bloody Mary right now. Let me change."

Eliza and Sara changed into jean shorts and T-shirts and rode their bicycles downtown. It was already scorching hot, but the sea breeze made the ride pleasant. They decided to go to the Boarding House, a casual spot a few blocks in off the water with a nice weekend brunch selection. Holly texted to say she'd meet them there. As they were parking their bikes in the rack outside, Eliza heard someone calling her name.

"Eliza! Eliza Benson!" She turned to see a familiar figure crossing the street towards her with open arms.

Eliza beamed and grabbed her old friend in a tight hug. "Maggie Manning! Oh my God, I haven't seen you in forever!"

Maggie was a little on the shorter side, with brown curly hair and a dazzlingly white smile. She ran her hand through Eliza's hair. "Ugh, I missed you. You were always my prettiest friend. You look ah-mazing! It's *so* good to see you. What're you doing back in Nantucket?"

Eliza smiled and gave the concise, rehearsed answer she'd been using whenever anybody asked her that question. "My dad passed away, so I took some time off work to come back and help my mom out." She saved the rest of her story for another time.

The corners of Maggie's eyes turned down in sadness. "That's right, I heard about that. I am so sorry, Eliza. My condolences to you and your family."

"Thanks, Mags," she said, hugging her old friend again. She and Maggie had been teammates and best friends throughout high school. College had taken them on separate routes, after which they'd fallen off into the occasional Christmas or New Year's Eve text exchange back and forth. It seemed like Maggie was back on the island now, though. And ... what was that?

"Are you engaged?" Eliza asked, her eyes wide.

Maggie grinned and wiggled the fingers of her left hand next to her face. "Just last month. I'm still getting used to the ring."

"It's beautiful," Sara chimed in. Eliza could swear she heard the faintest note of jealousy in her sister's voice.

"Thanks so much."

"Is it the same guy from before?"

"Yes," Maggie confirmed. "Gary. He's, like, perfect for me. He cooks, he sings, he's tall. My dream come true. We're so happy."

"I can't believe it! I'm thrilled for you guys."

Maggie batted her eyelashes playfully. "Thanks, girl. What about you? Is that a little baby belly I see? Oh my goodness!"

It was Eliza's turn to demur. She decided to nip the question in the bud. "Yes, but the father and I aren't together anymore. It's for the best."

Maggie straightened up and nodded solemnly. "I understand." Suddenly, her face lit up with something. "That gives me the best idea, though! What are you doing tonight?"

"Uhh ... no plans, I don't think. Why do you ask?" Eliza asked.

"Perfect! Then you *have* to come out with me. Gary's old friend is in town, and we were gonna take him out for drinks. It'll be so much better if we make it a little blind double date thing, don't you think?"

"Yes!" Sara chirped. "That sounds perfect for you, doesn't it, Lizzy?"

Eliza groaned. The last thing in the world she wanted was to get dragged along on a blind date. But Maggie and Sara kept bugging and bugging her until she finally caved. She and Maggie traded cell-phone numbers and set a time to meet at a bar whose name Eliza didn't recognize.

"I'm so excited!" Maggie squealed before leaving after another hug. "See you tonight!"

Holly rode up right on her bicycle just as Maggie disappeared around the corner. The sisters hugged. Holly looked sad, but Eliza figured they would have time to talk about that subject later, back at the house. Right now, she was starving.

"Guess who's got a hot date tonight?" Sara teased once the three women had all been seated at a corner booth.

Holly looked at Eliza in bewilderment. "Surely not the Benson golden child?"

"Guilty," Eliza blushed. "But it's not really a date. Just hanging out with an old friend and her fiancé's friend for some drinks."

"Sounds like a date to me," Sara mumbled mischievously.

"I'm not the only one out on the town though, am I?" Eliza shot back.

"Maybe Russell and I will see you out then." She winked.

Holly looked back and forth in confusion. "All right, I'm gonna need both of you to explain what's going on, ASAP."

Sara laughed and filled her in on everything. The Benson sisters talked and caught up on their respective lives over Bloody Marys—just orange juice for Eliza—and eggs Benedict. When they'd all eaten their fill, Holly headed for the inn to surprise Mom. Sara tagged along. Eliza wanted to go back to the house and take a nap—she was feeling really worn out by the heat, and her sisters encouraged her to be careful, given her condition. After one last hug, they all pedaled off.

There was someone waiting on the front step at 114 Howard Street when Eliza pulled into the lane on her bike. It was a mail courier in uniform. He was holding a bulky package.

"Are you Eliza Benson?" he called over his shoulder as she walked her bike the rest of the way in and leaned it against a post.

"Yeah, I am," she said, frowning. "Is that for me?"

"Yup." He set the package down. "Sign here please."

Eliza took the pen the man offered and scribbled her signature on his outstretched clipboard. "What is it?"

"No clue. Heavy as heck, though."

Eliza's frown deepened. Who in the world was sending her a heavy package? She racked her brain as she unlocked the front door for the messenger and he hefted the package onto the side table in the front room. "Thanks," she muttered as he left. She peered at the thing. It was huge and lumpy. She set her tote bag down and ripped the wrapping off.

Underneath was the most massive, extravagant fruit and flower display that Eliza had ever seen in her life. Even after years of working in finance, where the general theme was trying to outdo the person next to you by any means necessary, this floored her.

Sticking out from a gold-leaf-painted stake in the top of the display was a card. She plucked it off and opened it.

Eliza, it read. *I miss you. Come home. We can make this work. – Clay.*

She let the card flutter to the floor. Her mouth hung open in shock.

But she didn't have much time to even begin processing everything, because at that moment, her phone rang. She knew with a growing sense of dread who was calling her.

"Hello?" she said numbly as she accepted the call and held it to her ear.

Clay didn't say anything for a moment. He was breathing on the other end heavily, bordering on creepy. "Eliza?" he said finally. "Eliza, babe, are you there?"

It was her turn to stay quiet for a moment. She wasn't sure what she wanted to say first. *Why now? Why this? Why do anything?* Eventually, she settled on, "What do you want from me, Clay?"

He sounded surprised by her question. "I want you to come home, babe. Back where you belong."

She winced when he called her "babe." He had never, ever called her pet names before. Not babe, not honey, not darling. Just *Eliza.* Frankly, the cutesy stuff sounded plodding and weird coming out in his voice. She would've preferred his business tone to this smarmy BS.

"I am home," she replied curtly. "I'm not coming back to New York yet."

"Did you get the gift I sent?" he asked, ignoring what she'd said.

"You know that I did. Why else would you be calling now?"

"You're right," he chuckled. "Well?"

"Well what, Clay?"

"Do you like it?"

"Do I *like* it? What kind of question is that?" She was honestly taken aback. Was this supposed to make amends? Was this supposed to make up for what he'd done to her, to them, to the life she was supposed to have?

"It was crazy expensive, you know. I didn't even realize fruit baskets could cost that much. Pretty funny."

Eliza rolled her eyes and looked at the display. There was no denying that it had certainly cost her ex-fiancé a pretty penny. The whole thing was done up in gold leaf and white roses. The basket looked like it had silver filigree woven into the handle, and the chocolates studded amongst the ripe, sweet fruit were also dipped in gold. It was absurdly over the top. The old Eliza might have found the gesture touching, in a cold sort of way.

New Eliza found it disgusting.

"So this is a money thing."

"A what?"

She got angrier as she went on. "You can't buy me back, Clay. Jesus, what is wrong with you? Do you think you can just send me an expensive gift and I'll come swooning back into your arms? You lied to me. You were using drugs for God knows how long, and—"

"No, no, no," he said, cutting her off. "I wasn't, baby, I was just—"

"Do *not* interrupt me." She was all cold fury now. This was Finance Eliza. The ice queen who knew how to fight for herself in the cutthroat halls of Goldman Sachs and the streets of Manhattan. This was the Eliza who hit a leadoff double in the bottom of the ninth to ice a conference championship her freshman year of college. This was no-BS Eliza. And she was not about to kowtow to a drug-addicted narcissist like Clay Reeves. "This doesn't *work* for me anymore, Clay. It wasn't working for a long time. And it's not going to work again. So let me tell you what I'm going to do: I'm going to donate this basket to someone who needs it. I'm going to throw your card in the trash. And I'm going to delete your number. After I do all that, I want you to never call me again. Am I clear?"

There was a long, tense silence.

Then Clay hung up without saying another word.

26

BRENT

Brent hated the look of shock on his mom's face. It was only there for a second before she tucked it away behind a gentle smile—classic Mom—but he caught it, even if he wasn't sure that Mike did. It broke his heart. He'd disappointed her plenty of times in the last four months. He'd managed to hide some of his more egregious screwups from her, but she was his mom at the end of the day. She knew when her son was hurting. And she'd had loads of evidence if she wanted to look for it. The bruises on his face were pretty dang hard to hide if she chose to swing by his apartment or forcibly drag him to dinner at the inn.

"Morning, ma'am," Sheriff Mike said to her with a tip of the hat. "Brent asked me to drop him off here. Thought he could use a little motherly love this morning, I imagine."

"Is everything all right?" Mom asked with a tilt of her head.

"I'll leave that to Brent, if that's okay," Mike demurred. "Time for me to get going now. Hope you both have a wonderful day." Mike turned to Brent. "Take care of yourself, kiddo."

Brent nodded and swallowed. He was still hungover, and now he had a raw throat and a knot of sadness in his chest to go on top of that. He didn't like seeing Mom sad, and she'd spent a lot of the summer being sad, even if she refused to admit it. She thought she was sneaky, keeping all her cards clutched close to the chest. But he knew his mother as well as she knew him. And she was hurting just like he was.

He watched Sheriff Mike amble back down the sidewalk, climb in his patrol car, and cruise away. Only then did Brent look back at his mother. He expected a lecture. It wouldn't be amiss. Knocking on her door early on a Saturday with a cop in tow? It was a bad look, even for him. Heck, part of him even wanted her to lecture him. *Yell at me. Tell me I'm a mess. Tell me to clean my act up or else I'm getting the boot.* Since when was he, Brent Benson, such a beaten dog in mind and spirit? He was a proud kid growing up, a fearless daddy's boy. Now, all the fight had left him, and here he was, moping on his mother's doorstep, silently begging for her to put him down like he thought he deserved.

"Look at me, Brent Benson," Mae ordered softly. He could barely bring himself to make eye contact with her. When he did, he didn't see anger or disappointment in her eyes. He saw the same eyes he'd always seen: brimming with a mother's love. "Are you okay?"

He wasn't quite sure where to even start answering that. "I don't know," he said honestly after a moment's thought. "Probably not."

"Oh, honey," she murmured. She reached out to touch his face and then thought better of it. His bruises must look real bad if she was that hesitant.

"I'm sorry, Mom," he whispered.

She tutted. "None of that now. You look starved. Come get some breakfast." She shepherded him inside with a gentle hand on his back. He winced when she touched him. He wondered if she would notice that.

Inside the inn, she led him to the kitchen table. "Sit," she said, pointing to a chair. He sat. He still had his head hung low and his eyes rooted on the floor. The hangover was still present, but he ignored it like a check engine light on the dashboard.

Mae had moved into the kitchen and was bustling back and forth, getting who-knows-what going. She came back over a minute later with a tall, cloudy glass. "The patented Mae Benson hangover cure begins with a tall glass of room-temperature water, mixed with Himalayan pink salt, and a fresh-squeezed lemon. Drink."

Brent took the glass from her and drank. It was acrid going down his throat, but when it got to his belly, it seemed to take a tiny bit of the edge off the nausea.

She returned again from the kitchen a moment later with a steaming mug. "Cup of coffee, as hot as you can stand." He was about to ask for milk and sugar, but she shook her head and waved an index finger back and forth. "Black. No ifs, ands, or buts about it. Oh, and take these." She fished out a couple aspirin from her apron pocket and put them in Brent's palm. Her fingers lingered for a moment on his wrist, almost like she was taking his pulse. It was the first human contact that wasn't a punch to the face he'd had in Lord knows how long. It sent a shiver racing through his soul.

He swallowed the aspirin and darn near burned his tongue on the hot coffee. He'd always liked to let his coffee cool down to something approaching room temp. His sisters thought that was gross as all get-out, but he just figured that he only had one tongue and there wasn't much use burning the taste buds right off it.

A few minutes later, Mae was setting down a plate of six eggs fried over-hard and a mountainous stack of bacon. "Eat it all," she told him. "Dry, no ketchup. Sorry, hon. I know you hate that." Hate that he did indeed, but he was in no position to argue, so he just did as he was told. She sat across the table and watched him as he ate.

By the time he'd finished choking down the eggs and bacon, he was definitely starting to come around. But the guilt and the shame he'd felt when he first woke up at the Garden didn't seem to be going anywhere. Mom didn't say much, though he felt her eyes on him, never wavering, never leaving. She'd never had much of a temper, but surely this was a justified occasion to get at least a little bit angry? He hadn't even told her what had happened yet, though he was sure she could guess just fine. Bruised fingerprints around his throat, a lingering black eye, and the stench of booze radiating off him in waves pretty much told the whole story clear and simple. He just kept his gaze trained on his plate and waited for the yelling to begin.

"You know ..." Mom said quietly. Brent flinched in his seat but didn't look up. "I used to make this concoction for your father when he'd had a few too many. Here, this is next." She slid a half a grapefruit and a spoon over to him on a small side plate. It wasn't his favorite by any stretch of the imagination, but he dutifully picked up the utensil and started to pry a section of the fruit loose. "Your dad would wake up moaning and groaning like he'd just lost a prize fight. Lord, he was a whiner when he was sick." She chuckled under her breath. "But I'll tell you what—it worked, one hundred percent of the time. *You're my witch doctor,* he'd tell me with a grin, sitting at the kitchen table just like you are now. And I'd always laugh and then banish him outside to clean the gutters or something as punishment. He'd moan and groan about that, too."

Brent couldn't help but laugh. Just the tiniest, feeblest laugh, but it was more than he'd managed in months. He still hadn't really said much of anything since Mike dropped him off on the inn's doorstep.

"He would hate to see you like this, you know," she said.

Mike had told him the same thing. Both were right. Brent could tell she was shifting gears a little bit. The air in the room got a little denser, a little tighter, a little more sorrowful. Or maybe that was just the constriction in his throat at the thought of his dad seeing him looking like such a pitiful wreck.

"I know," he choked out.

"He'd hate it a lot. You were his boy, his youngest. He loved you more than life itself. Would've given you the world, if he could. Tried to, actually, if I remember correctly."

Brent laughed again at that, just a little bit more. "I know," he mumbled again through a mouthful of grapefruit.

Mom reached across the table and grabbed Brent's hands. "I need you to look at me when I tell you this, baby. Can I ask you that much?"

It felt like the hardest thing in the world to lift his head up and look at his mother. It felt like he was dragging his skull through quicksand or gravity had tripled when he wasn't paying attention. But he made the effort, until his eyes met his mother's. She was smiling sadly at him. Her eyes were full of concern and love.

"What I want to say is this: your dad loved you. And what happened to him was not your fault. He was stubborn as a mule and there wasn't a thing in the world you could've done to stop him. So it's not your fault. Do you hear me?"

"I hear you, Mom." Tears were running down his face. He forced himself to keep looking into his mother's face, even when he wanted so badly to tear his gaze away and go bury himself in darkness and booze until his chest stopped aching so much.

"So I need you to pick your head up for me. And for him. And for yourself."

"I know, Mom." He sounded like a broken record, but he couldn't say much more because the tears kept coming and coming and coming. It was like the rain on the night of the accident all over again, when it just would not stop pouring down. Brent felt as dark as those clouds had been.

Mae squeezed his hand with all her might as Brent gave into the tears. When he stopped fighting, the dam broke open and he started sobbing audibly. He put his forehead down on the table and wept. Big, choking sobs tore through him. He'd only cried once, in the hospital waiting room, since his dad had passed. Nothing since then. This was four months of tragedy coming out all at once. It hurt on its way out, but in the wake of the tears—when they finally began to slow some indefinite amount of time later—he felt lighter. Clearer. Mom kept stroking the back of his head until they eventually ceased altogether.

He looked up at her. "I'm sorry, Mom. For everything. I'm sorry I missed the funeral. I'm sorry I've been such a mess."

She shook her head and cut him off. "That's the one thing I'm not going to abide by, Brent. No apologizing. No moping. We're a forward-looking family. Always have been, always will be."

He nodded slowly. The tears were drying on his face, though an errant sob still rippled through him every minute or so. "Okay. I can do that."

"Good. Now, down to business."

Brent tilted his head. "Business?"

"Business," she affirmed. "I've spoken with Aunt Toni, and we're hiring you to do a renovation on the detached guesthouse in the backyard. You'll be responsible for demo'ing what's already there, and revamping everything to bring the quarters up to spec for future guests to stay in. I'll have Eliza set you up with a budget for the project, but you'll be responsible for procuring the parts and doing all the labor yourself."

"You want me to work for you?" he asked idiotically.

Mae smiled. "I do. But we're gonna have some ground rules. Ready?"

Brent hesitated, then nodded. "Uh, okay. Ground rules. Got it."

"No drinking. No fighting. No trouble. You start work at nine in the morning and you end work no earlier than five in the evening. And you go clean out that foul apartment of yours—today."

No drinking. No fighting. Those two things had been the bulk of Brent's days for a lot of days. The thought of the vacuum that would be left behind in their absence filled him with fear. There were a lot of hours in the day to think about what had happened and what he had become. Without alcohol to quiet those thoughts ... well, who knew what would happen?

But maybe it was time to stop running from his demons. He'd spent a whole summer doing it. The real question wasn't what would happen if he stopped. It was, what would happen if he kept it up? He'd be dead in a ditch somewhere before Christmas. That was no way to go. That was no way to honor his father's legacy.

He had to give this a shot.

"Do we have a deal?" Mae asked.

He stood up. "Yes, Mrs. Benson," he said with a sheepish grin. "We have a deal." He stood up and stuck out his hand for her to shake. She laughed and shook it, then walked around the table to pull him into a hug.

"I love you, son," she whispered into his ear. He felt the tears on her cheek brush off on his neck.

"I love you too. And Mom?" He pulled away from the hug but held her at arm's distance. "Thank you."

27

HOLLY

After breakfast downtown with her sisters, Holly and Sara had gone to the Sweet Island Inn so Holly could surprise their mother. Mae had been happy to see Holly and embraced her warmly, but she'd also been super busy dealing with the kinds of problems that only someone responsible for a house full of needy strangers can have. So, after a couple minutes of chitchat, the women had decided to come back later, after Mae's day had calmed down somewhat.

Back home, Eliza had gone down to take a long nap, saying the heat was getting to her once again. But Holly hadn't been able to sit still. She'd tried reading again—first in her favorite rocking chair, then in the hammock on the back porch, then on the couch—but everywhere was equally uncomfortable. Truthfully, it was her mind that wasn't letting her relax. Every time she started settling into a position, she would think about Pete, sitting sadly at the kitchen table with the newspaper in front of him, and her eyes would start to water.

She missed him, but this was for the best. Maybe they just needed this time apart in order to remember what they loved about each other. At the end of the day, love wasn't the issue. She loved Pete and he loved her. That hadn't changed since they had first started dating. But she couldn't be in love with an absent husband. She needed him with her. If he couldn't give her that, then it didn't bode well for their future together. He had to see where she was coming from on this, right?

Those were the kinds of thoughts that prevented her from unwinding. Finally, fed up with the silence and the stillness she was desperately trying to wrangle for herself, she gave up and set the book down. "I'll just be busy for a bit. Burn off some of this mental energy, and then I'll be able to spend the rest of the afternoon actually kicking back," she said out loud. She hoped that, by voicing her thoughts to—well, to nobody—that it would manifest them into reality. She'd always liked the idea of manifesting things into reality, even if she didn't truly believe in that woo-woo nonsense deep down. Maybe she just wasn't trying hard enough.

So, to take her mind off Pete and Plymouth, she started cleaning the house. Part of her was screaming to turn her Mom Mode off, but once she got going, she simply could not stop. She mopped all the hardwood, going so far as to yank the couches away from the places they'd spent decades resting and get under there, too. She scrubbed the crown molding. She dusted light fixtures and baseboards. She repotted three plants that had outgrown their homes. She even vacuumed the lampshades, which was getting a little bit ridiculous— even she realized that—but she was on a tear and couldn't hold herself back if she tried. A few hours went by in a flash. Holly felt like she'd just gotten going, but try as she might, she simply couldn't find anything else that really needed doing.

"I'll just go for a walk then," she said out loud, again to nobody. "A nice, brisk walk. It's a beautiful day. I should be outdoors anyhow." Then, realizing that she sounded like an insane person babbling to herself, she tucked her cell phone into her pocket, grabbed a hat from the hook by the door, and left the house.

She went down the street and swung towards downtown. Then, thinking better of it, she doubled back and went towards the beach on the south side of the island. When she got there, she slipped off her sandals and let her toes sink into the damp sand. She let out a long, exaggerated sigh. Maybe she could fool herself into relaxing. She closed her eyes and focused on the sensation of the sand suckling ticklishly at her feet. "Ah, there we go ..." she murmured. "That feels—"

Her phone started ringing.

"Oh, for crying out loud!" she bemoaned. She plucked it out of her pocket and froze when she saw the caller ID.

Pete.

She thought about not answering. She'd barely been gone for twenty-four hours, and he was already calling her. What happened to a trial separation? To *"some time apart to figure things out"*?

But then again, this man was her husband. Her first and only love. The father of her children. Maybe he had something he needed to tell her, maybe something had happened, or maybe he was just struggling. She couldn't just ignore him. That wasn't right at all.

So she answered, though hesitantly. "Hi," she said in a near-whisper.

"Hey." His voice sounded strained. Nothing like her normal, jovial Pete, the one she fell in love with way back in the hallway at Nantucket High. "What are you doing?"

"At the beach," she told him.

"Oh. Must be nice."

"I wish it was."

She could practically hear his brow wrinkling through the phone. "What does that mean?"

"I just can't relax. That's all. Thinking about—uh, the kids."

"Yeah. I'm sure they're having fun. The camp posted pictures online. They look happy. Grady is a mess. Rubbed a popsicle over every inch of his face, if the photo is anything to go by." Pete chuckled, but Holly didn't. She couldn't. She just felt sad.

"Are you at work?" she asked.

"No," he replied. "I went in a little bit ago, but I just couldn't get anything done. Couldn't focus. I ... I miss you, Hol."

"I know. I miss you, too. But we need this. I can't come home yet. You have to figure out if you can have this job and a family at the same time."

"I know," was his murmured reply. He sounded so pained. She thought about his face on the security cameras again. "I'll let you go then. You should relax. Enjoy the beach for me, okay?" Holly had to bite her lip to stop from smiling. Pete hated the beach; they both knew that. He was a winter guy, a mountain guy. She was the beachy one out of the two of them.

"I will." She hesitated then, not sure what else to say.

"I love you, okay, Hol? I love you a lot."

She didn't know how she should reply to that. She just decided to say the truth. "I love you, too, Pete. Get some rest if you can." Then she hung up.

That evening, Holly and Eliza walked over to the Sweet Island Inn. Sara was out on her date with Russell, so it would be just the two of them and Mae spending some time together. Holly had a bottle of her favorite chardonnay in hand. Mae welcomed them in and they went to the back porch to relax in some rocking chairs that were situated out there. The view of the sunset was nice, and the wine helped put a damper on Holly's racing anxiety. She wished Eliza could have some. It seemed like she needed it; she looked exhausted even after her nap. But when Holly asked, she just said she was tired and wouldn't offer up anything more. Holly knew something else was bothering her big sister, but Eliza didn't like to be pushed, so Holly left it alone. If she wanted to talk, she'd open up on her own time.

For her part, Mae looked weary, too. She said it was one of those days where everybody needed something from her at the same time. She hadn't had a moment to herself since opening her eyes. Holly knew that her mother loved nothing so much as staying busy and being helpful, but she was worried that she was wearing herself thin.

"You sure you want to keep doing this, Mom?" Holly asked as she poured wine into glasses for her and Mae, and a seltzer water with lime for Eliza. "The inn, I mean."

"Don't be silly," Mae dismissed. "I'm enjoying myself very much here. It feels like I was made for this. It's so nice to meet all different kinds of people and welcome them to Nantucket."

"We just want to make sure you're okay. That's it," Eliza said.

Mae gave them both a smile and a pat on the knee. "My girls, always looking out for me. Don't worry about your mother. I'll be just fine." Eliza seemed satisfied enough with that for the time being. Holly wasn't, but she didn't want to be a nag.

"So, my darlings," Mae went on, "how are we doing today?"

"Tired," Eliza replied at once.

"Tired," Holly agreed.

"Something troubling you?"

Holly looked to Eliza, figuring her big sister was going to take the lead and answer first, like she always did. But Eliza looked oddly reluctant. Eventually, she said in a soft voice, "Clay called."

That was surprising. He hadn't said much of anything to Eliza since she left—at least, to Holly's knowledge. Eliza was private by nature, but she would've shared something like that with her sisters, certainly.

"Why did he call?" Holly asked.

"I'm not sure, honestly," Eliza admitted. "Maybe he realized I was serious. Maybe he just thought enough time had passed that I'd change my mind. Either way, I told him not to call me again."

"I'm sorry, honey," Mae said, patting her knee again. "That must have been hard. It's always tough when the past reaches out like that, even when you're sure about your decisions."

"Oh, I'm sure," Eliza said without hesitating. "I don't want anything to do with him ever again. It is tough though, you're right. I just thought it was all figured out. Turns out I was wrong."

"I know what you mean," Holly offered. She didn't want to make this about herself, but she could certainly understand feeling like you'd had your life all set in place and then someone came along and yanked the tablecloth out from underneath it like a magic trick gone wrong.

"Did something happen with you?" Eliza asked her.

"Pete called."

Eliza laughed darkly. "Two tough calls today, then. Better tell Sara not to check her phone."

"Definitely should," Holly agreed. "It wasn't a bad call, necessarily. It was just ... hard. I know he's hurting, and I want to help. But I really feel like this is important. We can't keep going the way we were going."

Eliza nodded enthusiastically, but both women fell silent, thinking about where things had gone so wrong.

"Let me tell both of you girls something," Mae said. "Relationships are hard. As hard a thing as exists in this world. It's tough to share your entire world with another person. You have to rely on them at the same time that you have to make sure you're not wholly dependent on them. It's a tricky balancing act."

"You can say that again," Holly said.

"But you also have to see that love is so precious. Isn't it nice to know that there's someone who wants what's best for you, no matter what? Now, it's not quite a mother's love—" Holly and Eliza both laughed softly at that—"but the love of a good man is something special in its own right. I know that you both are grown and smart and brave. I raised you to be that way, and you've both made me so proud over the years. But, if a little old lady can be so bold as to offer you some advice, it's just this: if you find a good love, don't let it go."

Holly let those words sink in. *If you find a good love, don't let it go.* She was confident that what she had with Pete was a good love. The question was, did he feel the same way? He was so absorbed in his job, and though part of the reason for that was his desire to provide for his family, she knew that he also relished the difficulty of it and the challenge it presented. Could he be okay with letting that go in order to be there for her and their children the way they needed him? That was a tough ask. But it was essential.

She wondered what Eliza was thinking. Her sister was lost in thoughts of her own. She looked so sad sometimes, when she thought nobody was looking at her. That worried Holly perhaps more than anything. Eliza was as tough as they came, and if there was anyone who could handle the stress of being a single mother, it was her. But she worried anyway.

"Mrs. Benson?" came a small child's voice from the other end of the porch.

Mae turned to look. "Freddie!" she said brightly. "What can I help you with, honey?"

"I was just wondering if, if, if ..." the little boy stuttered nervously, "if you have any snacks? I'm real hungry."

"Freddie!" his mother chirped, striding onto the porch. "What did I tell you about bothering Mrs. Benson? I'm so sorry about him interrupting your private time."

"Oh, nonsense, it's no bother," Mae said as she rose from her seat. "I've got a special little snack waiting just for you. I'll be back in a minute, girls," she said to Holly and Eliza. She touched the little boy softly on the head as she went inside to the kitchen. Freddie and his mother followed.

"He's cute," Eliza muttered after everyone had gone, leaving her and Holly alone on the porch.

Holly was taken aback. "I don't think I've ever heard you call any kid 'cute' in your entire life," she said, laughing. "Not even mine!"

Eliza blushed. "Blame the little banana, I guess." She turned to look at Holly. "Your kids are cute, though. I'm sorry if I never told you that before."

Now, Holly was the one blushing. "Stop it. Don't get all sappy on me."

"I mean it, though," Eliza insisted. She had an unusual gleam in her eyes that Holly didn't remember ever being there before. "You have a beautiful family."

"Thanks, Lizzy," she whispered. Her throat felt tight all of a sudden. She wasn't sure why, but it felt like it was really important to Eliza that Holly take her seriously right now.

"Your kids are cute and your husband loves you and you just seem—I don't know, you just seem so *happy*. Content, like. Is that weird of me to say?"

"No, not weird at all. It's sweet. Thank you."

"I know you and Pete are a little rocky right now, but I really do mean what I'm saying. I'm ... a little jealous of you, I guess."

Holly's jaw fell open. "You? Jealous of *me?*"

Eliza laughed. "It's true. Very."

That was an astonishing thing to hear. As far as Holly knew, Eliza had never been jealous of anyone in her life. It was everyone else who was jealous of Eliza. She was the rock star, Dad's favorite, A+ student, effortlessly competent athlete. Everyone in her orbit could point to her and say, *"That's what I wish I was."* What did she have to be jealous of Holly for?

"Gotta say, I never thought I'd see the day. Not in a mean way or anything," she rushed to correct, hoping she didn't hurt her sister's feelings. "It's just ... I mean, you're good at everything. I know you're going to be a great mom, too."

"Thanks," Eliza said, looking down at her belly in a curious way. "I hope I'm as good a mom as you are. You are a great mom, you know."

"Now you're really going over the top. You feeling okay?" Holly teased. "Should I be worried?"

"I'm fine," she replied with a sad smile. "Just wanted to let you know that I love you and I'm proud of you. That's all."

Mae came bustling back onto the porch a moment later before Holly could answer. She was shocked. Well, maybe shocked was the wrong word, but it was something like that. She'd seen a side of Eliza she didn't know existed. Vulnerability, fear, uncertainty. She knew her sister was going through an unexpected rough patch in her life, but at the end of the day, she was still Eliza Benson. Everything she touched turned to gold.

Which was part of the reason why it felt so good to hear Eliza compliment Holly like that. It made Holly realize that she had a good life. One worth being proud of. Her kids *were* cute, and her husband *did* love her. Those were things worth protecting.

If you find a good love, don't let it go.

28

SARA

"Oh, you gotta be kidding me," Sara scoffed. Then she doubled over laughing.

Russell was standing on the front step of 114 Howard Street. He had a red rose in one hand and was wearing a bowtie over his collared polo shirt. He was grinning at her like an absolute fool. The image was ridiculous and hilarious and totally unexpected.

Sara had come downstairs when Holly had shouted up mischievously that Sara had a "gentleman caller" waiting for her at the door. She'd come down, dressed in black jeans and a flowing red tank top, but Russell had caught her totally by surprise with his goofy little getup.

"My princess," he said, whipping off an imaginary hat and bowing low to her.

"Change of plans," she said sarcastically. "I'm busy tonight. Gotta brush the cat's teeth or something like that."

He held his hand over his heart. "You wound me."

Sara chuckled again. "Are you gonna keep this up all night? You better buy me lots of drinks then."

Russell laughed and grinned. "No, that's about all I got, actually. Here, take this." He handed her the rose and undid the bowtie from around his neck. "I already stabbed myself on those stupid thorns a half-dozen times."

Sara took it from him and brought it to her nose to smell. She inhaled deeply, savoring the flowery scent. There was a dish they made at Lonesome Dove that used rose petals, and she'd always loved the —*no, none of that now*, she scolded herself. Eyes up, eyes forward. No dreaming about the past. That chapter of her life, the Gavin Crawford/Lonesome Dove chapter, was firmly closed. She had a good evening ahead with a nice guy who actually seemed interested in dating her, and she fully planned on having a fun time.

"This is beautiful. Thank you. Let me just stick it in a vase and I'll be right out," she told him. She went into the kitchen, filled up a little glass-blown vase, and stuck the rose in. It looked nice. She'd always been a fan of single flowers, for some reason. They looked more beautiful on their own.

When she was done, she went out the front door. She didn't bother shouting out to anyone that she was leaving. Holly had gone for another long stroll on the beach and Eliza was sleeping since she wasn't feeling too great. Sara thought the heat was getting to her and she ought to take it easy, but Eliza did what Eliza wanted. Sara shrugged it off. Her body, her baby, her problem. Nap the day away, as far as she was concerned.

"Ready?" Russell asked when she walked down the driveway towards where he was parked.

"Yep. Let's go."

They drove off towards the outer rim of downtown and stopped outside a casual-looking bar. "The Rust Bucket?" Sara asked in disbelief.

Russell laughed and shook his head. "I told Xander not to name it that, but he had a vision and wouldn't budge. It's nicer than it sounds, I promise. Great oysters." He looked panicked for a second. "You do eat oysters, right?"

"Of course," Sara said. "I'm a chef. I eat everything."

He smiled, that lopsided, dimpled smile. "Good. They're great here. Let's go, shall we?"

A few minutes later, they were seated in a corner booth with a pair of ice-cold beers and a tray of fresh oysters. "So, Sara Benson," Russell began when they were all situated. "We covered the past over a slice of pizza. Should we turn to the future over a plate of oysters?"

She giggled. "Seems reasonable. You really are in a grand mood tonight."

He ran a hand through his hair. "Sorry, I'll tone it down. The question stands, though. What's next for you?"

She took a sip of beer and leaned back in her seat, looking out the window next to her. The sun was barely clinging to the edge of the horizon. It was a nice night, warm and comforting. "That's a tough one," she said eventually. "I'm not too sure. I've been here all summer, helping out my mom at the inn. It's nice to cook without the pressure. Makes me remember why I started it in the first place, you know?"

Russell nodded. "Sure. Love of the craft and all that."

"Exactly. Brings me back to the good times. My mom and I have always clashed like oil and water, but she was the one who got me excited about the kitchen in the first place. When we were on good terms, I'd help her out. She's a hell of a cook."

"I remember that. She used to have me over for dinner on random Sundays, back when we were—back in high school, I mean. Great lasagna."

"And shepherd's pie, and filet mignon, and raspberry cheesecake. She's got all the moves."

"What does she think about you being back here?"

Sara played with the condensation on her beer bottle. "Hard to say. She keeps things close to the chest. Tries to put up a good front for the family a lot of the time. She's hurting inside, I know that, and it does help to have her kids around. But the Benson clan has seen better days, that's for sure."

Russell looked like he wanted to ask what exactly that implied, but he bit his tongue and sank back in his seat. It was touching, actually. Not that she had anything to hide from him, but her siblings' troubles were their own, not exactly hers to share with someone over a beer.

"So, cooking at the inn is the present," he summarized. "What's coming up, though? Headed back to New York?"

She sighed. "I really wish I knew. I was on a good path, you know? Maybe not earning international drug dealer money like someone I know, but I was starting to make a name for myself. As a female chef, that's tough. It can be a cutthroat industry."

"So I hear," Russell said, nodding. "You're tough, though. You've got backbone. I always loved that about you."

"Oh yeah?" Sara asked with a devilish grin. "What else have you always loved about me?"

Russell didn't blink or hesitate. "Your smile. Your sarcasm. The way you set your jaw when you start to do something challenging." He sat up then and shook his head like he was coming out of a daze. "Okay, whoa. Wow. That was too much. Way too intense by like, a thousand percent. Should we drink more? I'll order shots."

Sara laughed out loud. "No, no, not too much at all. It was cute. I like your smile, too, you know."

He grinned sheepishly. "I'm gonna order the shots anyway. But thanks."

She waved a hand. "Order away," she said. "I'm game if you are."

The night went by in the blink of an eye. By the end of it, Sara's cheeks and sides hurt from laughing. Russell had told her stories about his time backpacking through Europe after graduating college and how he'd ended up stranded in Berlin without a single euro to his name. They hadn't broached the topic of his divorce even once. Sara wanted badly to ask, but she could tell that he appreciated the reprieve from thinking about it. It made sense to her—if he worked from home and didn't get out too much, he probably spent a lot of time brooding on what had gone wrong between him and MaryAnne. Maybe he just needed a fun, relaxed night out without constantly dissecting the past. She could certainly relate.

Russell insisted on paying the bill when it arrived even when Sara balked. After bickering for a few minutes and flipping a coin, she finally relented and used the opportunity to get in another dig about his business. He'd explained it to her in detail—something about drop-shipping industrial plastic products from China to plumbing businesses in the United States, nothing shady about it—but that kind of thing never really clicked in her creative brain, so she just kept teasing him anyway.

They walked outside into the warm night afterwards, down to where they'd parked, and climbed in the car.

"I had a fun time," Russell said as they headed back towards Howard Street. "Thanks for coming out tonight."

"I had a good time, too," Sara replied, looking at him. He was looking straight ahead, two hands on the wheel. He was still a little nervous, apparently, even after a pair of beers and the shot of tequila he'd ordered. She felt bad for him. It seemed like his ex-wife had really done some damage to him. From little comments here and there, Sara had gleaned that she was really critical of a lot of things— Russell's goofiness, his big laughter, his warm heart. He was the kind of guy who would wrench his car across oncoming traffic to stop at a little kid's lemonade stand. Sara was hurt on his behalf that there was anyone in this world who would try to scold that kindness out of him.

"Think we can do it again some time?" he asked her.

"Once again, if you're gonna ask me on a date, you gotta say the words, Mr. Bridges," she teased.

He put the car in park outside the Benson house and turned his gaze on her. He ran a hand through his hair and smiled softly. "Sara Benson, will you go on another date with me?"

"I'd love to." She kissed him on the cheek, then undid her seat belt and got out of the car. He probably had wanted to kiss her, and she'd considered the possibility, but she was still a little gun-shy about it. Gavin had done some damage to her confidence just like MaryAnne had done to Russell's. She was wary of what this might be blossoming into. Excited, definitely, but also nervous.

She told herself to calm down. It was just one date. No big deal. She'd been on plenty of first dates that didn't pan out. Even if this felt different, there was no point in spinning it up into a big to-do. Just take things one night at a time. Tonight, that meant a kiss on the cheek and a sweet good night.

∽

She sang to herself softly as she showered and took off her makeup. The alcohol was loosening her up enough, though her eyes were getting drowsy. She'd been on old-person hours for most of the summer—bed by nine p.m. the majority of her nights—so staying out past eleven was really pushing her limits.

When she got out of the shower and toweled off, she noticed her phone lighting up with a missed call. It was from a number she didn't recognize. Frowning, she picked it up and hit the button to call back.

"Hello?" answered a familiar voice.

"Gavin," Sara breathed. The warmth of the beer and oysters vanished at once from her body. It was replaced by a cold sense of foreboding.

"How've you been?" he asked casually, like they were good friends who chatted all the time, rather than—rather than whatever it was that they were to each other.

"Fine."

"Good, that's good." He trailed off.

She bit her lip. Even through the phone, he still had an undeniable effect on her. That voice, deep and rich like caramel, made her think of those forearms, and those forearms made her think of the man himself, and that unlocked a box in her heart she'd thought that she had locked up and destroyed the key to.

The right thing to do was hang up the phone now. Before this got out of hand. It wasn't leading anywhere good, that was for darn sure. She'd taken a glimpse down that road, seen the sights, gotten a good enough look to know that it wasn't for her. *Hang up. Hang up now.* That's what she should do.

But she just couldn't bring herself to do it.

"How're you?" she blurted finally, against her better instincts.

"Great. Well, not great. But okay. We miss you around here."

"Yeah?"

"Yeah, big-time. It's just not the same kitchen without you. Carlo has been yanking his hair out trying to deal with all your replacements. They're good, but they aren't you."

"That's nice to hear." To her utter astonishment, part of her meant it. Gavin had never been one to lavish her with compliments like this. Even though she knew he was a liar and a jerk, she found herself— not quite swooning, but something in that vicinity. *Gross! No! Stop it,* she screamed internally. But she found herself instead sitting on the rim of the bathtub, still in her towel, as if settling into a conversation.

"When are you coming back?" he asked her.

"I quit, remember?"

She could picture him waving his hands dismissively as he said, "Yeah, but c'mon, you know you didn't really. You can always come back. Door's open forever for you."

She squeezed a section of the towel in a fist. Weren't these the words she'd wanted to hear from him? That he cared about her, that he valued her? They were, and she couldn't deny that it felt really freaking good to hear them now. Despite everything that happened, there was a part of her that was insanely drawn to Gavin Crawford. No matter how hard she wanted to excise that part and chuck it out a window, she couldn't. He spoke her language. He had her on a hook.

"What about—what about Melissa?" she asked. *Yes, you go, girl!* hooted the angel on her shoulder, the one who'd been pleading with her to hang up the phone.

But she heard the same hand-wavey tone in his voice. "She and I are taking some time apart." He didn't offer anything more than that, and despite the angel's pleas, she didn't press any further.

This was it. The window she'd spent an ungodly long time hoping for. Gavin was truly single. The Melissa Question Meter read "GO FOR IT!" All the stars were aligning. She could go back to the city and spark something up with Gavin. She could get her life back on track, with an unexpectedly amazing bonus on top of that. Back in the Lonesome Dove kitchen and in the arms of a man she wanted more than anything.

But then she thought about Russell. He wasn't anything like Gavin. He wasn't slimy or conniving. He was an honest guy, a good guy, someone who had proven that he cared about her already. They had fun together and she didn't spend the entirety of her time in his presence anxious over what he thought about her, wondering whether his words matched his intentions, or whether there was an ulterior motive lingering below the surface.

"I—I gotta go, Gavin," she said suddenly.

He sounded surprised. "Gotta go where?"

"I just … I gotta go. I'm not coming back to the city … yet. My mom needs me here for now. I'm sorry. I'll talk to you later." She hung up the phone before she could lose her nerve.

29

ELIZA

"Oh shoot!" Eliza said suddenly, bolting upright in her seat on the porch. "What time is it?"

"Uhh, about 8:15," Mae said. "Why, what's wrong?"

Eliza leaped up and grabbed her bag from the side table. "I completely spaced on that date I agreed to tonight. Argh! I gotta go home and get ready. Holly, can I borrow your car?"

"You're going on a date?" asked Mae. "With who?"

Eliza stopped and laughed. "Honestly, I don't even know. I ran into Maggie Manning downtown and she talked me into going on a blind double date with her, her fiancé, and some friend of theirs. Not my thing at all, but Sara wouldn't leave me alone until I agreed."

Mae smiled. "Well, that's very spontaneous of you! I'm sure you'll have a good time."

"Thanks, Mom," Eliza replied. She leaned over and kissed her mother on the cheek. "It was really good hanging out with you guys. I'll see you later!" They waved goodbye as she raced out the door and hurried home as fast as she could manage without sweating.

When she got back to Howard Street, she took the world's fastest shower, blow dried her hair out as quick as she could manage, and then gave her face a quick once-over with foundation, mascara, eyeliner, and her favorite dark red lipstick. She didn't have much time to pick out clothes, so she settled on a soft black dress that stopped just above her knees. She threw some wine-colored pumps on—nothing too high; she was pregnant after all—and then she was out of time. *Where are you??* buzzed her phone with a text from Mags. *Your mystery man is antsy!!*

Eliza rolled her eyes. She really hoped that Maggie wasn't setting unrealistic expectations for Gary's friend. She was fun but could get a little carried away sometimes. Eliza needed to make it clear that she had no interest in romantic relationships of any kind right now. *But what about Oliver?* chimed an annoying voice in her head. She shushed it. This was a fun night out with an old friend, nothing else.

She grabbed Holly's keys from the side table as she hustled downstairs and out the door. Firing up the minivan, she headed towards the restaurant where they had planned on meeting. Driving this Mom-mobile made her chuckle. "Is this what my life is going to be once this baby is born?" she mused as she checked her makeup in the mirror. The image of Goldman Sachs powerhouse Eliza Benson piloting a big minivan through the streets of Manhattan made her laugh.

She parked outside the restaurant and hurried in. She was out of breath by the time she saw Maggie and Gary in a booth towards the back. "I'm with them," she explained to the hostess, and then walked back towards where they were seated. Gary's friend was facing away from her, so she couldn't see what he looked like just yet.

Maggie met her halfway and pulled her into a tight squeeze. "Dang, girl! You really are a stunner. I love this dress on you, and that lip color is awesome too."

"Thanks, Mags," Eliza mumbled.

"This is my fiancé, Gary," Maggie said, stepping aside to let Eliza and Gary shake hands.

He was tall, with orange hair, freckles, and the slightest gap between his two front teeth. Eliza thought he looked like a handsomer version of the boy from the cover of *Mad* magazine. "Eliza, great to meet you. Maggie's told me a lot about all the trouble you ladies used to get into back in high school."

Eliza grinned. "Whatever she told you, it's a lie."

"Oh, I'm sure," he chuckled.

"You gotta meet his friend!" Maggie interrupted, grabbing Eliza's arm and steering her around Gary to where his friend was climbing out of the booth behind them. "You're gonna love him. Eliza, this is Oliver! Oliver, Eliza Benson."

Eliza froze in place. She looked up as Oliver, Pianist King of the Bar, rose to his full height and offered her his hand to shake. There was a smile playing on his lips and a fiendish glimmer in his eye, but he didn't give anything away as he said, "Eliza, it's a pleasure to meet you. I'm Oliver."

Eliza wanted to cackle like a maniac. What were the odds of this? Sure, Nantucket was a small island full of random connections between its residents. But even so, this was too funny to be real. Since when was there a rom-com writer pulling the strings of her life? Something about Oliver's expression told her to play along, though, so that's exactly what she did. Biting back her laughter, she took his hand and said, "Oliver, was it? Nice to meet you, too. I'm Eliza."

Maggie looked back and forth at them, pleased as punch. They probably held each other's hands just a moment too long, because Maggie's brow furrowed and she said, "Am I missing something here?"

"No, not at all," Oliver said quickly. "Just my normal social awkwardness, that's all."

Maggie shrugged and clucked, "Let's get something to eat, shall we?"

They all settled around the booth. Gary switched sides so that it was Eliza and Oliver sitting across from each other. It took everything in her to stop from smiling like a fool every time Oliver caught her eye, but somehow she managed.

"What brings you back to Nantucket, Eliza?" Gary asked politely after they'd put in orders for a couple of appetizers.

"Gary!" hissed Maggie. Eliza could hear her kick him under the table. "I'm so sorry," she turned to Eliza and explained. "I already filled him in on everything, and he should've known better than to ask."

"It's all okay." Eliza chuckled. "It's been a sad summer, yeah. But the future looks bright."

"Does it now?" Oliver asked, that same glimmer in his eye shining brighter and brighter with every passing minute. That same blanketing intensity that Eliza had felt when they first met enveloped her once again. It was the oddest thing. Like he was touching her without actually doing so.

"Tonight does, at least," she shot back with a wry smile.

"Agreed!" Maggie chirped.

"Sorry, Eliza," mumbled Gary with a hangdog look on his face.

"Don't worry about it at all," she reassured him. "Let's just have some fun, yeah?"

They hung out and noshed on half a dozen different appetizers. Maggie caught Eliza up on the babysitting/nannying business she'd spun up. It sounded like she was doing really well, with eight employees and lots of rich clients. The wealthy families who came to stay on 'Sconset during the high season were always eager to hire her employees to watch their kids so the parents could have nights out to themselves.

Oliver was mostly quiet, though he chimed in every now and then with little jokes and jests that seemed like they were meant for Eliza's ears only. He was as clever as she remembered, and very quick on the uptake. He seemed intent on keeping up the charade that they'd never met, too, which got funnier and funnier with every passing moment. It turned out that he and Gary went all the way back to high school, when they'd been in a band together.

"We would've made it big time, too," Oliver said, "if Mr. Square over here hadn't decided that his talents lay more in engineering than in shredding guitar solos."

"You played the guitar?" Maggie turned to her fiancé. "You never told me that! When am I getting serenaded?"

"That was a long time ago," Gary said, rubbing the back of his head like he was embarrassed as they all laughed. "But I'll serenade you anytime, darling." He started crooning some horribly off-tune old rock 'n roll number. Maggie groaned and threw a bread roll at his head.

Oliver leaned over towards Eliza and held his hand up to stage-whisper, "We never let him anywhere near a microphone, though." She nearly spit out her water laughing.

Eliza was stuffed after a while. They'd polished off an awe-inspiring amount of food between the four of them. "I don't know about you guys, but I'm about to burst," she said, looking around. "Do you want to walk off a little bit of this food?"

"That's a great idea!" Maggie agreed. "Why don't we go down Main Street and check out some of the shops?"

They gathered their things and went meandering down the main shopping drag. Gary and Maggie were strolling slowly hand in hand, so Oliver and Eliza drifted ahead of them a little bit. When she almost tripped on a curb, Oliver held out his arm. "Grab on," he said with a grin. "Can't have you falling on your head out here in the darkness."

She hesitated, but took his offer, looping her arm through his and holding on to make sure she didn't stumble again. Heels might've been a bad idea.

They chatted as they walked along, stopping every now and then to look into the windows of some of the cute shops that lined Nantucket's Main Street. The night was warm, but the breeze rolling down from behind them was cooling, with a hint of salt lingering on her tongue after each gentle gust. Oliver told her stories about some funny incidents that had happened in the bar over the last few weeks. Mostly drunk people getting up to drunk people antics, but the way Oliver told it made everything seem funny and dramatic.

"You're a big exaggerator," she said accusingly.

"Who, me?" he protested with a grin. "I would never. The truth, the whole truth, and nothing but the truth, so help me God."

"Mmhmm. Color me skeptical."

"What about you?" he asked after a beat.

"Don't change the subject. We were making fun of you."

He poked her. "Yeah, well, I'm sure we'll circle back around to that soon enough. What about you?"

"What *about* me?"

"What's next for you?"

Eliza stopped for a second. "That's a heavy question," she said.

"Only if you let it be."

She thought about what she might say to answer it. What was next for her—in her mind—hadn't ever changed. One way or another, she was going to go back to her life in New York. Minus Clay, of course, but all the other pieces would be in place. She'd have the apartment to herself, and soon a baby to fill it with joy. Aside from that, though, she was still going to work hard and make a lot of money and spend her days being endlessly successful. That was what her life had always been about. That's what had always been next. What other options did she even have?

"Back to New York, I guess," she said finally.

"Hmm," Oliver said.

"What's that supposed to mean?"

"Just, 'Hmm.' That's all. Nothing to it."

"Now who's full of secrets?" She poked him in the side like he'd poked her, drawing a laugh out of him.

He didn't get a chance to answer before Maggie and Gary caught up with them. "You two really seem to be getting along well!" Maggie said excitedly. Eliza was sure that she and Gary had been gossiping about her and Oliver throughout their whole walk. Maggie was always pretty good at playing matchmaker, but even she couldn't take credit for this one.

Eliza wondered what "this one" even was. She had just told Oliver that she had a life to go back to, and she meant it. That would happen sooner rather than later. Her whole summer had been like a dream, and she was bound to wake up any minute. She might as well start preparing herself for that mentally. In the meantime, though, she could enjoy herself tonight. Might as well. Real life loomed in the distance.

"Let's go dancing," she said suddenly. She looked up at Oliver. He still looked a little disappointed, if that was the right word, but he perked up a little at the prospect of keeping the night going. "I've got a feeling this guy knows his way around a dance floor."

Maggie raised an eyebrow and smiled. "All right! I'm in. You never used to be this fun!" she teased.

"I'm still not this fun," Eliza fired back. This was all an act, a vacation from her real life, which was very serious and important. She worked at Goldman Sachs and had a nice apartment in Manhattan and everything she touched was successful. "Serious" and "important" could not be reiterated enough. She was *not* fun. She was *not* spontaneous.

But maybe—just maybe—she could be.

PART III

AUTUMN

30

BRENT
ONE MONTH LATER

"Time flies" was an expression that always made Brent laugh. Sometimes it did, but a lot of times it most definitely did not. When he had been at the marina on the night of his dad's accident, every second had felt like a lifetime. But over the last month, time seemed to be running through his fingers like sand at the beach. There just wasn't enough of it to do everything he wanted to do. But he sure was trying.

He'd thrown himself into his routine with a newfound gusto. He started every morning the same way. Rising before the sun was up, he shoved his feet into his running shoes and got moving before his eyes were even fully open. He went slow at first, just jogging to loosen up his joints, until he got to the beach. Then he started to open up his stride. He ran four or five miles just about every day. He ended each run the same way, too—sprinting as fast as he could. Some days, the ocean wind in his hair and the sun peeking up over the horizon made him laugh like a maniac. It felt *good* to be alive. He'd spent a whole summer feeling the exact opposite. But gosh, he'd just forgotten how nice it felt to really feel his body. Sweat on his tongue, wind in his face, legs churning, lungs burning. Lord almighty, that was a good sensation.

He'd found a running partner, too. While cleaning up his worksite one night, he'd heard a noise. He took a peek in the small dumpster he'd rented for the job and found a little stray dog in there. She was absolutely filthy and stunk to high heaven. But Brent fell in love with her on sight. He coaxed her out with a spoonful of peanut butter and petted her until she was comfortable enough to fall asleep in his arms. Poor thing must've been exhausted, because she hardly even woken up when Brent took her upstairs to his mother's room at the Sweet Island Inn and gave her a bath. It took a good twenty minutes before the water coming off the dog's fur stopped sloughing off black and sludgy. It turned out that she was a soft blonde. When he'd showed her to Mae, his mother laughed. "Blonde, just like all of you children! She was meant to be a Benson." Brent couldn't agree more. He'd named her Henrietta, after his father, and when he'd told Mom about that, he could've sworn he saw the faintest suggestion of a tear in her eyes.

Once Henrietta was cleaned up, collared, and had been to the vet to get her shots, she stuck to Brent like white on rice. Wherever he went, she went. Henrietta loved running along the beach in the morning just as much as him. He loved racing her and seeing her gallop wild and free out there. She'd get to their beach exit a few seconds ahead, then stop and look back at him with her tongue lolling out. She had taken to licking the sweat off his face, too. Once upon a time, Brent would've thought that was gross. But, in his eyes, Henrietta could do no wrong. They were just two gutter dogs, loving on each other.

Henrietta liked to hang around while he worked, too. That was a good thing, because Brent wasn't doing much else aside from working. After he got back from his runs, he scarfed down a quick breakfast of toast and coffee that Mom always set aside for him, and then he got to work. The project Mae had hired him to do was no mean feat. The back house was in bad shape; Aunt Toni said she'd never been able to spare the time or expense to get it right. Transforming it into what Brent had in mind was going to be one heck of a task. But he was feeling up to the job.

He'd started by pretty much gutting it to the studs and then rebuilding it back up. New flooring, new tiling in the bathroom, new cabinets and fixtures in the kitchen. He grouted the tiled floors and fixed up the insulation in the walls where it had gotten messed up. He repainted the outside so it would gleam white in the Nantucket sun.

It felt like he was doing the same work on the house as he was doing on himself. Gutting his soul to the studs and building it back up. Days were easy, relatively speaking. There was always work to do. That kept his mind off things, even when it tried to stray towards unwanted memories of being on a job site with his father. He'd learned everything he knew about handiwork from his pops. What tool went where. How a responsible man kept his workspace clean. He'd learned to sing while he worked, too. *A song on your lips lightens the load on your back,* Dad used to say. Dad liked country. Brent sang Bruce Springsteen, mostly.

Nights were harder, though. There was nothing to distract him from the demons in his head. No singing, no hard labor. Just darkness, whether he closed his eyes or kept them open. He didn't sleep much the first night, nor the next, nor the one after that. Matter of fact, it took nearly two weeks before he slept through until morning without a night terror. Every time he woke up screaming, though, Henrietta woke up, too—she slept in bed next to him—and nuzzled him back to sleep. He was starting to think that she was his guardian angel.

So, mostly, he tried to keep working. It was best that way. He liked his days long and sweaty. Mom usually came out around noon with a sandwich and a glass of lemonade for him. She didn't linger very often. Just gave him his food and a kiss on the cheek and went back inside to keep up with her own work. She didn't peek at the work too closely, either. She kept saying she wanted to be blown away once it was all said and done.

One of the guests, Dominic, liked to come close to sunset when Brent was finishing up. He was some sort of writer, it turned out, working on a novel about something or other. He told Brent he'd decided to extend his visit at the inn indefinitely because he was liking it so much. The two men often shared a drink at the end of a hard day—beer for Dominic, but Brent stuck to just water or lemonade. He'd made a promise to his mother to stay on the wagon and he had every intention of keeping that oath. The shakes of withdrawal those first few nights were something that Brent never wanted to repeat again. He'd done it twice now—that was enough to last him a lifetime.

For his own part, Dominic seemed to be close with Brent's mom, too. Brent liked the idea of her having a friend, and Dominic seemed like a nice guy.

"Coming together nicely, isn't it?" Dominic said one evening. He and Brent were seated in a couple of ratty lawn chairs that Brent had found while scavenging through a back closet. The sun was on its way down, though it still had a ways to go before nightfall.

"I think so," Brent commented, eyeing the day's handiwork. "Still got a few things to throw together, but I like the progress I'm making."

"Well, you've certainly been putting the work in. It's admirable." Dominic clinked his beer against Brent's glass of ice water.

"Thanks." Brent chuckled. Dominic had a funny way of choosing his words. He wasn't sure whether to chalk it up to his profession or his nationality. Either way, Brent liked the way things sounded when Dominic said them. *Admirable* had a nice ring to it. It sounded like a real honor.

"How is your lady friend?" Dominic asked after a sip.

Brent blushed and wiped a bead of sweat off his lip. "'Lady friend' is a bit of a stretch," he mumbled, embarrassed. "We've never really talked."

That wasn't quite true. On one of Brent's first morning runs, he'd noticed a woman sitting at the foot of the dunes, looking out at the morning waves. She was there the next day, and the day after that, too. By the fourth day, they'd taken to waving to each other, and by the eighth, Brent worked up the guts to stop and say good morning to her.

"Good morning," she'd said with a bright smile. She had dark hair cut in bangs across her forehead. Her legs were long and tan where they stretched out beneath her jeans shorts. She looked like a yogi or a dancer, maybe.

"I see you here every morning," Brent said awkwardly. "So just, uh, thought I'd be, y'know. Neighborly, or whatever. Polite-like."

She'd laughed. It sounded like a wind chime. "Very neighborly indeed. I'm Rose."

"Brent," he said. She stood up, brushing sand off her thighs, and stuck out her hand to shake. Brent smiled and took it. He towered over her, and his hand swallowed hers. He kept his eyes fixated on her face the whole time. She was very pretty.

"It's nice to meet you, Brent," Rose said. "Should we do this again tomorrow?"

He gave her one more grin. "You bet." Then, not sure what else to do, he gave her a wave. "Tomorrow it is. C'mon, Henrietta!" he'd called, and off they went.

The next morning, she'd had a bottle of water for him when he stopped. "Thought you might be thirsty, Mr. Ironman," she teased.

Brent took it from her gratefully. It was awfully nice of her to think of him like that.

Over the next week, it became a ritual. They stopped and chatted every morning on his runs. She liked to watch the sun rise over the water, she said. That's why she was sitting out on the beach—to start her day in some peace and quiet. Brent liked that sentiment. He learned that she was a young, single mother of a four-year-old girl named Susanna, and a kindergarten teacher at the local elementary school. After a few days, he sussed out that Susanna's father was no longer in the picture. He didn't press the issue at all; he didn't want to make her uncomfortable. But the thought made him feel a little giddy for reasons he wasn't ready to confront.

"Well, you certainly seemed interested," Dominic said, snapping Brent back to the present moment. "Or have I misinterpreted things?"

"I suppose not," Brent admitted. "She's nice, and very pretty. I just ... gotta focus on my own stuff right now, you know?"

"I do indeed," Dominic said, falling silent. Brent liked that about him —he knew when to talk and when to just sit back and enjoy the moment quietly.

"Time for me to be moving along," Dominic said after a while, standing up. He was a night owl, he'd told Brent, and he did all his best writing late at night. The sun might be on its way down, but Dominic was just now getting ready to start work. "But, if I may offer some unsolicited advice, from an old man to a much younger one— it'd be a shame to let a nice, pretty lady spend all those mornings alone." He gave Brent a wink and a pat on the shoulder, and then walked inside, leaving Brent to watch the last of the sun's descent by himself.

31

SARA

"No. Freaking. Way!" Sara said in disbelief.

Russell laughed, bent over with his hands on his knees, guffawing until tears winked at the corners of his eyes. Despite her initial shock when she'd first walked into his house, Sara found herself laughing along with him. Both of them were clutching onto each other to stop from falling as they cackled and wheezed.

"Stop, stop! My sides hurt!" She swatted him, but he didn't stop laughing for another few minutes. Only when they'd both slid to the floor did they finally calm down and regain their breath.

"This is the most ridiculous scene I've ever come across in my life," she said, eyeing him. "What on earth got into you?"

They'd had a date night planned for a week or two. After their first date over beers and oysters a month ago, they'd hung out at the beach and gone on a few bike rides, but they hadn't had another proper date. Russell insisted that this time he would cook for her. "Problem is, I don't know the first thing about cooking," he'd admitted. "I burn soup. I mess up toast. I do make a mean bowl of cereal, though."

"No problem," she'd told him. "You just get the groceries, and I'll work my magic. You can just sit back and be pretty."

"Woof, that's a relief," he'd joked. "Being pretty is what I'm best at."

So, she'd shown up to his house that Saturday night, the first Saturday in September, wearing dark blue jeans and a white off-the-shoulder top, expecting him to have grabbed a few ingredients for pasta or something pretty simple like that. To her utter surprise, though, his kitchen counter, dining room table, both living room side tables, and half the floor were absolutely *covered* in heaps and heaps of plastic grocery bags.

He'd looked at her when she froze in place wide-eyed, shrugged, and said, "I didn't know what to get, so I panicked and got one of pretty much everything."

Thus, the laughing commenced.

"One of everything?" she said now, swatting him again. "Are you insane? Who *does* that?"

"I told you, I panicked," he said, still chuckling every now and then as he wiped the tears from his eyes. "I didn't want you to get thrown off your rhythm because I didn't have some ingredient or something like that."

"You are absolutely out of your mind," she replied, shaking her head. "There is no way on earth we are gonna be able to eat all this food. I'm gonna be a whale. You'll have to take me out of here in a wheelbarrow like Violet Beauregard."

"Violet who?"

Sara's jaw dropped. "You've never seen *Willy Wonka and the Chocolate Factory*?!"

He held his hands up guiltily. "Sheltered childhood. I watched *Star Wars* and *Indiana Jones* 'til the VHS tapes wore out, and that's pretty much it."

"Good Lord, we have a lot of work to do on you," she said, wheezing.

"Don't I know it. Should probably do some work on these groceries first, though. There's ice cream in one of these bags, and I can't in good conscience let that melt."

Laughing like fools, they commenced unloading all the groceries into the main refrigerator and pantry. They stuffed whatever didn't fit there in the backup fridge Russell had in his garage.

"We could open our own grocery store with all this stuff," Sara grumbled.

"I get it, I get it, I'm a clown. Sue me." He smiled ruefully.

Once they'd gotten everything in some semblance of organization, Sara went to work. She'd been cooking extravagant dinners for the guests at the Sweet Island Inn a couple times a week—lobster thermidor, coq au vin, sous-vide steak with twice-baked potatoes. It felt good to flex her culinary muscles and use all the techniques she'd learned at CIA and Lonesome Dove. Tonight, she decided to make a pretty simple garlic shrimp linguine in a red wine tomato sauce. She was going to make the pasta by hand, though, so she set Russell to work rolling out dough and cutting it into long strands as she started setting up the items for the sauce. Russell poured them both hefty glasses of a nice, buttery white wine.

"Looks like you're doing more drinking than working," she commented with a glance over her shoulder after they'd gotten going. "Caught ya red-handed." His cheeks burned and he pretended to roll the pin as hard as he could for a second, making her laugh.

"They say to share your gifts with the world, don't they?" he retorted. "Cooking is your art. Drinking wine is mine."

"You are in rare form this evening, Mr. Bridges."

"Always, Miss Benson. Always. Hey, what kind of music do you like?"

Sara shrugged. "Oh, I'm easy. Anything but opera, pretty much."

"Great," Russell said, wiping off his hands on a dish towel and walking out of the kitchen. "'Cause I've got a three-hour recording of me yodeling and playing the banjo that I've been *dying* to play for you."

She grabbed a bag of frozen peas that was near at hand and chucked it at his head as he walked into the open-space living room. He ducked just in time, laughing, so it hit the wall behind him with a *chunk* and slid to the ground. "You better not!"

"Yes, chef!" he barked. He spun around, clicked his heels together, and gave her a military-esque salute. She just shook her head and sighed, though she couldn't stop herself from grinning. Russ was a complete and utter goober, and his gooberness was turned up to an eleven out of ten tonight. Still, it made her laugh.

Against her better instincts, she found herself thinking of Gavin. Gavin was anything but a goober. He was stylish, composed, suave at all times.

She'd tried to deny it to herself as often and as loudly as possible over the last month, but the fact remained that Russell and Gavin were both warring for real estate in her heart. Gavin had taken to texting her every now and then since their unexpected phone call. Just a *Thinking of you* or a *What's up?* She didn't always reply, but even when she did, he rarely said anything back. What kind of game he was playing, Sara didn't know for sure, but she had to admit that it was effective. She felt like a fish chomping at a lure that kept moving out of reach every time she got close.

Russell, on the other hand, was ever-present. If she texted him, he texted back right away. He double- and triple-texted when he had something to say. He used emojis and sent goofy selfies when the mood struck. He was funny and warm and wide-open to her.

Polar freaking opposites.

She was shaken from her thoughts by the soft crackle of music coming from the other side of the room. She looked up and saw Russell sliding a record out of the sleeve and putting the needle in place.

"A record player, huh?" she asked wryly. "Old school."

He flashed her a grin. "Can't beat the sound. I know, I know, I'm a big snob. But my dad raised me on these things. He was a big Motown guy."

"How come you don't have any rhythm then?"

"I got the good-looks gene instead. My brother got the rhythm."

"Who said you're good-looking?" Sara teased.

"My reflection, mostly," he shot back as he walked back around the corner and leaned up against the counter next to her. "But I was hoping that, if I play my cards right—and pump you full of enough chardonnay—I might get you to agree with that tonight."

She laughed and pushed him in the chest. "Shush and go finish rolling out my pasta."

He gave her the mock salute again. "Yes, chef!"

They chitchatted about their days and various gossip around the island as the low-key jazz crooned from the speakers and their wine glasses kept getting filled and emptied and filled and emptied. Sara tossed everything she'd been preparing—shallots, celery, carrot, tomatoes, basil, parsley, lemon juice, and a hefty splash of Cabernet Sauvignon—into a sauté pan to let it simmer down for a while. Then she went over to help Russell finish slicing all the pasta into nice linguine strands while the pasta water got to a boil.

The forty-five minutes after that passed by just as easily. Eventually, the pasta was ready to cook, the sauce was almost done, and all she had to do was grill up the shrimp real quick and throw it all together.

"Bon appétit," she said when it was done, sliding a plate in front of Russell at the dining table.

He pouted. "Hey, I helped."

She leaned down and pecked him on the cheek. "Yes, you did. Like a pro ... crastinator."

He jabbed her in the side with a spoon. "Watch it, Benson. I'm highly respected in Nantucket culinary circles."

She backed up, hands held high in surrender. "Forgive me, Chef Bridges. I bow to your superior skill." Laughing, she took her own place at the table.

"Oh, this is heavenly," Russell said as he took his first bite.

Sara grinned. No matter how often she heard it, compliments about her food never got old.

Russell asked her about cooking in fancy New York kitchens as they both dug in. "What's that like?"

"Hard," she admitted. "Fast-paced. Loud. Can't make mistakes."

"Sounds intense."

"Definitely. I love it, though."

He looked at her quizzically. "You miss it all, don't you? That life."

She thought about it before answering. "I'm honestly not sure," she began hesitantly. "Part of me misses it, yeah. But it wears on you. Feels like you're in a pressure cooker when you're at work, and when you're not, all you want to do is get drunk or sleep. It's a tough way to live."

Her answer was the truth. New York was hard, and she really did love the ease of Nantucket. She'd grown up here, and she always used to joke to her colleagues back at Lonesome Dove that she had saltwater in her veins. Cooking in her mother's kitchen had been an unexpected source of fun and relaxation, too. It was like rediscovering why she'd fallen in love with the art in the first place. When the music was on and she had wine in her system and laughter echoing around her, cooking was pure bliss. She wondered if it was possible to recapture that sense of freedom at Lonesome Dove, knowing that Gavin would always be lingering around the corner.

The conversation wandered on from there, but part of Sara's thoughts stayed back on Russell's question. Could she ever go back to New York? In some ways, she'd resigned herself to that door being closed. But the more she thought about it, the less sure she was. Gavin seemed at least conversational these days, which made her think that maybe there was still a possibility of taking her place back in the kitchen at Lonesome Dove. Or at least getting his recommendation to get her hired at a different establishment.

"What's next?" Russell asked eagerly when they were done eating. His plate was scraped clean, Sara noticed, amused.

"Cleanup time," she said.

"Ugh, say it ain't so!"

"Such a drama queen," she tutted. "Come on, let's get it done."

He followed her into the kitchen, plate in hand. They set them down in the sink.

"Hey, Sara," he said quietly in a weird voice. She turned around to see what he was doing, when—*wham!*—he clapped a hand on either side of her face and absolutely coated her with loose flour leftover from making the pasta.

"Oh, no you did not!" she shrieked. Grabbing a handful of it herself from the cutting board, she hurled it at him with all her might.

An all-out war ensued. Flour went everywhere, puffs of it erupting back and forth, until they were both white from head to toe and panting heavily.

"I cannot believe you just started a flour fight with me. This is gonna take an eternity to clean up."

She could see his smile through the floating powder. "Couldn't resist," he said. It was tough to make out his facial expression, thanks to the flour caked on his face, but it seemed to her like he was looking at her strangely. When he spoke again, his voice was a little lower, a little huskier. "I hope I'm not pushing things too fast, but I gotta say, it'd be awfully nice to kiss you right about now." He stepped halfway to her. Just a foot or two separated them now.

Sara smiled shyly. "Russell, we've been working on this. You have to ask for things if you want them."

He grinned back. "Right you are. Sara, can I kiss you?"

She closed her eyes and kissed him first in response.

32

BRENT

The day had finally come: the big unveiling of Brent's renovation.

Everyone had come over to the inn for the ceremony. "Did we have to do this so early?" Sara grumbled, rubbing the sleep out of her eyes. "No human being should have to be up at this hour."

"Shush," Eliza said, poking her sister in the ribs.

"Be nice," Holly reprimanded.

"Sorry, sis, but you gotta see it with the morning sunlight coming through. It's way better that way, trust me." Brent was wringing his hands in front of him nervously. That was a Mae habit he'd picked up somewhere along the way. Speak of the devil, his mom came bustling out right then. She had a steaming cup of coffee that she handed to Sara, who took it gratefully, and a cup of tea for Eliza, who murmured her thanks as she took it by the handle.

"Honey, before you start," Mae began, "I just want to say how proud we all are of you."

"Agreed," chimed Holly and Eliza at the same time.

"Definitely," Sara added.

Mae continued, "You've been working your tail off on this thing, and that's all well and good, but I'm proudest of how you have gone about it. It's been a tough summer for our family; we all know that. And things were rough for a little bit for you especially. But you've poured yourself into this and—well, I'm just grateful. And proud of you. I know without a doubt that your father would be proud of you, too." Mae was crying now, just a little bit. Brent found that he was, too. He hadn't expected that. He didn't have time to check if his sisters were as choked up as he and his mother were, because Mae pulled him into a hug. He closed his eyes to hold her tight.

"I'm proud of you, son," she repeated in his ear. Said like that—just for his ears alone—it made him shiver. It felt like his dad was speaking through her.

Everything she'd said was true. He had committed himself to this renovation mind, body, and soul. The work itself wasn't important— he knew that, his mom knew that, everyone knew that. This was just a guesthouse at an inn.

But the work represented something that words couldn't really capture: his turnaround point. Maybe part of him would always blame himself for his father's passing, but Brent was starting to realize that he couldn't ever really control those thoughts. That was fine. He was learning to live with it, and in the process, he was learning more about himself. He'd always known he was a concrete guy, a man of *things*. Perhaps that's why these long days of physical labor had felt like doing repair work on his soul. He was using the things his father had taught him—how to swing a hammer, to measure twice and cut once, and on and on like that, the million little Henry aphorisms that had bubbled up throughout each day over the last month since he began this project. It was a little on the nose to say that he was exorcising his demons one nail at a time, but so be it —Brent had never been much good at metaphors anyway.

"Thanks, Mom." He wiped the tear tracks off his face and straightened up. It felt as though the sad moment had passed like a cloud over the sun and left in its wake was pure pride in what he had done. "Now, time for the big show! Come on, follow me."

He turned and opened the door of the guesthouse. Everybody filed in after him.

"Brent!" Holly gasped when she got her first look. "You gotta be kidding me. This is ... this is *amazing.*"

"I don't even have the words," Sara chimed in.

Even Eliza, whose tastes for interior decorating had never quite lined up with the nautical Nantucket aesthetic, had her jaw hanging open.

Best of all was Mae's face. She'd clapped her hands to her mouth and was looking around, wide-eyed.

Brent couldn't hide the smile that crept on his face. "Enough, you're making me blush," he joked. "Let me give you guys the tour. So, this is the living room." He swept his arm around. The fresh white paint on all the doors and trim was gleaming and flawless. It was a nice complement to the soft gray he'd picked for the walls, the same color as the ocean in the wintertime. The floors were a blonde wood with a nice lacquered finish, and he'd hung new curtains over the windows in a weathered gray that looked lovely against the lighter gray of the walls. The black iron hinges and door handles he'd installed stood out sharply and added some contrast to everything.

"I kept most of the original furniture," he explained, pointing at the robin's egg blue couch and armchair in the living room, "though I also built a new coffee table and stained it with this dark wine color right over here."

The women trailed after him, still in shock, as he led them into the kitchen.

"In here, we got new cabinets, courtesy of Fredo's Fixtures downtown, and new countertops."

"Where on earth did you get this marble?" Mae asked in astonishment.

"Scavenged it from a buddy working a demo on the other end of the island," he admitted sheepishly. "The one question I was hoping you weren't going to ask! But, don't worry, I did a thorough job of cleaning it and cutting it to fit and all that."

"It's beautiful," Holly declared. Brent agreed. He was partial to the whites and grays that swirled through it, looking almost like they were liquid.

"Let's go to the bedroom." In there, he pointed out more new curtains and the same fresh flooring, along with some picture frames he'd knocked together to hold a few dozen pretty seashells he'd found during his morning runs. "New nightstand and linens shelves in here, too."

The bathroom, which they went to next, was his favorite part of the house. It, too, was gleaming white, with a dark sealant running between the tiles. He'd placed a soft teal-colored tile at regular intervals throughout the tiling to give everything a true Nantucket feel.

"And that's pretty much it!" he announced when they'd all made their way back to the living room.

"Brent, you've got serious talent," Eliza said. She was smiling at him like his dad used to do. Like, *Look at what you're capable of!* He didn't think he could feel any warmer, but at the sight of her smile, his own ticked a notch wider.

Stone-cold sober for a month, running every morning, and working his butt off to do the best possible job he could—this moment made it all worth it. All the nights when he wanted nothing more than a drink, when he'd wondered if this was a stupid vanity project and he ought to go back to drowning himself in booze ... those seemed so utterly distant. He felt *big*.

"I want to hear about how you did all this," Holly added. "I mean, seriously, you need to start hiring yourself out around the island. I never even realized you knew how to do all this stuff on your own!"

"Dad taught me a lot when I wasn't even paying attention," he explained with a shrug.

"I want to hear, too," Sara said. "Maybe you can do the inn kitchen next. It could use a little TLC."

"Why don't we all go sit down to breakfast?" Mae suggested.

Eliza's stomach rumbled and they all laughed. "Sounds good to me," she joked, "since I'm eating for two."

Brent looked out the window. The morning light coming in was as beautiful as he'd hoped for. But he still had one more piece of unfinished business.

He turned back to his family. "I'll be a little late to breakfast," he said. "I gotta go take care of something first."

"You're late, Ironman," Rose accused teasingly as he ran up to her huffing and puffing, Henrietta close on his heels.

"Sorry, I was busy working up the courage."

Rose frowned. He liked how her button nose wrinkled up when she was confused. "The courage for what?"

"To ask if you wanted to go out with me sometime," he blurted. He winced. Not his smoothest moment, that was for sure. But he was a little out of practice. It would have to do.

When she comprehended what he'd asked her, she smiled. "I'd love to."

Brent felt like he could do a backflip then and there, though he'd never attempted one before in his life and now probably wasn't the time. "Awesome," he said, finally catching his breath. "I'd love that, too."

33

ELIZA

Everyone was still chattering about how well Brent had done when they sat down to breakfast in the inn's kitchen. Holly kept saying that Brent ought to start up his own handyman business like Dad used to have. Eliza was inclined to agree. That level of craftsmanship demanded a big payday. She thought Brent could do really well for himself if he decided to embark down that path.

After crab and spinach omelets for everybody, Eliza and Sara decided to take a walk down to the beach. Holly said she wanted to go back to the house on Howard Street to do some laundry and take care of a few odds and ends, while Mae had some similar work to do around the inn. They all hugged and parted ways.

Eliza and Sara were mostly quiet on the way to the beach. It was a nice day, finally cooling down a little bit after the scorching hot summer, so both of the women were content to just enjoy the fresh air and exercise.

"Have you thought of a name yet?" Sara asked, nodding towards Eliza's pregnant belly. She was showing more and more every day.

"What? Oh, no. I don't want to. I think I'm just going to be spontaneous when the day comes."

"That's a bold move for you, sis," Sara teased. "Eliza the planner is never spontaneous."

"Yeah, well, it's a new chapter in my life, I guess," she said with a grin. Truer words had never been spoken. She'd been thinking a lot about chapters in her life lately. The baby would definitely change a lot of things, that was for sure. But she wondered whether she ought to make an effort to keep other things the same.

For instance, maybe it was time to return to New York.

She'd been reluctant to even consider it, but over the last few days, it had been buzzing in her head nonstop. Even when she was hanging out with Oliver, like they'd been doing most nights, just watching movies or taking long walks on the beach, she had thoughts of Manhattan and Goldman Sachs in the back of her head. She was set with savings for a while, so it wasn't about the money. Part of her just craved the power and importance of her job. She liked feeling needed, strong, essential. Nantucket was ... not that. Life was good here in its own ways—slower, calmer, a little slice of backwater paradise far away from the honking taxi horns and pretentious people who populated New York. But she just couldn't shake the desire to be back in the midst of things.

Whenever Oliver caught her lost in thought, he'd say the same words he'd said to her when they first met: "What's your story, Eliza Benson?" Usually, she demurred and changed the subject.

When the women settled down, Sara turned to her. "Do you miss New York?"

Eliza decided to answer honestly. "Yeah. I do. I miss the ... just the New York-ness of it, you know? I miss my job. I miss being surrounded by people. I miss feeling like the whole world revolved around me. I know that sounds selfish and silly, but I can't think of a better way to explain it."

"No, I know what you mean," Sara said.

She'd been on a journey of her own this summer, Eliza knew. It seemed like things were going really well with her and Russell, but Eliza had caught Sara staring at her phone on more than a few occasions. Once, when Sara was in the shower and her phone buzzed, Eliza had taken a guilty big-sister snoop and saw the contact name "GAVIN" lighting up her screen. She felt certain that that path held only trouble for Sara, but she also knew that there was no dissuading her little sister when she wanted something. Gavin was bad news. But if Sara was set on pursuing him anyway, not a soul on earth could convince her not to. It was a tricky situation.

"I've been thinking of going back too, you know," Sara added after a long pause.

"Really?" Eliza pretended to be a little bit surprised. She knew Sara would not appreciate learning that Eliza had snooped on her phone. If she wanted to talk about Gavin, Eliza would be all ears, but she was going to let Sara come to that decision on her own terms.

"I just ... I miss it like you do. I miss my job. I miss my—"

"Your Gavin?" Eliza blurted. Welp, so much for letting Sara come to that on her own. It was unlike her to be so loose-lipped. Nantucket had softened her.

But to her surprise, Sara just blushed instead of getting defensive. "Have I been that obvious?"

"No, no," Eliza reassured her. "But you're my little sister. I know you. I can see when you're conflicted."

"'Conflicted' is exactly the right word. I feel like Gavin and Russ are boxing each other in my head all the time."

"Well, who's winning?"

"Both of them. Neither. I don't know. It's hard. They're complete opposites."

That certainly seemed to be true. Eliza had never met Gavin, but from the way Sara had described him on the few occasions when she opened up about him, she could tell that he was a photo negative of the goofy, warmhearted Russell.

"I can definitely see that. Maybe just take some time to yourself and see where your heart leads you."

"Where my heart leads me?" Sara chuckled. "I think Nantucket is getting to your head, Lizzy. You never used to care about hearts."

Eliza smiled inwardly. "You might be right about that."

"Speaking of hearts, how's yours? I still think it's super weird that He-Who-Must-Not-Be-Named hasn't tried harder to patch things up." It was true—since the fruit basket debacle, Clay hadn't reached out to Eliza even once. She supposed she should be grateful—she'd been the one to tell him not to try anything again—but she had to agree with Sara that it was a little bit strange. Clay wasn't the type to just let things go so easily.

"Maybe. I'm happy with my heart these days, though. Oliver is—he's … I like him."

"I can tell. I've never seen you this happy, Lizzy," Sara said with seriousness in her eyes. "Ever." The waves crashed before them, licking at the white sand as Eliza weighed her sister's words.

She couldn't deny it. Oliver did make her happy. It was far too soon to call it love. Eliza would hardly be the first person to make that designation anyway. But there was something there between them, something real and palpable that made her nervous and excited all at once.

It was the uncertainty of him that did it, she'd decided. Everything else in her life had always been rigid. A place for everything and everything in its place. Oliver refused to fall in line like that. He was unpredictable and funny and constantly surprising her. An enigma wrapped within a mystery, like a Magic-8 ball with unlimited possibilities for what might bubble up if you shook it just right. Like Sara with Gavin and Russell, Eliza was finding herself caught between two men who couldn't be more different. The big difference between her and her sister was that Eliza was very, very sure which route she intended to take—anything that led away from Clay.

"C'mon, let's walk a little," Sara said. "My legs are falling asleep."

They left the serious conversation behind as they got up and walked down the beach a little farther. When they'd gone as far as they wanted, they turned around and strolled back to the house.

Eliza was woken up from her nap that afternoon by her phone dinging with a new email. That in and of itself was strange—she hadn't been getting many emails these days. Most of them got filtered into her out-of-office autoresponder that said she was taking a leave of absence from the firm. But this one got through. That must mean that it had been marked as urgent.

Rolling over and groaning, she grabbed her phone with one hand while rubbing her eyes with the other. It took a moment for her vision to adjust enough to read the email at the top of her inbox, but when she finally comprehended what it said, she sat bolt upright in her bed.

It was from Janine, the head of human resources at Goldman Sachs. The subject line read, "!! FIRM SEPARATION PAPERWORK [Time Sensitive]."

"What the ..." Eliza muttered. She opened the email. It was the standard documentation that Goldman Sachs gave to any employee who was leaving the firm. A release of liability, information on 401k and health-care policies, and a letter from the managing director informing them of their termination and thanking them for their service.

She was being fired.

Her hands were shaking as she opened her contacts and found the contact number for Marty Fleishman, the MD. It felt like her vision had narrowed down to just her phone screen.

Buzz. Buzz.

The line rang and rang and rang, but Eliza was determined to keep trying until someone answered. She got his voice mail, hung up, dialed again.

Buzz. Buzz. "Hello, this is Marty Fleishman—"

Hung up. Dialed again.

Buzz. Buzz.

Finally, he answered. "Eliza ..." he began.

She cut him off. "You need to tell me right now what is happening, Marty," she said icily.

"I stepped out of a meeting to take this call, Eliza. I have to go back in."

"Don't you dare, Marty," she hissed. She was all cold fury, an Amazon queen enraged. "Tell me what is happening. Now."

He sighed. She could picture him shuffling back on forth on his feet. He was an older man, mid-fifties, classic New Yorker. His paunch hung over his belt, but everything he wore was immaculately tailored. The watches he wore everyday cost more than the net worth of Eliza's entire apartment building.

"Marty," she repeated. "Talk to me."

"We couldn't hold your position open anymore," he said finally. The words sounded limp and lame coming out of his mouth. Eliza knew instantly that they weren't true.

"Bull. I made more for the firm last year than the rest of the department combined. If you couldn't hold my position, then you must have decided to just stop making money. What is the actual explanation?"

"Look, Eliza ..." He sighed again.

She wanted to grab him by his tie through the phone, yank his face into hers, and scream until he spoke the truth. "I'll ask one more time: What. Happened?"

There was an uncomfortable silence. But Eliza was prepared to wait as long as necessary. "Clay told us," he said.

Eliza's blood ran cold. "Clay told you *what*?"

"That ... if you came back ... you'd have to leave again soon. I can't say anything more, and I shouldn't have even said that much. You know we're in delicate territory here."

Eliza couldn't remember a time in her life when she'd ever been angrier. Not when the Harvard pitcher decided to throw three consecutive pitches at her head during conference play her junior year. Not when Nora Simmons tried to make out with her prom date back in high school. Not even when a drunk college kid had thrown up on her shoes on the subway fifteen minutes before she was supposed to meet the CEO of a Fortune 100 technology firm to pitch them on her firm's services. All those events paled in comparison to what was happening right now.

Clay had told the firm she was pregnant. And those spineless goblins were using it as an excuse to fire her. It was patently illegal. She knew that, they knew that, and they knew that she knew that. But what Eliza also knew was that, if she brought a lawsuit or raised a fuss, she'd never work in finance again. Every bank, hedge fund, and private equity firm in the country would slam its door in her face. She'd be blackballed permanently. No more sitting in the seat of power. No more feeling like she could move millions of dollars with the click of a mouse. She'd be shut out. Iced out. Left out.

Forever.

How could they?

A different woman might have cried in this circumstance. The old Eliza would have marched into the Manhattan headquarters of Goldman Sachs and crucified every man who dared look at her wrong, from the janitor all the way up to the chief executive officer.

But the new Eliza just hung up.

She let the phone fall from her hand onto the bedsheets. Her eyes drifted up to the ceiling fan. It needed to be dusted. How had she not noticed that? She'd been staying in this room for almost four months now, and she'd just now noticed the thick layer of dust coating the tops of the blades. It was one detail out of a million that she'd missed. She'd been too busy thinking about what—Clay? Work? New York? Oliver?

Oliver. Now there was a jolt to the heart. Just a few hours ago, she'd been sitting on the beach with Sara and contemplating what it would feel like to go back home to New York and leave Oliver in her past. If she'd done that, he would be nothing more than a fun memory. He'd go on to sweet talk some other woman in the bar, maybe, or a different bar. Maybe he'd marry that woman and they'd have beautiful, green-eyed children with slender pianist's fingers. He and Eliza would probably never cross paths again.

But now she had a choice. Well, a choice forced on her by the absence of a choice, if she wanted to get technical about it. New York wasn't a home anymore for her. That door had been closed. Slammed. She thought about calling Clay. But she knew already what he would say, as if the conversation had already happened.

I had to get through to you somehow, didn't I?

You told me not to call you, so I didn't. I called Marty instead.

Her fist curled in anger.

But then, just as suddenly, she let it go.

Try as she might, she couldn't find any hate in her heart for Clay. He wasn't a bad person, at least not in the way that most people thought of bad people. He wasn't outwardly malicious or cruel for the sake of being cruel. Cruelty implied that he'd had a choice between doing good and doing bad, and he'd chosen the latter. That wasn't the case. Clay was just a shark. He feasted when there was blood in the water and he could not wrap his head around the idea of caring for children and he had never been physically or emotionally capable of loving her in the first place. She had merely deluded herself into thinking there was even a possibility of that.

The only real possibility left to her had sharp, sparkling green eyes and liked to ask her what her story was. Oliver was a possibility. Maybe nothing more than that, and maybe he never would be. But right now, where Eliza sat—in the bedroom in the house on the island where she'd grown up—the path that Oliver was offering to her seemed sunny and well-lit. The alternatives were dim at best.

She made up her mind. She was going to stay on Nantucket, and she was going to walk that path with him.

She picked up her phone again, found Oliver's name in her contacts, and texted him.

Hey, she typed. *Wanna hang out?*

34

BRENT

Brent closed his eyes and let out a long, rattling sigh.

He was nervous. He was finally willing to admit that much, at least. He'd spent the whole afternoon telling himself that he wasn't nervous, but that was a bold-faced lie. That whole "do a backflip" sensation of pride he'd been feeling when he ran towards Rose on the beach this morning was long gone. In its place was the same gut-churning nausea he'd had back in sixth grade, when he'd waited after school with a ring pop and a handmade card to ask Cristina Suarez to the school sock hop. He felt like puking. He'd put on too much cologne. This outfit—a Nantucket red button-down and jeans—was so ridiculously stupid that he might as well just turn around and go home now because—

The door opened.

Brent's eyes flew open, too. But he found himself staring at empty space. He was confused for the briefest of moments. Then he adjusted his line of sight a little lower and realized there was a little girl standing in the doorway.

She had her mother's dark hair, pulled back into pigtails and tied with violently pink scrunchies. Her dress matched her hair tie, and she had a half-dressed Barbie in one hand. She looked up at Brent with nothing but pure curiosity in her eyes. "Who're you?"

Brent opened his mouth to speak, but no words came out. He closed his mouth, opened it, tried again. Still nothing. He was sweating, he realized. The night wasn't even that hot. Good Lord, what was happening? He'd been smooth once upon a time, hadn't he? He was no hermit. He'd been on his fair share of dates. He'd had girlfriends —nothing serious, but still, it wasn't like he'd spent the last twenty-two years cloistered like a monk. But here he was, babbling and befuddled by the first female he encountered tonight. And this one happened to be four years old.

He swallowed hard, bent down on one knee, and gave Rose's daughter a big smile. It felt forced and fake, but he stuck with it anyway. *No one likes a quitter,* his dad used to say. Brent wanted very badly to start liking himself again, and that started here. He wasn't gonna quit on anything.

"Hi, you must be Susanna," he said. "I'm Brent. It's nice to meet you." He held out a hand for her to shake.

"My mom says I'm not supposed to talk to strangers," she said solemnly. She rocked back and forth from toe to heel and clutched her Barbie doll to her chest.

He nodded. "That's smart. I'm not a stranger, though. I'm a friend of your mommy's. Hey, do you like puppies?" He winced as soon as the words were out of his mouth—it sounded like he was trying to entice her into an unmarked van and kidnap her. But there was no turning back now. He drew his phone out of his pocket and showed her some pictures of Henrietta. "This is my puppy."

"She's pretty," Susanna replied. She was still uncertain about him, he could tell. He supposed that was a good thing.

"I think so too," Brent said with a wink. "Her name is Henrietta. I found her behind our house. She's my best friend now."

"Can I meet her?"

"Absolutely. Tell you what—next time I'm in the neighborhood, I'll bring Henrietta by, and you guys can be best friends, too."

"Suz! Suz!" called a voice from the back. Rose came hustling out, fixing one earring. She saw it was Brent standing at the door and relaxed. But she wasn't going to let her daughter get away without a lecture. "Susanna Maria, what have I told you about opening the door when I'm not around?"

"You said don't do it." Susanna looked at the ground with sad eyes.

"That's right. You don't know who's on the other side."

"But Mr. Brent said he's your friend!"

Rose looked over at Brent and grinned. "Four-year-olds, am I right?" She chuckled. She turned back to her daughter. "He is my friend. Well, I'll let it slide this time. But no more, okay?"

"Okay," murmured the little girl.

"Go play now, hon." She shooed Susanna into the interior of the house and turned back towards the front door. "Sorry about that," she said.

Brent rose from his half kneel, groaning. "Oof, I forgot how hard it is to get up and down from their level."

"Tell me about it. I do it all day long at school. They oughta issue kneepads to kindergarten teachers."

"My kindergarten teacher probably would've preferred a helmet," he said. "She told my mom I was, and I quote, 'an unholy terror.'"

Rose smiled. She had on a bright red lipstick, and Brent was having a hard time looking at anything else besides that. "Well, good to see that nothing has changed then."

Brent smiled and rubbed the back of his neck. "You look great," he murmured.

"What'd you say?" Rose asked. She'd been turning back into the house.

"I said, uh, you look amazing."

"Oh! Thanks. I'm scarily out of practice for this. You wouldn't believe how many times I had to wipe off my makeup and start over. It's been ages since I went on a date."

For some reason, that put Brent at ease. "You and me both."

She laughed. It was such a musical sound every time. "I don't believe that for a second, wise guy. Good-looking man like you on a vacation destination like this? You must be a big hit with the ladies."

He wandered in, shutting the door behind him and leaning up against the wall while Rose stocked up her purse for the night. He took a second to admire her. She wasn't very tall, more like petite. But she looked great in slim black jeans that ended with a frayed hem at her mid-calf. The knit, salmon-colored top she was wearing showed off her arms, which were toned and tan. "You've got me pegged all wrong," he said. "I'm just a lonely guy looking for love in all the wrong places."

"Well, keep looking elsewhere then," she said with a wry smile. She tapped him on the nose as she walked past him. "I'm just using you for the free ride to the movies."

The babysitter rang the doorbell before Brent could think of anything clever to reply to that. He hung back while Rose gave the girl instructions. Rose had initially thought that she wouldn't be able to get anyone to watch Susanna for the night while she and Brent went to the quaint drive-in movie installation that someone had erected for the summer. But then Brent had remembered that Eliza's friend Maggie ran a babysitting company, and everything had come together nicely.

"Ready?" Rose said to Brent once she'd wrapped it up.

"Ready," he confirmed.

They went outside to his old truck. He'd scrubbed the heck out of her and she was shining as good as he knew how to do. Brent opened Rose's door for her and helped her up. "Careful, it's a steep one," he said, holding her hand to get her into the seat.

"No kidding. This thing has seen a lot, huh?" She blanched. "I didn't mean for that to sound rude. I'm sorry. Jeez, I'm nervous."

Brent laughed out loud and patted the hood as he walked around to the driver's side and clambered in. "No offense taken. This old girl has definitely seen a lot. She was my dad's old ride. She and *Jenny Lee* were both his."

Rose gave him a weird look. "Wait a second. Jenny Lee? Do you have a wife or a girlfriend or something?"

Brent suddenly realized what had confused her and burst out laughing. "No, no! Nothing like that. *Jenny Lee* is my boat."

Rose pretended to mop some sweat off her forehead. "Woo, that's a relief. This was about to set a world record for the shortest date of all time."

"You ain't getting out of it that easy," Brent said with a wink as they pulled out and headed down the road.

They chatted about all kinds of things on the ride over and while they waited for the movie to start at the drive-in. As a kindergarten teacher at the local elementary school, Rose was up on all the parental gossip and had loads of funny stories about kids saying the darndest things.

Dad's truck was as old school as they came, old enough that it still had a flat bench seat that ran all the way across the front. After they'd parked and gotten some popcorn from the stand at the entrance, Rose slid over towards him.

"Can I put my arm around you?" Brent asked her sheepishly.

She smiled, then curled up against him with her head on his shoulder. Right then, the movie started—an old-school John Wayne cowboy flick, one of Brent's favorites—and they fell quiet.

It felt more right than Brent could ever have imagined to have Rose curled up against him. She'd come virtually out of nowhere, but now that she was next to him, breathing softly and smelling like perfume and with her skin so soft against his fingertips, he wasn't quite sure how he'd ever gotten by without her. Nothing had ever felt so right so fast. He knew he was being delusional. "Love at first sight" was a Hallmark marketing slogan, not a real thing that happened in the real world. Anyone who believed otherwise was a sucker, and his dad hadn't raised him to be a sucker.

But there was no denying that it felt good. He loved how easily they'd fallen into a banter. He liked that she was as nervous as him—she'd turned to him halfway to the theater and admitted she was already sweating—and that she laughed at her own goofs. He liked that she laughed at anything, ever, because her laugh was maybe the sweetest sound he could ever remember hearing.

Brent Benson, you are being a dang fool, he scolded himself. *Pull yourself together.* She was just a woman, yes, but then again, he was just a man, and maybe it was okay for them to enjoy each other's company more than expected at such short notice. Maybe the universe had conspired to throw them together at exactly the right moment. Brent had never believed in that fate garbage before, but he'd also never had a reason to believe it. If fate was real, then it had dealt him an awful hand—up until now. Maybe now it was making up for what it had done to him before. If fate was real, it had taken his father and

given him Rose. There was no weighing those two against each other
—they were each their own separate thing—but he decided to just
stop thinking in circles and enjoy the moment.

After all—life was meant to be enjoyed, wasn't it?

They talked throughout the second movie, some 1950s noir with a
quippy, fast-talking detective delivering awful puns to a blonde
bombshell. "*A dame walked into my office one rainy night. She had legs
longer than a bad date*"; that kind of thing. Eventually, the clock struck
eleven, and Rose reluctantly said that she had to be getting back
home to relieve the babysitter.

"Fun can't last forever, I guess," Brent said as he fired up the truck and
took them back towards Rose's place.

It was a short drive, less than twenty minutes before they were back
where they started. Brent killed the engine in the driveway and they
sat still for a minute, just looking at each other with silly grins on
their faces.

"I had a good time tonight, Ironman," Rose said. She bit her lip like
she was anxious.

"Me too."

"I'm glad you worked up the courage to ask me out."

He smiled. "I just happened to call tails."

She punched him in the shoulder playfully. "If you actually flipped a
coin to decide whether or not to ask me out, I'm going to be very
upset."

"Of course not," he said, laughing. He paused, then said, "I threw a
dart at a board."

She whacked him over the head gently with her clutch, both of them giggling. Before she could lean away, though, he grabbed her wrist softly. The laughter died quickly. Both of them stared into each other's eyes. His throat felt tight.

"You know, I think you're special," Brent whispered. Her face was so close to his. He couldn't stop staring at those lips.

"I might think the same about you. Not telling, though," she whispered back.

"Can I kiss you?" he asked.

She bit her lip again. "I think that'd be for the best."

So that's exactly what he did. Her lips were as sweet as he'd known they would be. But the kiss lasted just a moment before she put a soft hand on his chest and pushed him away. "Brent ..." she began.

"Uh-oh," he said. "This is where you tell me that you have a boyfriend and he's about to come storming out here with a shotgun." He expected her to laugh, but she just looked downcast for a second. When she looked back up at him, he could swear he saw the ghost of a tear in her eye.

"Susanna's father was ... not a good man. It took me a long time to pick up the pieces after he left. He—shoot, I don't even know where to start with it. It wasn't good. It just wasn't."

Brent leaned back. "I understand. I'm sorry. I shouldn't have crossed the line."

"No, it's not that. It's just—I like you. More than I should. More than anyone should like a guy after one date and some sweaty chitchat on the beach in the mornings. And that scares me. Can ... can you promise me something?"

He hesitated. He wanted to make sure he said the right thing here. She'd said she liked him. That alone was enough to put the biggest, dopiest smile on his face. He felt the same warm sensation in his chest that he had while revealing the renovation that morning.

But he knew this was a critical moment. A lot hung in the balance here. What exactly was hanging, he couldn't say, but he could sense the importance, the tension in the air. "Whatever it is, I promise," he said.

"You don't even know what I'm going to ask you yet."

"It doesn't matter. It's yours."

She touched his jaw. Her eyes flashed. "Just don't break my heart, okay? That's what I'm scared of. Promise me you won't break my heart."

He laced his fingers through hers, just below his chin. "I promise."

He meant it.

35

SARA

Sara was alone in the kitchen at the Sweet Island Inn. She had her elbows deep in sudsy sink water as she scrubbed plates, pots, and pans. She'd just finished cooking another dinner for the inn guests. On the menu tonight was Nantucket baked cod. She'd taken a few pounds of fresh cod fillets, bought earlier from fishermen who'd caught them offshore that morning, and brushed them with melted butter, lemon juice, and a top-secret blend of spices she'd sworn to her mother she would never reveal to another living soul. Once those were ready to be baked, she'd added tomato slices and a fine dusting of high-quality Parmesan cheese, then put them in the oven to cook perfectly. While they cooked, she whipped up a sautéed vegetable medley and rice pilaf for sides. Dessert was a Nantucket cranberry pie—another island specialty, and a recipe she was sworn to take to her grave. Mom didn't take much seriously, but family recipes certainly qualified.

She was singing softly under her breath—some silly pop song she'd heard on the radio while she was cooking—when her phone dinged. She looked over to where it sat on the countertop next to her. It was a text from Russell. She rinsed the soap suds off her hands, dried them off, and opened it up. *Whazzzzupppp!* it said.

You know that joke is older than I am, she said.

He sent back a smiling emoji. *Just trying to stay relevant, lol.*

And failing.

Comes with the territory. What're you doing?

She took a sip of wine. She was feeling a little buzzed. She'd been drinking while cooking and during dinner and now during clean-up, and she hadn't kept track of how much of the Pinot Grigio she'd consumed. *Oh, you know, just living the Cinderella life over here. Cook, clean, repeat.*

Sounds like you need a Prince Charming to come carry you away to your happily ever after.

She grinned. *I'd like that :)*

Roger. Gonna finish up my work and come by to scoop you. Ice cream?

Sara rolled her eyes, laughing. Leave it to Russell "Sweet Tooth" Bridges to talk her into getting ice cream after she'd just eaten enough cod and cranberry pie to feed a grizzly bear. She sent him a thumbs-up emoji and set her phone down to finish the dishes. She resumed her singing as she washed. With the alcohol flowing through her system, the warm and fuzzy prospect of hanging out with Russell invigorating her, and the undeniably catchy pop track bouncing around in her head, she was feeling good. She even started to add some dance moves. Nothing major—a little shimmy here, a hair flip there. But it was enough so that she didn't even notice when someone walked into the room.

"Nice moves," said a voice that was sickeningly, horribly, jaw-droppingly familiar.

Sara screamed and dropped a pot in the sink water. It hit like a cannonball and sent a geyser of water shooting everywhere, including all over Sara. She froze in place.

"Gavin! What are you doing here?"

He was leaning against the doorframe of the kitchen. He was in his Gavin Uniform, as per usual. The same scuffed boots, the same dark jeans. The shirt didn't look like one she'd seen him wear before, but it fit his standard theme, and of course, the sleeves were rolled up. It looked like he'd gotten a small tattoo on one forearm. Sara couldn't quite make out what it was.

"I came to see you, Sara," he said. She was sure that she was dreaming. Maybe she'd had a *lot* more wine than she realized and she was actually slumped on the hammock out back right now, having a very, very strange dream. Because there was no way that Gavin Crawford—the real, in-the-flesh, good-smelling and good-looking and sweet-talking Gavin Crawford—was standing in the doorway of the Sweet Island Inn, looking at her and telling her that he'd come to see her.

"You're joking," was all she could think to say. If this wasn't a dream, then it was a cruel practical joke. It had to be. It couldn't be real.

He shook his head and gave her a soft smile. He had a light beard growing in. It looked good on him. Very masculine. "Not joking. I ended things with Melissa. We're done for good. I missed you."

"Shut up," she blurted.

"What?" His brow furrowed.

"Sorry, not—just, I mean ... How? Why? What? You ended things with Melissa?" She knew darn well that she sounded like an absolute idiot, but she was still having an extremely difficult time coming to grips with this new reality. She could taste the soapy water that was dripping down her face. It was gross. She pinched her thigh. It hurt. This was real. There was no way she was dreaming.

He exhaled. "Yes. We're over. I know I haven't always been the most, shall we say, attentive to you. But I just didn't realize how much I liked seeing you in the kitchen. Talking to you. Even just texting you over the last few weeks made me realize it. I missed you."

Sara blinked. Surely, any second now, this would all resolve itself into something that made significantly more sense. But she blinked and blinked and blinked again, and nothing changed.

She honestly had not the faintest clue what to make of his words. He was saying the things she'd spent years hoping and praying he would say. He *missed* her?! *Earth to Sara, this is your dream come true!*

So why didn't it feel that way? Why did it feel a heck of a lot more like a nightmare?

"Gavin, I … I don't know what to say."

He stood up straight and crossed the distance between them. Coming up to her, he put his hands on her hips and pulled her into him. That was too much by about a hundred-fold. Her nose was full of his scent now. Citrus and cedar cologne, a mint aftershave, and that ineffable Gavin-smell. It lit her up like a Christmas tree. His smell was like a lightning bolt to her brain. It brought her rocketing back to the past. Back before Russell and before the inn and before Brent's downward spiral and before Eliza's baby and before what happened to Dad … It brought her back to standing in the half-completed guts of what would become the Lonesome Dove, and looking to where Gavin sat and thinking, *Oh no.*

That was exactly what she thought right now: *Oh no.* This couldn't possibly be a good thing. It might seem like it—a rich, successful, attractive man saying he missed her? How could that be bad? But she knew, deep down in her heart, that this was a wish-on-a-monkey's-paw scenario. Even if it looked good on the surface, there was a dark and unfortunate catch lingering in her near future, just waiting to trip her up.

"Then don't say anything," he said. "You don't have to. I'm sorry for what happened before, back in Boston, but now ... I'm here. I want to be here, with you. I want you to be here with me. So you don't need to say a word. Just ..." He trailed off. Suddenly, his face was looming closer and closer to hers. Her head was swimming with wine. This was wrong and right and messed up and perfect all at once. Like reality had become a Rubik's cube, and every time she looked at it, she saw a different color, but each was as puzzling as the next, and she didn't even know which place to start turning to get where she wanted to go.

A thought came ricocheting from deep in the recesses of her brain, like the only rational part left in her had been chucked down a well but was still screaming as loud as it could: *Don't. Do. It! Remember Russ!*

She thought about Russell. She thought about his goofy dad jokes and his horrendous cooking abilities and how he looked at her like she was the only thing in the world that mattered in any given moment. She remembered eating pizza with him and biking downtown and hurling flour in each other's faces, then kissing as it whirled around them like an indoor summertime snowstorm. She felt safe when he kissed her, and seen, and wanted, and loved. They hadn't used the L-word yet, but she knew that they could both feel that emotion baking slowly in their respective hearts and it was just waiting for the right time to emerge.

She'd spent a summer caught between the idea of Gavin and the reality of Russell. Back and forth she had gone, imagining two futures branching away from her. Both had seemed tempting. Both had seemed good. Both had seemed happy. But suddenly, she knew with unyielding certainty that she wanted the one with Russell. She would only ever be a shiny bauble to Gavin. The fact that she had "gotten away" was no doubt half of her appeal to him. Russell, though ... Russell saw her as essential.

She chose him.

But before she could make up her mind to say those words out loud, Gavin was kissing her, and holy cow, it set off a fireworks show in her stomach and her brain. Her heart fluttered with the twin rightness and wrongness of the kiss. He was a good kisser, and his torso was brawny and lean as he pulled her close to him, and that *smell* was so freaking overpowering, and, and, and ...

"Sara!"

She broke away. Her hair was still dripping with soapy water, and her shirt was similarly soaked. Gavin still had a hand on her hip, she noticed, even though she'd shoved him back when she'd heard someone call her name.

She closed her eyes, too, if only to exist for just one more second in the universe where she hadn't been kissing Gavin. Because she knew that, the second she opened them, she was going to see something in front of her that would break her heart.

When she couldn't escape it any longer, she took a deep breath and opened her eyes.

Russell stood in the doorway. He looked back and forth, back and forth, between Gavin and Sara and Sara and Gavin. Then, without another word, he set a single rose down on the dining room table, turned, and left.

36

HOLLY

After the morning's unveiling at the inn, Holly had spent the day taking care of some things around the house on Howard Street.

There was a closet full of mismatched knickknacks that she'd been itching to organize, so she chucked a load of dirty clothes and linens in the washer and got to work. She separated out Christmas ornaments, a set of china plates that went back four or five generations in the Benson family—her dad used to swear that they came over on the Mayflower, though not a living soul believed him —"The Pilgrims ate their Thanksgiving dinner off these guys, kid you not!"—and a variety of other things, including Dad's old baseball mitt and some of the freakishly lifelike Norman Rockwell doll collectibles that Holly's great-aunt had always loved. Holly, on the other hand, had been terrified of those things since she was a little girl. She resolved to quadruple-duct-tape the box that contained the dolls and bury it in the farthest, darkest corner of the closet. The rest of the things were put into bins and labeled, then stacked up again neatly.

That took a few hours, during which she let her mind wander away pleasantly, thinking about not much of anything. She realized with a pang halfway through that she missed her kids. She hadn't picked up a toy or heated up a bowl of dinosaur-shaped mac 'n cheese in so long that it was starting to feel like a distant dream. Their time at sleepaway camp had ended the week before. Holly felt like that would've been the time to come home, but she and Pete had texted about it, and he'd told her that he would take care of everything. If she wasn't ready to come home yet, then she could stay there as long as she needed. She felt horrifically guilty—her kids needed her, didn't they? But Pete had been adamant that he wanted to handle everything; he wanted to pick them up from Vermont and bring them back home. Holly reluctantly did as he asked.

They hadn't talked much about *them*. Holly could only imagine what he had been thinking, what he had been doing. It was the longest they'd spent apart since they first started dating. Every morning, Holly woke up and reached out towards his side of the bed, only to realize that there was no "his side of the bed." It was just her, in Nantucket, while he did who-knows-what nearly a hundred miles away in Plymouth.

She missed him. She wanted him. But she was still unsure about their marriage. Was it going to survive? She'd never been less sure about anything. She wasn't sure anymore that this separation was a good idea to begin with, or whether it would even fix any of the problems that had bubbled up between her and Pete when neither of them seemed to be looking.

Those thoughts circled in her head like a merry-go-round. When she got nowhere productive in fifteen minutes of brooding on the topic, she resolved to stop thinking about it. She cranked up the music on the stereo and buried herself in finishing up the closet organization task she'd set out on.

An hour after that, her stomach rumbled loudly like a volcano threatening to erupt. She was starting to get a headache, and she knew that she needed to eat something soon or she'd spend the evening miserable and bedridden—her headaches had always been nasty affairs. The problem was, they didn't have much in the way of food in the fridge. With Eliza spending most mornings at the inn helping her mother by handling the inn's business tasks and Sara helping out more and more with cooking for the guests, it was pretty much just Holly left in the house on Howard Street. So it fell to her to keep the fridge stocked. But she hadn't been to the grocery store in over a week. So, sighing, she got her keys and drove down to the Stop & Shop to pick up a few things.

Her mind wandered back to Pete while she drove and then wandered the grocery store aisles. She'd fallen into a habit of checking the house security cameras every night before bed, even though she felt like a crazy cyber stalker while doing it. Still, she couldn't resist. But she'd set a five-minute timer and limit herself to that. Once the timer went off, she closed the app and went to sleep. Night after night since she'd left, she'd found Pete home earlier than she expected. Holly couldn't say for sure, but it seemed like he spent an awful lot of time staring into the distance. They texted every now and then—not often, just enough to continue managing the household together. Though, without the kids at home, there wasn't much to manage.

Right now, she was missing him so much that she pulled out her phone. She stopped with her thumb hovering over the cameras app. Just a peek couldn't hurt, right? It wasn't her bedtime ritual—it wasn't even six p.m.—but she was desperately craving just the tiniest glimpse of her husband. "Thirty seconds," she said out loud, like she was making a promise to herself. Moving fast, she brought up the cameras. The kitchen was empty, as were the dining room, living room, and backyard. That was odd. Frowning, she pulled up the front-yard camera. Pete's car wasn't in the driveway. She sighed and closed the app.

So he was at work. On a Saturday evening. The kids must be at his parents'. Maybe nothing had changed after all. She'd spent so many minutes and hours convincing herself that this was going to be the cure-all for the problems in her marriage. Just a little short break from things, like a quarantine, and then they'd be able to get back to it and rekindle the love and partnership she'd been needing and missing.

But it looked like she was wrong. Pete couldn't cut back his hours. He didn't want to give her what she needed from him, and she was so weary of trying to do that for him. It felt like her heart was sinking in her chest. Before she could start crying, she straightened up, grabbed her cart, and marched out of the store.

By the time she got through the checkout line and climbed into the driver's seat of her minivan, though, the tears wouldn't be held back any longer. She sat in her empty car and cried. She cried for what she'd once had, which was love, and what she had now, which was not much of anything at all. She loved her kids and she loved her husband, and yet she didn't see how she could keep going forward with things the way they were now.

Eventually, a few long minutes later, the tears dried up, though the sadness remained. She felt like she'd passed a fork in the road. There was no going back now. This separation had shown that there wasn't any hope of salvaging her marriage. She'd be a single mother for the rest of her life. Struggling at best. She hadn't gone to college and she didn't have much of a resumé, so getting by would be a daily challenge. She'd probably have to come back home to Nantucket on a permanent basis so her mother could help her with Alice and Grady. What else would change? So many, many things, both the ones she could predict and the ones she knew would take her by nasty, vicious surprise.

She had failed.

She put the car in gear and drove home. Upon arriving back at Howard Street, she unloaded the groceries and walked into the house, balancing the paper bags precariously in her arms.

But when she set the bags down on the counter, she noticed something that hadn't been there when she left.

It was an envelope bearing her name. Whoever wrote it had printed it in neat, capital letters. *HOLLY.* She thought for one bizarre second that it was Pete's handwriting—he always wrote in all-caps—but then she shook that thought out of her head. It didn't make any sense, and she knew it was probably just a result of her sadness leaching into her thoughts.

Frowning, she tore open the envelope and retrieved the letter inside. It was a small section of white cardstock, unmarked except for a few lines written in the same blue ink and handwriting as her name on the outside had been. She had to reread the message a few times before it finally started making an inkling of sense.

A hacky sack, a high school hall.

A clumsy slip and trip and fall.

The place we met, you dropped your book.

A gift is there.

Now go and look.

When she'd read it twenty or thirty times, she set it down and slumped onto one of the barstools that lined the kitchen island. This made no sense whatsoever. It was Pete who had written this ... right? Maybe she was hallucinating. She had to be. Because there was no way, no how, no chance on earth that Pete—who had never written a lick of poetry in his entire existence, as far as Holly knew—had composed a poem that actually rhymed and flowed well. And not only that, she understood it! It was referring to Nantucket High, where they'd met. That didn't exactly make her Sherlock Holmes, but still ... Someone was playing a prank on her, right? Which corner was Ashton Kutcher hiding behind?

There was a smile threatening to steal across her lips, but Holly wasn't quite ready to give it free rein. First things first—she was going to go down to the high school, like the poem told her to do, and see what was waiting for her there. If it was Pete trying to be silly, she was gonna tear him a new one. If it was one or more of her sisters playing some sick practical joke, she was gonna tear them *two* new ones. And if it was something else ... well, she'd figured that out when she got there.

Snagging her keys, she went back out to the minivan, doing her best to stay calm, cool, and collected, even though she wanted to sprint in and do one hundred miles an hour down the road. She got in the car and drove the ten minutes down to the high school campus.

When she got there, it was dark and quiet—duh! It was a Saturday, after all; what had she expected? The only lights shining were spotlights illuminating the sign that read, "NANTUCKET HIGH, HOME OF THE WHALERS." Holly pulled her car up to the chain-link fence that had been pulled across the main drive into the school to keep people out over the weekend. She sighed. There was nothing here. This had been a wild goose chase. Whichever sister was behind this—it had to be Sara; Eliza would *never*—was in deep, deep trouble. How could she be so cruel? And why?

She leaned forward to rest her forehead on the steering wheel and try to gather her emotions. In doing so, she accidentally hit the lever to turn on the high beams. She sat up straight. That was when she saw it: stuck in the chain-link fence was another envelope. She'd almost missed it.

She leaped out of the car and ran over to tear it out. This one, too, had her name printed on it in the same neat, block letters. She ripped it open. Again, another piece of cardstock, another poem.

A slice of heaven, extra cheese.

A date that brought me to my knees.

An angel sent from the heavens above.

The night that first began our love.

"The pizza shop!" Holly yelled. She looked around as soon as the words escaped her lips, embarrassed that someone might hear her. She wanted to cackle like an insane person. She and Pete had had their first date to go see a movie—Holly always swore that it was something with Arnold Schwarzenegger, and Pete was equally adamant that it had been Bruce Willis; how they mixed up those two, neither of them were ever sure, but they'd spent an ungodly amount of time arguing about it. Whichever one it was, after the movie, they'd gone to get pizza.

God, that was a lifetime ago. She remembered how hard Pete had been trying to seem cool and laid-back. At one point, he'd been trying so hard that he wasn't looking where he was going and he'd tripped over a curb and had darn near done a somersault on the sidewalk. *A date that brought me to my knees.* Holly wasn't sure whether to laugh or cry at the memory. Right after he'd fallen, she'd blurted out loud without thinking, "Are you gonna stop trying to act all Rico Suave now?" Pete had laughed and hung his head and said he was glad she called him out, because then he could stop trying and actually be himself. She was grateful for that, because she loved him. Even then, she probably knew it. He was cute and he held doors open for her. She loved him and he loved her.

She needed to get to the pizza shop.

She drove like a madwoman there, and when she arrived, she didn't even bother finding a parking spot, or even locking the car behind her. She just jumped out, caution lights flashing and door wide open, and ran into the pizza shop with a lunatic's smile on her face. "Where is it, where is it ..." she mumbled under her breath as she looked madly around the shop.

"Oye! Chica!" Alejandro, the owner, smiled and whistled at her from behind the counter. He had a piercingly loud whistle. Holly felt the redness flush in her cheeks as the whole shop looked at her. She smiled, embarrassed again, and jogged over to where Alejandro was waving another envelope at her. She thanked him, and he gave her a wink. "Drive fast," he said.

She tore open this envelope on her way back to the car. This time, she read it out loud to herself.

"The kiss that launched a thousand ships / I leaned but almost missed your lips / It was the first, but there'd be more / As we watched the boats return to shore."

It clicked at once for Holly.

"The marina!" She raised her fist up in the air triumphantly, like she'd just won a gold medal at the Olympics. Again, everyone inside and outside the pizza shop looked at her with concern in their eyes. She'd better get going—someone was bound to call the police soon and report a crazy woman yelling nonsense in downtown Nantucket.

She couldn't get to the docks fast enough. As she drove, she remembered the memory that Pete's poem was about. This must've been their third, or maybe their fourth date. They'd had dinner—lobster, of all things—at a white tablecloth restaurant downtown. Pete had proudly paid with crumpled five- and ten-dollar bills he withdrew from a Batman wallet. Savings from summers cutting lawns, he said, and Holly remembered being so touched that he would use that on her for this silly, overly fancy, perfect, perfect dinner. Fifteen-year-old girls are impressed by the littlest of things. But even now, more than a decade later, she didn't think it was such a little gesture. It was love in the form of sweaty, triple-folded cash, spent on something that neither of them needed but both of them had remembered forever.

After dinner, they'd gone for a walk, and meandered down to take a seat by the docks and watch the fishing boats come back into harbor. He'd looked at her then with such goofy, Pete-like intensity in his face, the moon lighting up his eyes, and he'd leaned in to kiss her. But she'd already been leaning in to kiss him, because she didn't see how they could go a single second longer without kissing each other. They'd bumped noses on the way in. They'd laughed it off, and then Pete had said, "Try again?" They had done just that, and the second time had been magical. One of the fishermen had hooted and hollered as his boat passed them, but they hadn't stopped kissing.

She parked at the marina—properly, this time; she'd had quite enough public attention for the evening, thank you very much—and half jogged down to the docks. There! At the end of one of the small wooden piers, she saw an envelope sticking out from between two planks. She scurried down the stairs and retrieved it.

Like the others, she ripped this one open and scanned it eagerly.

I waited here on bended knee.

Between the moon, the stars, the sea.

The words were said, the question spoken.

A promise that would never be broken.

I love you now. I loved you then.

I swore our love would never end.

There's one more thing that's left to say:

Come back to me, my Hollyday.

~

Pete was waiting for her at the beach. She hesitated at the mouth of the dunes. She could see him, outlined against the dark ocean by the moon at his back. He was facing away from her, towards the waves, but when he heard her approaching, he turned around. There was just enough ambient light for her to see him smile.

He had stuck a candle in the sand at his feet. She could swear she saw a half-dozen broken matches dropped on all sides of it. She laughed to herself. For some unknown reason, Pete had the hardest time lighting matches. He'd always just hand her the package and say, "You do it."

This was a quiet beach, not quite secret but close to it, tucked away at a non-touristy part of the island. Few people came here. But Holly had on the day Pete had asked her to marry him. He'd had one of her friends invite her on a casual sunset walk. When they'd arrived, he was waiting for her, with a path of rose petals and candles leading from her to him. He'd said some sweet things that she'd been far too overcome with emotion to commit to memory the way she should have. She mostly remembered pulling him up and kissing him and squeezing him tight. He was *hers*. She was *his*. Her Pete. His Hollyday.

"I missed you," he said as she walked up. She stopped about a yard short of him, just out of arm's reach.

"I—"

"Let me go first, if that's okay," he interrupted with a soft smile. She fell silent and let him continue. "I've had a lot of time to think while you were gone. I know you needed this time, and I think I did, too. But it wasn't hard to make up my mind. I choose you, Holly. I choose you over everything. You and our kids are the only thing that matters to me. I chose you back in high school, and at the pizza parlor, and at the docks, and I chose you here. I'll keep choosing you, every day for the rest of our lives. I love you. I want to be with you. Whatever you need from me, you have it. It's yours. I'm yours."

Holly didn't trust her voice to say anything. The tears coursing down her face would have to be answer enough. She ran and jumped on Pete. She had just enough time to see his eyes widen in surprise before she tackled him into the sand and kissed his stupid, silly, perfect face as if her life depended on it.

In so many ways, it did.

37

BRENT

ONE WEEK LATER

Brent woke up on Sunday morning, a week after his first date with Rose, with a big smile on his face. He'd been waking up with a smile on his face every day since their night at the drive-in theater. A big, doofusy smile, but one that he couldn't wipe off if he tried.

Life is meant to be enjoyed, isn't it?

Yes, Dad! he wanted to shout from the rooftops. *Yes, it is.*

Life was *good*. He had spent the week going over the renovation once more with a fine-toothed comb, making sure everything was shipshape, and then helping his mom out with a few dozen other little handyman tasks around the inn and the house on Howard Street. It felt *good* to be needed. To be useful. To be wanted. He still dreamed about his dad most nights, but that was fine, because it didn't have the same sheen of terror over it, and he no longer woke up in a panic in the darkness. He'd started dreaming about Rose, too, though that was a whole can of worms he wasn't ready to crack open quite yet. He told himself every time he looked in the mirror to take things slow, one day at a time, and that seemed like good advice for sure. No need to rush anything, slap a label on it, or start layering expectations on top of whatever little spark had been kindled.

They hadn't seen each other too much. With school starting up again soon, Rose was spending a lot of time down at the elementary school getting ready for the fall semester, so she'd been very busy. But she and Brent still spent all day every day texting back and forth. He laughed out loud at least a half-dozen times a day. All the women in his family had commented multiple times on how he was just radiating happiness. He'd told them enough about Rose to keep them off his back, but as with his reluctance to put a label on his relationship with her, he didn't want to spoil anything by talking her up too much to his mom or sisters, so he kept the details sparse. He'd swung by on an evening run so that Henrietta and Susanna could meet. They'd gotten along like gangbusters. Henrietta liked just about everybody, so Brent had been confident that she and Rose's daughter would get along. But Susanna must have been something extra special, because Henrietta took to her the second they first laid eyes on each other. She'd jumped all over Susanna, smothering her with doggy kisses. Susanna had squealed with laughter and promptly declared that she and Henrietta were best friends now, so Brent would have to back off. Rose had scolded her, telling her to be polite to Mr. Brent, but he had just laughed.

Speaking of Henrietta, she was lapping at his hand right now. He'd snoozed just a few minutes later than normal—it was a Sunday, after all—and she was anxious to go for their normal morning jog on the beach. "All right, all right, girl, calm down," he said. He yawned and got dressed to head out. He smiled to himself. Maybe Rose would be out on the beach catching the sunrise like she usually did. She'd taken to bringing Susanna along every now and then, and the thought of his dog and her new best friend getting along so well encouraged his smile a little wider.

He filled Henrietta's water bowl in the kitchen so she could get a drink before they went exercising. When she'd had her fill, they set out at an easy pace towards the beach. The sun had already climbed over the water's edge and it looked like it was about to be an absolute stunner of a day. The summer heat had been fading more and more, leaving a gloriously nice autumn in its trail.

Life was *good*. It couldn't be said often enough.

When they reached the sand, Brent started to go a little faster. He took a deep inhale of the ocean's breeze, letting it fill his lungs and rejuvenate him. About a mile down the beach, he rounded the bend. He was full of expectation—from this point on, he could usually see Rose sitting in her spot, waiting for him.

But she wasn't there.

He tried not to get too disappointed. He was a little late, after all, thanks to him sleeping in past his alarm. He'd text her when he got back and see if she had a little bit of time to hang out today. Maybe they could take Susanna and Henrietta to the beach for the afternoon. Could even make a picnic out of it, perhaps.

As he got closer and closer to her spot, though, he thought he could make out something sticking out of the sand. When he got a few dozen yards away, he saw that it was a bright pink envelope. He slowed his pace as he approached. To his surprise, he noticed something written on the outside in loopy, precise teacher's handwriting—*Brent Benson, Ironman*. This had to be from Rose, then. A smile stole across his face. He wondered what it would say as he plucked it out of the sand and opened up the letter.

The smile didn't last long.

Dear Brent,

This wasn't how I wanted to do this. But I practiced in the mirror a bunch of times, and I couldn't get through the whole thing without breaking down. So I had to write it instead. I'm sorry for that.

What I spent all week trying to find the words for is: I can't do this.

You are special. I knew that the first time I saw you running on the beach. Don't ask me how—maybe it was the smile or maybe it was something else, I'm not sure. But I just knew right away—that's a special guy right there.

Perhaps that's part of the problem. You are special—too special for me. I'm too fragile for you. I had my heart hurt by the stuff that brought me to Nantucket. And, after just that one date with you, I knew with one hundred percent certainty that there was something between us.

That's why I have to do this. I can't expose my heart again. It hurt too badly last time. I can't be a good mother to Susanna and I can't keep living my life like a responsible adult if I'm broken beyond repair. It's taken a long time to even get this far in my recovery. I can't afford to take a step back.

I know I made you promise that you wouldn't break my heart. The crazy thing is, I believed you when you said you wouldn't. I think you believed yourself, too. But there's always a chance. It's unavoidable. There's nothing guaranteed in this life. Not even the love of a good man like you.

I'm rambling now. I'm sorry for that, too. I know this is going to hurt you. But believe me when I say it's for the best. Better for me to stop things now, before they get too far, then realize down the road that I'm just too broken and scared to open my heart again.

I'm sorry. I'm sorry. I'm sorry a thousand times over, and I can't say it enough.

I wish you the best. You deserve happiness. I wish I could be the one to give it to you.

With all the love in my heart,

Rose

By the middle of the afternoon, Brent had read the letter perhaps one hundred times. He'd also had eight beers and six or seven strong chugs of Jack Daniels whiskey straight from the bottle, and he was getting very, very drunk.

His dad was a liar after all. Life wasn't meant to be enjoyed. If he was ever enjoying life, that meant it was just setting him up for another fall. Happiness just meant he wasn't paying attention to what lay beyond the next curve in the road.

He took another glug of whiskey. Screw it. Screw this. Screw everything. Henrietta looked at him mournfully. He couldn't bear to look back at her. He needed to get out of this house right now, because if she kept looking at him like that, he was liable to start crying, and he just did not want to do that right now.

"Don't look at me that way," he snarled at her.

She just tilted her head and looked back.

"Stop it," he ordered again.

She nuzzled his hand with her nose.

"All right, I'm gone," he said with finality, standing up suddenly. Henrietta leaped back, tail wagging. Maybe she thought the two of them were going out. She was half right—*he* was going out. He wanted to go talk to his damn father.

He was going to go down to the marina and take *Jenny Lee* out to the Garden of Eden, and he was going to yell at Henry until the SOB spoke back to him. He'd stay there all day and night if he needed to. He wanted an answer, and his father was going to give it to him.

Brent was unsteady on his feet, but still sober enough to hear the voice in his head telling him that this was a bad idea. Unfortunately for that voice, he was drunk enough to ignore it outright. He snatched his keys off the coffee table, dropped them, bent down to pick them up again. Then he marched out the door to where his truck was parked around the side of the house. He climbed in and took off down the road, growling under his breath.

Rose. She had led him on. She had set up him just to rip everything away. He tried to muster up some anger at her, but he couldn't. The truth was that he understood. He knew how it felt to have your future suddenly and irrevocably shattered. He was sure that, on some level, she thought it was her fault that Susanna's father had left her. Just like he was sure that, on some level, he still thought it was his fault that his father had died.

He had spent over a month believing that he'd exorcised that demon from his soul. But it turned out the sly devil had just been waiting in the shadows for the right moment to rear his ugly head again. And boy, now that it was back, it was back with a vengeance. *Your fault, your fault, your fault,* it said again and again like a wicked chorus. *You did it. You deserve this. You deserve to be miserable.*

Right now, Brent was having a hard time disagreeing.

He flew screeching into the marina parking lot, though now that he was here, he barely remembered the drive over. He was much drunker than he'd realized when he left the house. *Bad idea ...* said that cautionary voice again, but it was much weaker and quieter now and even easier to ignore than it had been before.

"Go to the Garden. Talk to Dad. Go to the Garden. Talk to Dad." He mumbled it under his breath over and over. Whether it was convincing himself that this was a good idea or simply trying to remember what on earth he had come here for, Brent wasn't sure, but he kept saying it as he fumbled his keys out of the ignition and started to stride unsteadily towards the docks.

He was halfway across the parking lot when he saw a face. Now, why was that face familiar? He stopped in place, swaying, and racked his brain trying to remember. Where had he seen that man before? Fat face, sunburned, wearing fishing gear that looked like it had never been ... Bingo. That was the jerk who'd insulted Brent back in early August. Right around here, actually. What had he called him? *Son,* that was it. He'd called him *son.* Brent didn't like that. He didn't like the memory, either. In fact, he liked it so little that he walked up to the man where he stood right now fueling up his boat, cocked his fist back, and swung it as hard as he could towards the man's face.

Time slowed down as his fist went through the air. He was vaguely aware of someone shouting his name in the distance. "Brent! Brent! Stop what you're—" It was Roger. Just like last time, as if this was some sickening replay of the same event that had happened almost six weeks ago.

But Roger was way too far away to stop him. Besides, the fist was flying already. It was going to make bloody, violent contact in three, two, one ...

Boom. Boom.

Two hits in quick succession.

The first hit was Brent striking the man in the jaw. The second hit was Sheriff Mike Dunleavy, pile-driving Brent into the ground with a tackle like a middle linebacker. Brent's head smacked against the gravel, and he blacked out.

He came to in the jail cell. He was surrounded by slick concrete. It smelled pretty awful in here. Like blood. Or, wait—that *was* blood. Brent's own blood. The side of his head throbbed something terrible, but when he tried to reach up to touch it, he realized that his hands were handcuffed behind his back. That explained why his wrists and shoulders were aching, too. He could feel bits of gravel still ground into his cheek where he'd hit the ground after Mike had tackled him. He was still pretty drunk, though a little less than he'd been before.

What on earth had he been thinking?

He looked out through the cell bars and saw the fat man sitting on a bench outside the holding area. He had an ice pack pressed against his jaw. Brent could see a trail of dried blood looping down from the man's nose. He also had fury surging in his eyes. Brent could hear him saying, "Of course I want to press charges! That crazy guy walked up and socked me hard. It was a sucker punch! A freakin' sucker punch!" He jabbed a finger towards Brent. Sheriff Mike was sitting in a chair across from the man, nodding and taking scribbled notes on a little yellow legal pad.

"All right, Mr. Fitzgerald, I've made a note of that. I'm gonna have Officer O'Leary here finish taking the rest of your statement, if that's all right with ya."

Another man in a sheriff's deputy uniform came over and escorted the man away. He gave Brent one more withering look before he disappeared through the door. Sheriff Mike sighed and rubbed his temples. Then, standing, he walked over to Brent. He unlocked the jail cell and slid it open, then dragged the chair he'd been seated in over in front of Brent and took a seat on it backwards.

"Brent, kid ... You messed up, man."

Brent had to lick his chapped lips twice before he could speak. "I know," he finally croaked. His head was still swimming—with pain, with alcohol, with Rose's words. *"You deserve happiness,"* paired with the image of his father. But he was aware enough to look into Sheriff Mike's eyes and realize that he could feel tears running down his face.

"Mr. Fitzgerald over there wants to press charges this time, and I can't say I blame him. You cold-cocked him, man. I told you you didn't have much rope left. What were you thinkin'?"

"I ... I don't know. I wasn't. I was ... I don't know. I just don't. I'm sorry. Can you tell him I'm sorry?"

Mike shook his head. "He doesn't wanna hear that, sport. Trust me. You're gonna need a lawyer. Brent ... Your father was my friend, you know. And I know that I've told you this and I'm sure you've heard it a million times from other folks, too. But he would hate to see you like this. He'd just hate it."

"I know," Brent repeated dumbly. He looked down in his lap. The tears were running down his cheeks, mixing with the dirt and blood, and splattering on his knees. He didn't want to look at Mike anymore. He just wanted it to be dark in here. He wanted to sleep for a long, long time.

"What happens next?" he asked after a long minute of silence.

Mike was in the midst of exiting the cell, chair in hand. He stopped. Brent could hear him sigh again. He didn't turn around when he spoke. "A few things. There'll be a trial. I expect you'll take a plea deal. Can't say for sure what the judge'll do. Maybe jail time, maybe just community service, considering the circumstances. It just depends."

"No," Brent interrupted, "I mean, what happens now?" He looked up.

Mike sighed a third time. "Right now, you probably oughta call your mother."

38

MAE

It was another heart-wrenching call in a summer that had been full of them. Sheriff Mike didn't say much when Mae picked up. He just said, "I'm handing the phone to Brent now," and then there had been a long pause while Mae held her breath and wondered what on earth was going on.

She heard Brent breathing on the other end of the line. And, call it crazy or call it a mother's intuition, she just knew that he was hurt. He hadn't even said anything and yet she was ten thousand percent sure of that. He was hurt—her youngest, her baby, her soldier—and he was bleeding, and crying too most likely.

"Brent?" she said when she couldn't bear waiting for him to talk.

"Hi, Mom," he rasped. His voice was thick with sorrow.

"Brent, honey... what's going on?"

He didn't answer for another agonizingly long moment. "You should probably come to the police station," he said finally. "I don't expect you to bail me out or anything. But I—I just... It'd be good to see you."

That was all he needed to say. She told him she'd be there right now and she went racing off that way.

Sheriff Mike met her in the lobby. "Where is he?" she said. It sounded like a snap. She didn't mean to be rude to Mike—he had been friends with Henry for a long time; she knew him and his wife well, they were good folks. But terror had a nasty grip on her heart.

"Mae, breathe," Mike counseled.

"Where is Brent?" was all she said.

Mike sighed with the air of a man who had been doing an awful lot of sighing lately.

"C'mon, this way."

She followed him back through the little Nantucket police station to the set of four cells in the back room.

And there, behind bars—oh, God, what was her baby doing behind bars?—she saw Brent. He was seated and looking down, rubbing his wrists gingerly. Had they cuffed him? Why on earth would they need to cuff him? He was a little lost right now, everyone with eyes could see that, but did he really need to be handcuffed?

She broke loose of Mike's calming hand on her shoulder and ran to Brent. He looked up and saw her coming. Standing, he met her at the bars.

She touched his hand through the gaps between the bars. He was dirty and bloody. There were tear tracks leading down his cheeks and his eyes were red-rimmed and raw. He looked like hell warmed over.

He looked like he needed his mother.

"I'm here," was what she decided to say, though that much was obvious. Maybe, though, it wasn't quite obvious. Maybe she was telling him she was *here,* not just here in the cell, but here in this downswing with him, here in his sadness with him, here in mind, body, and soul with him. Maybe that was what she needed to hear. Lord, she hoped that it was.

"I know, Mom," he said, his voice thick with unshed tears.

She squeezed his fingers in hers as tight as she could and said it again. "I'm here, Brent. I'm here, I'm here, I'm here."

He rested his forehead against the bars. "I know," he repeated.

"And we're going to get through this. Together. Do you hear me?"

"I hear you," he echoed numbly, like a little kid in school repeating after the teacher. "I hear you."

Where they would go from here, Mae wasn't yet sure. But she meant what she was saying with every fiber of her being. They were going to get through this. All of them, all of the Benson family.

As long as they stuck together.

The Benson family saga continues in Book 2 of the Sweet Island Inn series, NO BEACH LIKE NANTUCKET. Click here to get it now!

(Or keep reading below to get a sneak preview.)

Mae Benson needs a fresh start. Can she find peace and happiness on the beaches of Nantucket?

Last summer, a storm blew Mae's life to bits.

It's been almost a year since that fateful day.

Since she learned that life at the beach isn't all sunshine and rainbows.

She and her children are doing their best to pick up the pieces.

While Mae is running the Sweet Island Inn,

Eliza is learning what it means to be a mother.

Sara is rediscovering her passion in the wake of heartbreak.

Holly is searching for stability in her marriage.

And Brent is—well, Brent isn't doing so great.

Despite these challenges, the Bensons just might make it—if they can stick together.

But right when it seems like they're going to be okay, terrible news strikes.

A call from Aunt Toni changes everything.

And suddenly, Nantucket doesn't feel quite like home anymore.

Come book your stay at Nantucket's Sweet Island Inn—where the water is warm, the sun is shining, and everyone welcomes you like family—in this heartwarming, inspirational women's fiction beach read from author Grace Palmer.

Click here to start reading NO BEACH LIKE NANTUCKET now!

FRIDAY, APRIL 2—MORNING

"More coffee?"

"That would be lovely, thank you." Dominic looked up at Mae and gave her a broad smile.

It had become a morning ritual between the two of them—sitting on the first floor wraparound porch of the Sweet Island Inn and sharing the first cup of coffee of the day. Half the time, they didn't even say much of anything. Instead, they just sat there, soaking up the sunrise and each other's presence. The company was nice, as was the stillness, before the hustle and bustle of an innkeeper's never-ending work began.

It was strange to Mae to start her days in tranquility. After all, she'd spent most of her six decades on this earth hitting the ground running, bright-eyed and bushy-tailed. Maybe this was a 'growing older' thing. A new chapter of her life, so to speak. She still felt young at heart, but she couldn't deny that her knees and wrists tended to get a little cranky at her if she got them going too abruptly first thing in the morning. Slipping into the day, like going one toe at a time into the first ocean dip of the spring, felt nice and right.

Eventually, though, the time came when the rest of the Inn's guests would start to stir and she'd have to get up and going. She always felt just the slightest pang of nuisance when she heard a noise from upstairs. She still loved running the Inn—she'd told everybody who asked that it felt like this was the job she was born for—but she just loved these quiet morning moments with Dominic, too.

"Is today the day?" Dominic asked with a wry grin as he took a sip of the fresh coffee.

She settled into the rocking chair next to his. "Perhaps tomorrow," she said with a teasing grin of her own.

That little exchange was a ritual, too. A running joke that had started some time ago and seemed determined to persist. He'd asked her suddenly on one of their first mornings sharing coffee on the porch if today was the day she kicked him out of the Inn. And, just like she'd done on that first morning and every morning since, she had said, "Perhaps tomorrow." She didn't mean a word of it.

It was true that he'd been here for quite some time now. Nearly a year, actually. He'd extended his stay in Room 1 indefinitely. Mae was hardly upset about it. She liked his company, she liked his politeness, she liked how he knew when to ask a question or make a joke, and when to just smile and enjoy the sunshine or the snowfall.

"Can you believe it's been nearly a year?" she said suddenly after a moment.

"Time certainly passes with haste. More so, the older I get, despite my protests."

Mae loved how Dominic spoke. Elegant, poetic, even when he was doing something as simple as remarking on the weather or some new dish Mae had whipped up. "What a year it has been."

"That it has. That it has."

What had happened? So much and so little at the same time. Her old life had been irretrievably shattered by the tragic loss of her husband, but she had found a new and beautiful one inside of that, like a Russian nesting doll broken open. The Inn was a blessing she had never anticipated. She was newly a grandmother once more, and it gave her such pleasure to see Eliza blossoming into motherhood that she knew her eldest daughter had given up hopes of long ago. There was happiness in so many places in her world.

There was a little corner of happiness seated with her on the porch just now. Dominic was a source of happiness in her life; there was no denying that. Theirs was a comfortable and pleasant friendship. She had come to rely on it whenever sadness reared its ugly head.

They heard a big yawn come from upstairs. It was a warm morning, so the Robinson couple in Room 4 must have opened their window to greet the dawn. "I should get hustling," Mae said with a tinge of sadness. Again, she felt that little irritation at having to spoil this nice, quiet moment. But such was her life and her duty to her guests. Once she was in the thick of her errands, she didn't mind so much. The hummingbird side of her personality that so loved flitting from task to task to task wouldn't ever leave her.

"And so begins another morning," Dominic smiled. "Time for me to go back to sleep then, I believe."

Mae chuckled at that. She knew—though she didn't particularly like to acknowledge it, whether to herself or anyone else—that Dominic only got up for these mornings for her sake. He worked late into the night six or seven days a week, tapping out the beautiful words of his novel into his laptop. So, once they'd shared their coffee, he went back to bed for a few hours before getting back up and beginning his day proper. Sara had made one or two sly comments about it ("He wakes up that early just to hang out with you? Oooh lala!"), but Mae had just swatted her youngest daughter with a dish towel and told her to hush. No need to read anything into it. Dominic was a treasured friend. That was good enough for Mae.

They bid each other goodbye and went their separate ways. Mae went into the kitchen to pop her blueberry muffin mix into the oven in time to serve breakfast once the Robinsons came down, along with the Inn's other weekend guests, and put a fresh pot of coffee on to brew.

The rest of the day went by in a hazy blur. A trip to the grocery store to restock the Inn's pantry, a long overdue deep clean of the bathrooms in Rooms 3 and 6, and then hanging up some new pieces of art in the living room that she'd purchased at Winter Stroll and had been meaning to take care of ever since. She particularly liked one of them, a blurred watercolor of a Nantucket lighthouse. The color palette was soft and muted and the scene it depicted was a frigid beach in the dead of a harsh winter, but there was something indescribably beautiful about it anyways. If Nantucket could be pretty in the midst of a blizzard, then it could be pretty any time at all.

Before she knew it, the late afternoon rays were slanting through the kitchen window, and it was time for the other event on today's calendar. She'd been ignoring it all day long, trying not to expend too much mental energy on it. But now, here it was, up close and personal, and there was no avoiding it any longer.

One year since the accident aboard Henry's boat, *Pour Decisions*. One year since everything had changed forever for the Benson family. It had gone so fast—"with haste," as Dominic had said. Thinking back on it now, she knew that this year had been so full of many moments both happy and sad. But try as she might, she couldn't remember many of them. Only a few stood out: the return to Nantucket of her daughters, one by one, each for their own challenging reasons. The birth of her granddaughter. The Inn, of course. The journey of her youngest son, which had been full of switchbacks and turnarounds and many, many difficult times. She hadn't spent much time looking backwards. Onwards and upwards, as the saying went. Mae was particularly good at keeping her eyes rooted on the future.

But today, a year to the day since the accident that took her husband away, it was time to reflect. This night, at sunset, she and her children would be honoring Henry. Mae took a deep breath. She felt tears brewing deep down inside, but it wasn't time for that yet. First, she would get ready. Then, she was going to meet her children at Henry's favorite beach and remember him.

Click here to keep reading NO BEACH LIKE NANTUCKET.

ALSO BY GRACE PALMER

Sweet Island Inn

No Home Like Nantucket (Book 1)

No Beach Like Nantucket (Book 2)

No Wedding Like Nantucket (Book 3)

No Love Like Nantucket (Book 4)

Willow Beach Inn

Just South of Paradise (Book 1)

Just South of Perfect (Book 2)

Just South of Sunrise (Book 3)

Just South of Christmas (Book 4)

JOIN MY MAILING LIST!

Click the link below to join my mailing list and receive updates, freebies, release announcements, and more!

JOIN HERE:

https://readerlinks.com/l/1060002